IN CLOSED TERRITORY

IN CLOSED TERRITORY

EDGAR BEECHER BRONSON

ISBN: 978-1-963956-52-8

Contents

PREFACE

"CLOSED TERRITORY" is a phrase that inspires longings and expresses conditions of the sort that, in one form or another from the days of Adam, have served out to mankind most of the sweetest pleasures and bitterest pains experienced between earliest sentient childhood and feeblest senile age. Never are we so old or so young that we are entirely safe from the allurements it suggests, the novel charms and new intoxications with which our imagination close hedges every sinuous turn of forbidden paths. The pitfalls it holds, alike for toddling infancy, firm-treading prime, and halting, stumbling age, we never think of until into them we are deeply and more or less hopelessly plunged.

Happy indeed, then, he who may be so fortunate as to win free franchise to "Closed Territory," to traverse it untainted, and to leave it unscarred.

A personal acquaintance with the British East African Protectorate can scarcely fail to make any observant, thoughtful Briton or American proud of his AngloSaxonhood, of its boldness, its actual audacity.

This newest of British Colonies comprises 400,000 square miles of territory. It has a native black population of 4,000,000, divided among something over a dozen different tribes, each widely differing in language and tribal customs from all the others, all warrior races perpetually battling with each other until brought under measurable discipline by British authority, the most powerful the Kikuyu, the Masai, and the Wakamba.

And yet this vast new apanage of the Empire is occupied and held for the Crown by a numerically puny handful of about two hundred and fifty Englishmen!

This includes the Governor and his staff, the various administrative departments, the military and police departments—in fact, the entire civil list of the Protectorate, except the Post, Telegraph, and Railway Departments.

Troops? No troops? Oh, yes; but what? A few companies of East Indian Sikh infantry, doing police duty along the Uganda Railway, and two battalions of native Soudanese and Nubian Askaris! That is all!

And of this little group of two hundred and fifty white men charged with the task of holding four million raw, savage blacks in check, nearly four-fifths are stationed at Mombasa, Nairobi, Kisumu, and other railway points, while the outlying districts are held by a scant sixty men, posted in little bomas (garrisons) scattered along the coast and parallel to and never more than seventy-five miles from the Uganda Railway, divided up into "bunches" of three, two, or often no more than one white man to each boma, often remote from support, never with more than a handful of native troops under their command!

It is a distinctly sporting proposition in government, is that of British East Africa, with every man in the game playing against what would appear superficially to be, and what may at any time become in cruel fact, hopelessly overwhelming odds. And yet one never hears a hint of a thought of anything of the sort from the men themselves. Quietly, coolly, and usually most efficiently are they doing their work. "Playing the game," they themselves would call it, in ultra-British idiom—and playing it in a way to make a man proud to claim racial kinship with them.

Four years ago there were not as many as a dozen white farmers in the Protectorate. Now the white population has risen to a total, including all officials, of perhaps 1,200, and of these 550 are resident in Nairobi, the capital.

Settlement, trade, sport, and travel are rigidly restricted, by the Outlying Districts Ordinance, to the narrow policed belt lying along the railway, entirely within the outer lines of boma outposts. Entry into the vast areas comprising the "Closed Territory" lying to the north and south of the "open districts," without a special permit therefor from the Governor, is a penal offence. And very rarely are such passes issued for fear any holding them may in some way incite or become the victims of voluntary aggression by the shenzi (savages), and thus cause disturbances the slender forces of the Protectorate might easily prove wholly inadequate to handle.

It was for me, therefore, a stroke of rare good luck, for which I shall always feel deeply indebted to him, when Lieut.-Governor the Hon. F. J. Jackson, C. B., C. M. G., consented to issue me a pass for entering certain "Closed Territory," that enabled me to make a three months' safari through the countries of the Loita Masai, the Wanderobo, the Kavirondo, the Kisii, the Sotik, and the Lumbwa, the more for that both the Sotik and the Kisii had been in open, bloody revolt only a few months before the date of my pass.

Lying midway between the two old Arab caravan routes from the coast to Victoria Nyanza, one starting from Mombasa and the other from Tanga, in what is now German territory, most of the country I traversed under the pass still remains unmapped. It had never before been entered by white men save by the Anglo-German Boundary Commission, whose work of locating and marking the boundary line between British and German East Africa had been finished roughly four years earlier, and six months earlier by the man I was fortunate enough to secure as a mate for the trip, George H. Outram, himself formerly a Government official and a member of the Boundary Survey party of 1894. E. B. B., NEW YORK CITY,

January 1, 1910.

INTRODUCTION

THE story of the big game of Africa has been many a year in the telling, but it remains ever new. The freshness of it is perennial. To a lover of the physical aspects of nature, the book of the average African hunter contains such a wealth of wild-animal hunting adventures that the physical geography and the plant life suffer from lack of attention. It is not strange that in his effort to portray the marvellous abundance of wild-animal life in the most richly stocked game fields on earth, the landscapes, trees, and plants seem to the hunter like "trifles light as air."

I am glad of this opportunity to urge upon my brother sportsmen the assurance that he who devotes all his attention to the game and its pursuit, and ignores the remainder of Nature's open books of wild places, necessarily loses much that rightfully is his. It is not all of hunting to kill game. I would rather find a few animals amid grand or beautiful scenery than many animals in dull places. To every wild creature on earth, Nature has given its own special and appropriate stage setting, of rock and tree, or of field and stream. At least one-half the time the accessories are, to the comprehending eye, as interesting as the animal itself.

So long as the big game of Africa holds its own upon the veldt, just so long will the public welcome new books that strive to portray its moods and its tenses. I hold it to be the duty of every right-minded gentleman-sportsman, who shoots wisely and not too much, to publish an account of his observations, no matter whether he includes his shooting records or not. From such dreadful tales of sordid slaughter as those of Neumann, the ivory-hunter, all people who care for the beasts of the field may well pray to be spared.

Mr. Bronson's story is very much to my mind; and on hearing that it was to appear in permanent form, I was heartily glad. Through the chapters previously published I had followed him with interest and delight. He gratifies my desire to know the on-the-spot impressions of the explorer and hunter; for it is this personal equation that always brings the reader in closest touch with the hunter and his surroundings. His careful and clear descriptions of landscapes and the component parts of his African geography are delightful; and his frequent touches of humor, phenomenally rare in books on Africa, are most welcome exceptions to the African rule. Surely, a story of the Dark Continent need not by necessity be sombre.

In perusing this and other recent tales of the great game herds of the East African plains, the reader naturally asks the question, What has the future in store for the game? Will the onslaughts of sportsmen and residents soon reach such a point of frequency that the game will be killed more rapidly than it breeds?

It is upon the answer to this last question that the future of the big game depends. As a rule, it is not by any means the gentlemen-sportsmen, taking a modest toll of the wilds, who exterminate the game. In the first place, they are easily checked and regulated; for all their acts are known. In about ninety per cent of all the extermination cases that are fully known, the commercial hunters, and the resident hunters who kill game all the year round, are the real exterminators. I think that in most localities one case-hardened resident who is determined to live on the country can be counted upon to destroy more animal life each year than five average, sportsmen who visit the same territory for brief periods.

In those portions of the East African plateau region that are suited to agriculture, stretching from Bulawayo to Uganda, the wild herds are bound to be crowded out by the farmer and the fruit-grower. This is the inevitable result of civilization and progress in wild lands. Marauding herds of zebras, bellicose rhinoceroses, and murderous buffaloes do not fit in with ranches and crops, and children going to school. Except in the great game preserves, I think that the big game of British East Africa is foredoomed to disappear, the largest species first.

Five hundred years from now, when North America is worn out, and wasted to a skeleton of what it now is, the great plateau region of East Africa between Cape Town and Lake Rudolph will be a mighty empire, teeming with white population. Giraffes and rhinoceroses are now trampling over the sites of future cities and universities. Then the game herds, outside of the preserves, will exist only in memory, and in the pages of such books as "In Closed Territory" by Bronson, and in other books by hunters who shoot for themselves and write for the pleasure of their friends. For myself, I am glad that I live in the days of big game, in Africa and elsewhere; and as a natural corollary to a sportsman's life, A. D. 1910, it is his solemn duty to do his level best to insure that a good supply of wild life is left for the sportsmen of 2010. W. T. HORNADAY. NEW YORK, January 15, 1910.

I. THROUGH PATHLESS DESERT

My safari caravan was organized at Juja Farm early in December 1908. George Henry Outram an old Australian prospector of wide experience a veteran of Coolgardie of Kimberley and Johannesburg had recently come in from a prospecting trip in the ranges lying between the Mau and Kisii Escarpments close to the German border from which he brought back fine specimens of copper graphite and other ores and stories of lion elephant and rhino so thick and troublesome they left him scarcely half his time for work. The ore was in itself a potent lure and the added temptation of a chance of two or three months in a country still unoccupied save by wandering Wanderobo hunters and known only to perhaps a half dozen white men teeming with the best specimens of many types of central plateau big game extinct in most other sections and rare in all quickly decided me to go with him to his new diggings.

Our third mate on the trip was William Judd probably the most experienced and capable hunter of African big game now living, a man who hunts to get his own best loved fun when no chance offers to go out professionally as safari leader for visiting sportsmen, a man who has shot from the Pungwe River in far southern Portuguese East all the way north to Abyssinia and to whose rifle have fallen one hundred and fifty elephant and more lion rhino and big game of all kinds than he has been able to keep count of. Indeed the trio of us made a rather strong three of a kind perhaps not so very far below aces for each was pretty well trained to a finish in every sort of wild life hardship and had a few laughs up his sleeve for any and all difficulties that might be handed us. The staff consisted of Regal Wassama, William Northrup McMillan's head cook, a splendid old Somali wiry and active as a youth with the keen eye and dignity of an Arab chief and the culinary skill of the best French chef who barring the time devoutly spent in saying his five long daily prayers gazing and genuflexing towards Mecca was unremitting in his care of us, Awala Nuer a slender middle aged Somali shikari whose one good eye was ever picking up game before mine had noted it, my own boy Salem a Swahili so constantly thoughtful of my every want and so alert to fill it that but for his sex I would back him to make the best conceivable high ideal of a wife, and Molo a Herculean shaven crowned Kavirondo table boy who while trying his best to please was ever chucking plates and knives and forks about as he was trained to hurl the assegai and knob kerri he was carrying when I had first seen him a few months before. To carry our camp kit supplies and general outfit for a three months trip required seventy wapagazi porters all of whom were picked from the farm forces thirty five stalwart Unyamwezi and Kavirondo all trained men unflinching on a trek and thirty five raw shenzi(savage) Kikuyu, the former good for sixty pounds to the man, the latter for no more than forty pounds.

At daylight of December 9, Outram started for Nairobi with the safari, which also included seven little Abyssinian mules for our own use, and twenty-two donkeys to pack native food, chiefly beans and corn posho for the wa bagazi, for the country to which we were going was devoid of any form of native food except the meat of wild game, which Kikuyu do not eat.

But the season was that of the "little rains," which at the moment happened to be a steady all-day downpour that turned the Athi Plains into a sticky marsh and compelled camping short of town. When morning came, Outram found that the Kikuyu, always faint-hearted, had bunked to a man, timid of a long trek away from their own country or sick of the weather.

To our disgust we found Nairobi stripped of fit porters by the thirty safari outfits sent out in November, so that we were compelled to take on another lot of Kikuyu to fill the places of the deserters, and to get them delayed us till the twelfth.

And the first day's march was quite enough to stop and turn back any but an old-timer or the warmest of raw enthusiasts, for throughout the day rain poured in torrents, turning the alternating bush and rich meadow lands of the Kikuyu hills into fields of sticky mud nigh impossible for our porters to travel in. Thus at the end of seven hours our men were dead beat, and still we were out only nine miles from Nairobi. However, safari life in Africa is the best possible post-graduate course in patience, and this was only a hint of probably a lot more annoying delays ahead, so we made the best of it, hastily pitched our tents on the Ambagathi River, and huddled into them.

The next day the rainfall continued so heavy we decided it would be folly to try to move except for a halfmile plod through the mud in the afternoon for tea with Lord Cardross, whose farm is the outermost one south from Nairobi.

On the fourteenth the weather cleared sufficiently to enable us to move at daylight. At 7:30 A. M. I made an almost unpardonably early call on District Commissioner McClure and his charming wife, who from his Southern Masai Reserve Boma rules a district nearly as large as New England, with thousands of wild Masai and Wanderobo, the ancient lords of the domain, who still remain practically its only tenants, rules it, punishes its marauding raiders, and checks its savage feuds with no help but his own nerve and wits, a scant half-hundred native police, and the ominous spectre of British Imperial authority. Indeed, that very morning of my call he was just starting out on a punitive trek after a band of

Lenani's Southern Masai, who the day before had raided a neighboring Kikuyu kraal, killed a number of Kikuyu warriors, and looted two hundred and seventy-eight cattle.

Here at Mr. McClure's boma, a scant twelve miles from Nairobi, we left civilization behind us, for one might travel straight away a full thousand miles to the south without finding any white man's habitation,—and entered the great Ukamba Game Reserve, which for its western half is also the home of the Southern Masai.

Early in the morning we crossed the west shoulder of the Ngong range at an altitude of 6,500 feet, and then began a rapid descent from the cool verdurous central plateau to the arid, volcanic wastes to the southwest, camping at Ngong Spring, a feeble trickle of sweet water that within a few hundred yards of its birth disappeared in the burning sands of a deep, yellow-grassed, rocky gorge. Here at this spring we met scores of practically naked Kikuyu porters, men and women, loaded with three-foot cakes of carbonate of soda from the vast natural deposits of this salt in Lake Magadi, for the development of which a ninety-mile railway is planned if the samples then coming out prove satisfactory.

The meeting of these Kikuyu coming up out of the south augured ill for our journey, for between Ngong Spring and the Guaso Nyiro River, sixty-four miles to the south, there is not a drop of living water. For this five days' ordinary safari marching, the trail traverses a horrid arid country hot as Death Valley, isolated black volcanic uplifts rearing here and there high into the sky their rugged, grassless slopes, the plains everywhere strewn so thick with sharp fragments of volcanic rock the traveller rarely has a chance to set foot upon soil, while the thin growth of grass and thorny scrub on the levels and lower hill slopes is for nine months of the year burned gray as ashes and brittle as straw by the fierce equatorial sun blazing twelve hours a day out of a cloudless sky, and making the volcanic rubble so hot one can hardly hold a hand on it for a second. Indeed, the route from Ngong to Magadi is only possible after the season of the big rains of the early spring months or after occasional heavy intermittent showers, when, at four points on the way, natural tanks worn by the brief torrential downpours in the iron-hard volcanic rock are filled and afford a supply of fairly pure water until evaporation, occasional soda porters, and the nomadic Masai herdsmen and their flocks have exhausted it.

Hidden in rocky, trackless gorges or on the very edge of lofty escarpments, the position of these tanks remains to this day unknown to more than half a dozen white men, but luckily for us, we had with us in Outram the first white man to find these natural tanks, when, attempting a trek across this country with a section of the AngloGerman Boundary Survey Commission, five years before, he had been forced to find water or perish.

So, doubtful if we should find any water short of the Guaso Nyiro, and taking our chance of a complete wreck of our safari in the next two days, we bore away into the south at dawn of the fifteenth.

Within the first hour and a half we dropped two thousand feet, from 5,400 to 3,400, and it really seemed that with every foot of drop in altitude there was a rise of a degree in temperature.

But in the matter of water we were lucky. Seven miles out we found a tank with just barely enough left to freshen up our porters, mules, and donkeys, and twelve miles farther on, the head of the safari at two o'clock reached the "Big Water Holes," but only after a march across a lava-strewn plain that seemed absolutely molten with heat. There we found an abundance of water in three huge natural tanks forty to fifty feet deep and one hundred feet in diameter, that looked like miniature amphitheatres of some pigmy race, buttressed without with tall basalt columns, terraced within by varying stages of water-level erosion—the level then very low, no more than four feet at the deepest.

Muddy the water was, to be sure, and, worse, thick with the wash of the gulch above it, the higher crevices of the tanks incrusted with dry donkey dung washed down from soda caravan camps, and representing earlier high-water levels; but if not luxury, it meant life to us literally, for not a third of our porters would have reached camp but for the water we were here able to send back to them. And even at that the tough native porters came crawling in with feet, indurated nearly to hoof hardness, blistered, cracked, and bleeding from all-day plodding over the ragged, burning rocks, an utterly wretched, suffering, exhausted lot that made me wish I had never heard of a safari.

But the two old-timers with me took it as a matter of course and ministered as best they could to the real sufferers, and then kept me roaring over their weird prescriptions for the shammers, one of whom was forced to take a strong whiff of an ammonia bottle, while another was given a mixture of pepper, salt, and a spoonful of oil from a sardine tin, and within half an hour each vowed he was cured of all that hurt him, whatever it was.

At sunset the three of us strolled down to the tanks for a bath. Our boys brought us buckets of water, and each selected and retired to a niche in the face of the cliff, which just below the tanks fell away a sheer seventy feet, disrobed, and got busy with his sponge, to the immense entertainment, apparently, of a tribe of blue monkeys that sat on high pinnacles about us, chattering madly over our droll doings.

Obviously another midday journey in the infernal heat would completely cripple half our men, so the morning of the sixteenth we broke camp at 2:30 A. M. and with no better light than a moon well along in its last quarter, marched away through thorn scrub, up and down rocky hills almost impassable in daylight, but safely and truly piloted by the indomitable, never-hesitating Outram. About 4 A. M. we jumped three rhino, that in the dusk loomed up black giants twice their natural vast bulk, but, luckily for our porters, they scampered away, for it was far too dark to see a gunsight.

By 8 A. M. Outram led us up and across a lofty range, whence to the west opened such a magnificent view as I have never before seen of volcanic action on colossal scale. West of us, and as far as eye could reach to north and south, extended a series of six vast lava ridges or terraces, one rising behind the other, with valleys from five to fifteen miles wide between them, terraces approximately level of top, perpendicular of face, with scarce any points of access to their summits, black or dull red of color, the nearest and lowest probably 1,200 feet high, the others ranging to the rear and rising higher and higher, up to probably 3,000 or 4,000 feet. Like gigantic steps they rose to the lofty summit of the great Mau Escarpment, from which they appeared to have been rent away and dropped to lower levels, the intervening valleys representing tremendous sinks of surface caused by some frightful terrestrial convulsion that must have shaken this continent from end to end, and so fractured and crushed the old underlying formations that throughout British and German East Africa living streams and springs do not represent fifteen per cent of the volume of those of like rainfall in other parts of the world of less volcanic disturbance, and so condemned this region to virtually complete aridity.

Shortly thereafter we descended to a broad, grassy plain full of zebra and Granti buck, almost the first game we had seen, by the way, since leaving Nairobi, and Outram led us a mile off our true course, where, hid away beneath a high rocky ridge and immediately on the edge of a lava cliff several hundred feet high, we found several natural rock tanks of sweet rain water the Kikuyu soda porters had not quite emptied. Already, at 9 A. M., the rocks were so hot one could scarcely hold a bare hand on them, and porters and animals were exhausted, so we camped for the day.

Far down beneath us, at the low altitude of 1,980 feet, and at the lower end of the great Rift Valley or basin that stretches hundreds of miles away north into Abyssinia, lay Lakes Magadi and N'garami, pinkish white fields of soda winding away beyond eye, reach toward the southern horizon, and looking like the winding-sheet they have often in the past proved and must many a time again become for unlucky adventurers into this veritable Valley of the Shadow of Death.

At 4 A. M. of the seventeenth we were on the move, descending the escarpment by a semi-perpendicular trail toward the lake. Here a party of three East Indians with a lot of natives and donkeys, soda freighters, tried desperately to pass us, the leaders carrying water vessels. Suspecting they knew the water below to be scant, Outram raced ahead to the tanks a mile short of Lake Magadi, and held them against the Indians until our safari arrived about 7:30; and lucky it was for us he did, for one rock basin of perhaps sixty gallons of fairly clean water and four others of semi-liquid mud represented the total water supply, and the last drop of it was exhausted in watering our men and animals.

The situation was desperate. Ahead of us lay twenty-five more arid miles, utterly waterless, before we could reach the Guaso Nyiro River. Men and animals were exhausted and footsore. Two or three carefully hoarded quarts of water in our canvas bags was all we had left. The men were ugly and wanted to turn back. After a conference, we decided to lie there for the day and attempt to win through by a forced night march.

The forenoon hours were tolerable within the shade of the rocks, but after eleven the ravine became a blazing inferno of heat, dull, breathless, that parched the skin and seemed to dry up the very fountains of life. A tent fly so little stopped the sun rays, one could not sit beneath it without a helmet on, remove the helmet a moment and one's brain felt a-crackle with the heat.

Shortly after eleven things began to happen, first bad, then good. The bad was the next worst thing, after the prevailing drought, that could have struck us. Our nia para (native headman) reported that, under excuse of hunting water up the gorge, thirty-five of our Kikuyu porters had deserted, and were racing up the cliffs towards the tanks we had camped at the night before. At first this seemed nearly our finish, for scattering like quail and climbing cliffs like goats, one might as well try to catch a shadow, while their going meant the loss of over a fourth of our transportation. However, when we came to figure that over seven hundred pounds of our supplies were already consumed, and when we found that our other porters remained stanch, we realized that by packing our seven saddle-mules we could take care of the excess loads our remaining porters could not carry.

Then a corking bit of good luck befell us. One of ourloyal porters found, a mile away, a fine tank previously unknown to Outram, that furnished sufficient water to give all our men and animals an afternoon drink and perhaps ten or twelve quarts besides for our twenty-five-mile march, meagre enough for forty-five men, but still far better than none.

So at 5 P. M. we loaded the donkeys and Outram and I led out across the lake, Judd following on the rear of the porters.

Crunching over wide pinkish white desiccated areas, slipping about in ashen gray slime, wading shallow channels, a mile and a half brought us across the lake and to the foot of a steep gorge that led to the top of the next escarpment. South or west of Magadi no paths exist but the game trails, so Outram led on and I remained till Judd arrived, just before dark, and then pushed on ahead to try to connect gaps in the straggling line of porters and prevent their straying and getting lost.

Stumbling over grass-hid rocks and through belts of thorn thickets, keeping in touch with the fore and aft sections of the moving column only by constant calling back and forth, it was desperately hard going. Once for an hour Judd lost connection with our advance section, and I sat alone on a hilltop, shouting vainly for him, until I had lost all touch with the section ahead of me. At last, however, by rifle fire we signalled each other, and his tired and crippled men slowly crept up and joined me, and we stumbled ahead as near the course as we could guess, until finally a swinging lantern signalled us to the camp Outram had chosen, and glad we were to reach him about 10 P. M.

No tents were pitched or beds made, but down we dropped among the luggage and slept till the moon rose at 2 A. M. of the eighteenth, when loads were again resumed and the march continued.

Outram's work that night was the most remarkable piece of night travel I have ever known. Travelling by the stars, in a country where we were seldom able to keep a straight course for a quarter of a mile, turning sharply to right and left, on long detours to keep to ground that would not pitch us over a cliff or bump us into an insurmountable escarpment, the quarter-moon overcast most of the time, the ground covered thick with loose volcanic stones and often by solid walls of thorny scrub we had to push through or wind around,— he brought us just at dawn to the mouth of the one narrow gorge in fifty miles that enables ascent to the next escarpment! It was astounding.

Then came again the infernal sun, and men and animals began to weaken. The footing was frightful, no footing, in fact, just slipping, wrenching, spraining over loose ragged rock masses, until about 9 A. M. we sighted far below us, in one of the deep valleys of the interescarpment region, the line of tall green timber that marked the course of the Guaso Nyiro, and then began descent over smoother country.

But the last five miles were terrible, three across a level plain through grass shoulder-high and dry as tinder, and two through dense thorn thickets that made slow winding going, and yet offered little shelter from the scorching sun. The lead of our column reached this plain in fair form, but full a third of them would never have won through had not Outram and I hurried to the river with the ten strongest lead porters and sent water back to the stragglers.

We reached the Guaso Nyiro at 11 A. M., Judd and about half the porters got in about 1 P. M., and ten more straggled in during the afternoon; but it was midforenoon of the next day before the remaining fifteen found strength to push in across the plain with their loads, a haggard, footsore lot that needed a day's rest, heavy sleep alternating with long sousings in the river, before we were able to resume our march.

The camp was ideal. Superb big thorn and ficus trees, vine-clad, alive with monkeys and bright-hued, sweet-voiced birds, a swift-flowing fifty-foot stream of pure water teeming with fish (kumbari), and game everywhere about us, so thick that all through the valley and at convenient stream approaches, paths wide as wagon tracks were worn deep into the soil, giraffe, Granti, gerenuk, oryx, lesser Kudu, rhino and buffalo, guineafowl, pau, spur-fowl, and partridge.

In less than an hour the three of us caught forty-five fish, one-half to one-and-a-half pounders, while the boys caught them by scores. That night we feasted on kumbari à la Regal, that Frederick's sole à la cardinal could not beat, and on roast guinea-fowl.

II. OLD JUNGLE WARRIORS AT BAY

MOVED out well beyond the game reserve to the west of the Guaso Nyiro, the three of us were out before dawn of the nineteenth after rhino or buffalo. Within twenty yards of my tent we found where a rhino had passed in the night, and lucky it was he had not winded us. Only two months before, and at the same place, Outram's camp was charged at night by a rhino that actually trampled over one side of the blankets in which his mate, Robinson, was sleeping. All about us in the earlier morning hours buffalo had trailed in to and out from water, but we did not see one; all had trekked back into the thickest jungle, and were comfortably sleeping off their night's jag of food and water.

All sorts of other game we saw by hundreds, but at nothing did we shoot until, about 8 A. M., the sun became unbearable and we decided to return to camp. Then I stalked and was lucky enough to kill a bull giraffe that measured fourteen feet, eight inches, from hoof to horn end, and fifteen feet, nine inches, from tip of nose to tip of tail, a bull I later learned from R. J. Cunninghame to be a true "Kilimanjaro giraffe" (Giraffa camelopardalis tippelskirchi), a species of which no specimen then existed in the United States. Ordinarily I should never have thought of killing a giraffe, for they are wholly harmless, but our boys' feet were in such bad shape that marching unshod must remain impossible for some days, and the giraffe's three-quarter-inch hide makes the best sandals they can get. However, giraffes are so wary, their colors when in timber blend so perfectly with prevailing hues, their long necks are such convenient lookout towers for their high-perched heads, that stalking them successfully is so difficult that, as a rule, any sportsman who gets one has a handsome run for his money.

My bull proved no exception. We first sighted him, with two cows, at a distance of about four hundred yards, and in an open clearing where effort for nearer approach was useless. My first shot, with a .405 Winchester, broke his left hip and ranged forward, and then the three were off at the rolling, side-wheel, drunken-looking gait of their kind. But before they disappeared into the bush I put two more shots into him and Judd one.

Then we raced across the thicket and took up his spoor. And a rare chase he led us, through thickets one would never venture into in cold blood, for fear of face-to-face encounter with and certain charge by rhino or buffalo, bush so thick we often could not see the length of a gun barrel on any side of us. Once, on our right and not ten feet from us, we heard the whistle of startled buffalo and threw up our rifles for snapshots. But instantly brush began to crash and hoofs to thunder over the rocky ground, fortunately at right angles to our course. Had they come our way, we were so tightly shut in by thick bush that nothing could have saved one or other of us from a collision that would make butting into a freight train feel like a gentle bump. How many there were we never knew, indeed, neither of us had even a glimpse of one of them.

Within a few hundred yards the spoor became difficult to follow, for it by turns followed or crossed scores of other giraffe tracks, but what with occasional drops of blood upon the ground or smears upon grass or bush, we managed to stick to him.

Finally, after two miles at killing pace, streaming with sweat and racing a foot ahead of my mates, not because I was faster, but by their courtesy, I sighted him through a thicket just as he started off from a brief rest, and gave him two more shots before he again got out of sight. But, blowing like a finisher in the Marathon, I placed the shots badly, and it was not until yet another two miles had been covered at heart-breaking gait that I again got him in range and brought him toppling down with a shoulder-shot through the heart. His mates we never saw again after their first disappearance.

The hoofs, tail, skull, and head, and a few feet of the neck skin, were the only trophies I could manage to save, for even had the boys not needed the hide for sandals I could not have packed its tremendous weight.

Leaving a boy to guard the carcass from the marabout storks, that in a short time would have left nothing but clean-picked bones, we hurried back to camp and sent the boys out, and a happy lot they soon returned, loaded with meat and hide with which their stomachs and feet were soon stoutly reinforced.

The twenty-first of December we moved camp eleven miles south, parallel to the course of the Guaso Nyiro, to camp on the N'gari Kiti (clear water) River, traversing a wide plain level as a floor, the last third of the journey across alkali-incrusted, ashen-gray stretches in which our mules sank to the fetlocks.

The N'gari Kiti is a roaring, rollicking, bold stream, plunging down from a source near the crest of the Mau; but four or five miles after leaving the south shoulder of N'guraman Mountain on a brave dash for union with its elder sister river, the Guaso Nyiro, it falls a pathetic victim of its venturesome spirit, drunk dry by the thirsty plain and then spewed up a mile farther down in the form of a swamp that harbors every deadly thing, winged, reptilian, quadruped, that Central Africa produces, fever-charged mosquitoes, python, rhino, buffalo, leopard, lion. Outside of it few of its denizens are ever seen in daylight.

The last mile of approach to the N'gari Kiti is through a jungle absolutely impassable to man, without use of bush knives, except along game trails, but the bush is cut in all directions by the trails of rhino, buffalo, and giraffe, and, literally, almost wherever one can see the ground there are the footprints of scores or hundreds of the Big Ones. But the droll thing is that while these big fellows have deep-cut paths along which they easily race beneath low-arching, heavy-branched thorn and other scrub, nevertheless a man can only follow them crouched or on hands and knees half the time, and even so he generally finishes with arms and ears torn and bleeding.

This was the first really gay night about any of our eight camp fires. The day's march had not been hard, the porters were at last well shod, a clear, cool stream rippled merrily by, and the camp was full of meat. Donkeys and mules were bomaed in a thorn zareba in the centre of the camp, for the big bad ones were so thick about us it was more than an even chance something would charge through us, and the stampede of one's animals so caused is even more troublesome than the actual kills, our three tents were pitched on three sides of the boma, and the porters' seven fires were ranged in an outer circle about ours.

Then while we ourselves dined luxuriously on giraffe tail soup and a ragout of giraffe tongue with tinned tomatoes and potatoes that would make a gourmet sniff at even green turtle soup, all our men were alternately minding huge chunks of meat and fish roasting on sticks at their fires, gorging themselves, singing and dancing, cutting long strips of zebra meat for smoking and curing on great square platforms of green boughs built for the purpose over each fire, and calling the Kikuyu all sorts of terrible pagan names for their stupidity in deserting at the very door to this land of plenty.

And while we three white men of a Christian race stuffed ourselves without preliminary or postprandial grace, and our shenzi porters gracelessly gorged themselves like beasts, scarce thirty feet from our table stood the noble form of old Regal and the spare, ascetic-faced Awala, musically intoning their evening prayer to Allah, oblivious to all about as if alone in a monastic cell. It was a majestic rebuke to us, a weird mystery to the shenzi, whose voices were always lowered when the Somalis began to pray, and who sat contemplating them in wideeyed wonder to the end of each prayer, awed, almost silent, as were we ourselves silent out of sheer respect for a religion that can give men such perfect self-control that no danger daunts them and no hardship or suffering wrings from them a plaint.

Five times a day do they so pray, at dawn, at high noon, at four, at sunset, and before retiring, nor can anything interfere to delay these prayers, not even hungry masters. And before addressing Allah, mouth, face, and hands are carefully washed, the best turban wound about the head, the freshest garments donned, the feet bared; then, with a glance at the sun, if by day, or at the stars, if by night, to get their compass bearings, they spread their rugs, face toward Mecca, and begin a low droning chant that at a little distance might easily be mistaken for a well-intoned litany.

If I could find it in my heart to envy good old Regal anything, and he is himself, in himself, a lot of things I should like to be, it would be that profound faith in the efficacy of his prayers which has served to endow a man born a wild Somali warrior nomad and now for years a cook, with the dignity of a cardinal and virtues that would put no end of so-called "good men" to shame. In my judgment, all lucky enough to reach the real heaven of really good men, no matter what their faith, will find there Regal Wassama.

The night passed without incident, save that toward morning lions were heard grunting some distance away.

By dawn of the twenty-second, as soon as we were able to see our gunsights, we had finished our coffee, bread, and bacon and were out with our rifles; for here was a rarely good chance of record trophies, here where the game is as undisturbed by hunters, bar the hidden pitfalls and the silent spear and poisoned arrow thrusts of the Wanderobo, as it was in the beginning of time, here where trophy hunters had never come before.

It was an ideal morning, for heavy rain had fallen throughout the night, making easy the spooring of fresh tracks and softening dry grass and twigs until one's footsteps were noiseless.

From the moment we left camp our advance was slow and cautious-on foot, behind us, the gun bearers with our spare rifles, behind them the syces leading our mules — on winding game paths so low we had to crouch most of the time, where each turn of a bush might bring one face to face at arm's length with any old jungle warrior that would carry in his system as much of one's lead-unless it was particularly well placed could comfortably pack in a bandolier.

We moved down river towards the swamp and out toward the wide alkali plain that extends south from the swamp four miles to Lake Natron.

And it was a bit odd, our so going out in such infernal country, for only the day before each of us had vowed that any fool who liked, could go after rhino and buffalo in the thorn jungle of the river and the tall grass and vine tangle of the swamp, but he would have none of it; and now there were we three plunged into it, as if just a matter of course, prey each to the lure of the chase!

While the ground was covered with footprints made the day before, apparently everything had gone out to the open to feed or retired to the more secluded recesses of the swamp, for it was not until we reached the edge of the plain just at the upper end of the swamp that we found the first spoor made since the rain had stopped.

But it was spoor worth while, a giant rhino whose footprints in the soft ground were a full twelve inches in diameter. Evidently he had been out for a night's ramble and feed in the plain, and had probably entered the swamp no more than half an hour ahead of us.

Leaving mules and syces outside, we at once started into the swamp on his spoor, easy to follow as a highway, Outram in the lead, I next, and then Judd.

Sometimes the rhino followed paths, sometimes crushed haphazard through the tangle, just as the fancy struck him. Luckily the wind was quartering, across the general line of his advance.

We were not hurrying any. In fact, our pace would have made a passing funeral look like a Derby finish. Feet fell silent as the very dew itself. The least unusual sound reaching him meant either our losing him or his charging us, about an even-money bet which.

It is droll, but in this sort of stalking big game I always find myself having to fight a persistent inclination to hold the breath to listen, one seems to hear better when not breathing, which, if not resisted, keeps me as hopelessly blown and unsteady for close shooting as if I had just finished a hundred-yard dash, until I have now long made it a practice, under such conditions, to keep saying or thinking to myself, "Breathe deep and slow!" Keep the lungs full and the hand is pretty sure to stay steady.

I don't know just what time we entered the swamp, but I should think it was within fifteen minutes of our entry that about fifteen yards ahead of us we heard the crunch of huge jaws and a mighty sigh of surfeit. The old giant had apparently found shade to his liking and was meditating a nap. Plainly he was unwarned of our presence. Sound told us he stood beneath a large, wide-spreading tree whose drooping branches met the thick mass of tall grass and bush that lay between us and completely hid him from our sight. After perhaps four or five minutes' waiting, nerves tense and every sense alert, we thought we heard movement to his left and Judd turned to me, bronze cheeks white as paper, but square jaws set and eyes blazing battle, and whispered, "I believe there are two or three with him, if so, it's apt to be hell here."

And then a moment later another whisper came from Judd, "I think I can see his rump; shall I stir him up a bit?" and no more had I nodded assent before the roar of his heavy .450 cordite rifle was followed with shrill squeals of rage and pain, twigs cracked, great limbs snapped as the monster whirled toward the sound coincident with his injury, plainly swinging for a charge.

Then I caught a glimpse of his neck, just back of the ears, and sent two .405 hard-nose Winchesters into it, and, an instant later, sighting the upper half of the head, gave him a third. At this third shot he swayed about in the bush for a few seconds and then crashed to the ground. While I was shooting, Outram fired once with his .303.

All was now still beneath the tree, and after a few seconds we started clambering in to him, but, just as the vast carcass came in view, he tried to rise, and Judd gave him another .450.

But his effort to rise proved, when we got to him, to be only the death throe. Judd's first shot had hit him in the left hip and probably angled through the kidneys; his last had landed far back in the neck and below the spine. Of my two first shots one was four inches behind the ears, over and probably reaching the spine, the second two inches back of and an inch below the first, while my third had landed full in the curve of the head between eye and ears, about three inches below the left ear and a inch to the left of the centre of the "forehead." Outram's .303 was a few inches lower in the head, crumpled up in the bone.

It was my third shot that killed him, and at the same time exploded a fallacy I have read, to the best of my recollection, in every book I have ever perused on rhino shooting, viz., that it is folly to try to kill or even stop a rhino with a frontal head shot,—that no rifle ball will penetrate its massive frontal bone structure. For when we came to remove the scalp and chop away the horns, we found my .405 had driven through the frontal bone and smashed the inner skull structure to fragments.

And it was a prize I had! Not a "record," but close to it, a splendid old bull close to 3,000 pounds in weight, with an absolutely perfect front horn of graceful shape, 23 inches long and 24 inches in circumference at the base, while the back horn was 10 inches long and 24 inches at the base. His length from tip to tip was 12 feet, 7 inches, his height at withers, 5 feet, 9 inches, while the circumference of his foot was 30 inches. He was killed at 7:15 A. M., little more than two hours after leaving camp. To cut away his mask and horns, remove the hoofs, and cut strips from his full inch-thick hide for kibokos (whips) and canes, took us about two and one-half hours.

The foregoing horn measurements were made the night the rhino was killed. Thoroughly dried, the front horn measured 22 inches on the outer curve and 22 inches in base circumference, in length and 23 inches in base. Rowland Ward records only one black rhino horn above records 24 ½ inches in base (and that one 24 inches) and only seven better than 22 inches, and no rear horn above 23 ½ inches in base and only two above 22 ½ inches, thus placing my N'gari Kiti giant high among the top-notchers.

As soon as the trophies were secured and started for camp we clambered out of the swamp, and then ambled away south to the much larger swamp lying between Shombol Mountain and Lake Natron, wherein the Guaso Nyiro River finishes its career. There, Outram told us, were buffalo in hundreds. A high ridge of dry ground near the centre would, if we could reach it, command a wide view down into the long grass where by day the buffalo were browsing or asleep. To negotiate the four miles of intervening alkali plain, floundering through deep pools made by the previous night's rain, and laboring through mud into which our mules sank half-way to their knees, took more than two hours.

To the east of us the majestically buttressed summit of Shombol, and to the west the lofty uplift of the southern extremity of the Mau Escarpment, stood as a giant gateway, a worthy southern entrance, about five miles wide, to the great Rift Valley, there immediately guarded, as by a colossal fosse, by Lake Natron. This winding along the foot of the Mau in its northern reaches, bends east to and past the southern flanks of Shombol, perpetually sentinelled by Sonya's beautiful volcanic cone rising, midway of the gateway but miles to the south of it, to a height, I should think, of at least 9,000 feet.

As we neared the swamp, scores of acres of slightly raised and dry ground were found to be covered thick with buffalo "sign," trampled and littered like a farm barnyard. But try as we would, never a black back could we see. So presently we started for a try to reach the tall ridge in its midst that lay about three-quarters of a mile from where we struck the swamp.

Here there was no bush, only tall swamp grass and rushes, eight to fourteen feet high, and along the deeper water channels a still higher and thicker growth of cattails. For a few hundred yards the ground was boggy, but not very bad, nor were the channels very deep.

When in about a thousand yards we heard the shrill whistle of a buffalo a short distance ahead of us, but at first could not see him. Presently, however, as he crashed away past us, Judd caught a glimpse of him and tried a snapshot, but apparently missed.

Then we chugged on through the marsh, a short distance farther finding ourselves compelled to dismount and wade, and then bumping into a broad, sluggish, onehundred-foot channel that fell away to a depth nearly over one's head at the very edge and looked too ominous of crocodiles to be attractive. So we back-trekked and circled the north end of the swamp and finally found a place where we could flounder through the channel without quite swimming our mules. Then we prospected along its western edge without result, until one of our boys volunteered to try a crossing, won through, and poked about for nearly two hours, finally returning with advice of plenty of buffalo a half-mile away but a lot of hopelessly bad going intervening.

While the boy was gone, Outram whipped out a hook and line, found a boy who was treasuring a titbit of the rhino, and, commandeering it for bait, in a short time landed about twenty pounds of fine kumbari, ranging from one to three pounds in weight.

The boy back and the fish wrapped in green grass and stowed in our saddle pockets, about 2 P. M. we started for camp, on a wide circle to the west in hope of getting quicker out of the soft alkali plain to hard ground. In an altitude here below 2,000 feet, the heat on the open plain was terrific. Great herds of Wildebeeste to the west of us in the mirage looked big as elephants, while in the shimmering heat waves Natron itself looked more like a mirage than real water.

After about two miles we reached slightly higher ground and better footing, along which we proceeded for another half-hour without incident. It was then about 3:30 P. M. and we had come near to the southwest corner of the N'gari Kiti swamp.

Tired with ten hours' constant going afoot and a-mule, and drowsy with the heat, for some time I had been dozing comfortably in the saddle, unmindful of game of any sort, when suddenly I was roused by a low whistle from Judd, to find him gazing, face muscles tense, into the tall grass on my left. It needed only a glance to see that there before us, a scant one hundred and forty yards away, stood at last the royal quarry we had been seeking since morning, two splendid big buffalo bulls, their noses up, pointed, sniffing to precisely locate a scented enemy, their great heads and thick horns obscuring even their massive shoulders!

Instantly we bounced off the mules, and scarcely were our feet on the ground before here they charged, straight at us.

All three of us opened fire together, but despite the rain of lead, on they came without swerving until, at about thirty yards, they turned to our left, toward Lake Natron, for a few jumps, when the old fellow again started to whirl upon us, but as he turned, Judd gave him a .450 in the mid ribs that made him change his mind.

Within fifty yards of their first turn they disappeared over a low ridge and we raced after them. When we reached the top of the ridge, there below us, perhaps twenty yards away, the two grim old warriors stood at bay, badly wounded. But they were still full of fight, facing us, and the moment we appeared again they started a charge, but before they had made half a dozen jumps, Judd downed the young bull with a .450 in the shoulder and I the old bull with a .405 in the centre of the chest. And there, down and practically out as they seemed, they still showed so much fight on nearer approach that Judd advised, for safety, giving each a careful finishing shot, which we did.

One of my .405's was found crumpled up inside the skull of the younger bull, my first shot at him, and that it had not bowled him over at once was remarkable, while my first on the old fellow had caught him aft of the shoulder and ranged back through the lung. Judd's first had hit the young one in the hip. The old one also proved the tremendous toughness of their fibre, for Judd's .450, which had entered the mid ribs and turned his second charge, protruded but did not puncture the skin on the opposite side, we cut it out and I have it, almost unblunted, after traversing a great seventeenhundred-pound carcass, that even a .450

cordite cartridge could not drive a hard-nose ball clean through. Outram had landed in the pair three .303's, but they were only flea bites to these giants.

The two bulls fell and lay dead within precisely nine feet of each other, both, as seen in the photograph, falling headed the same way, toward their enemy.

They were splendid specimens of two types of bull, one absolutely in his prime, perhaps seven or eight years old, with perfect, symmetrical, unbroken horns, and the other a hoary old warrior, goodness only knows how old, grizzled, and with both horns short by five to six inches of their original length, broken and worn blunt and smooth in battles unnumbered with the doughtiest of his race.

The horns of the younger bull measured 41 inches on their widest spread and 27 inches from tip to tip, while the breadth of the boss was 15 inches.

The old bull measured 39 inches from tip to tip and 42 inches on the widest horn spread, with a 12-inch boss. They showed hard use and long, honorable service, did these old, worn Nature's weapons, smooth and polished like ebony from tip to base by mighty fence, wrench, and tussle with the best metal of their kind, whereas half the length of the younger bull's horns were rough and corrugated, their fine, sharp points intact.

But the old bull brought me another trophy rarer and that I prize even more than his splendid mask and horns. While the men were working on the head, Judd noticed a small black shaft about the diameter of a small slate-pencil standing perpendicularly out of his right loin, near the spine and six inches in front of the hip. Asking the boys what it was, one answered, with a laugh, "Other hunters have been out long before you, Bwana, but their resas (cartridge) was not as good as yours; that is a Wanderobo poisoned arrow." And so indeed it proved when, after five minutes' cutting and tugging, the arrow head was withdrawn from the bull's tough back muscles.

It was a remarkable and probably unparalleled example of the great power of the Wanderobo bow. From its sharply barbed point to its base, the arrow head was 5 inches long, and 4 inches of its length had been driven through the half-inch hide and on into the heavy muscles of the loin!

Since it stood perpendicularly in the loin, it must have been shot into the bull while he was passing beneath a tree, or when he was drinking directly below some overhanging bank, both methods of attack favorites of the light-armed Wanderobo.

While the Wanderobo poison is deadly to beasts within five to twenty minutes when fresh, applied to arrow heads in this dry climate it cakes to the hardness of enamel in a few weeks and becomes harmless.

Luckily for the old bull, it was evidently such an old disenvenomed arrow that had perhaps by mistake or as the last in the quiver, been driven into him. The poison is made from the bark of a bush much like a laurel, which is boiled down and down until it becomes a thick, gummy, concentrated extract. So prepared, it is thickly smeared over the barbed head and three or four inches of the arrow's shank or shaft. How the plant is known botanically, or whether it is known at all, I am unaware, but it bears a purple fruit, quite the shape and about the size of a small olive, which I understand is not itself poisonous.

So armed, the Wanderobo tackle and kill anything, from the tiniest buck up to elephant, their favorite tactics a silent shot from a brush shelter built within five to ten yards of a much-used watering place. Such primitive-shooting covers one sees daily above springs and along streams in mountains and plains of the Wanderobo country.

And precisely as the Wanderobo is an artful economist of energy in making his kills, so also is he a cunning laborsaver in dealing with the meat he takes; for directly a beast is so struck, off goes a runner to whatever near-by forest glade or bush recess is for the moment harboring his nomadic, houseless family and kin, and up they come on a run, young and old, like ravening wolves, and there stop until no scrap is left that even a vulture would covet, packing comfortably away in their stomachs what a white man would first laboriously carry somewhere on his back before getting the good of a bite of.

And this particular arrow head the old bull carried would plainly have gone much deeper had it not struck a rib, for as found the thin head was bent almost to right angles with its shank by contact with bone!

That it was a very old wound was obvious, for not only was it entirely healed, bar local irritation about the head, but in places where the hard black enamel-like coating of the poison was worn away, the shank was much rusted.

While at the time I realized I had a superb trophy in the head of the younger bull and a fine one in the older bull, I never dreamed I was crowding records until, upon my return to Juja, I got hold of the fifth edition of Rowland Ward's "Records of Big Game," a short perusal of which showed that of all the known best specimens of Cape buffalo ever shot, over their entire range past and present, from the Cape to Somaliland, very few have exceeded 11 inches in breadth of boss and none have equalled the 15 inches of my younger bull, excepting a head shot by F. C. Selous, whose measurements were 41 inches on widest spread of horns, 24 inches from tip to tip of horns, and 16 inches in measurement across face of boss, against my 41 ½, 27 ½ , and 15 ½ inches for the same measurements, thus giving my fellow second place in this particular, while only seven bulls reported have equalled the 12-inch boss of my older bull. This record pertains only to the big Cape buffalo proper; as for the smaller type of Abyssinian, while only one boss is returned of more than 10 inches, nevertheless one splendid fellow killed by Mr. R. A. Colvin had the breadth of 30 inches, obviously a magnificent freak.

It was 7 P. M. when we reached camp that night with our buffalo trophies, for we were forced to do an extra two miles by losing our way in the dense thorn jungle of the N'gari Kiti valley, in fact, we only regained camp at all by exchanging rifle-shot signals. And while most happy, a more tired and hungry trio would be hard to find, for we had been out fourteen hours in the blistering sun on scant water rations and without a morsel of food since our daylight breakfast. However, a wash, a tot of whiskey, a delicious giraffe tail soup, boiled buffalo tongue, and beans done as your Boston aunt used to cook them, made us fit for a pipe each, and then we tumbled into our blankets and a sleep that needed a deal of waking at four the next morning.

III. KUDU, COBRA, WILD DOG, AND ELAND

FORCED to remain in our N'gari Kiti camp the twenty-third, to clean, cure, and dry the skins and heads, I started out at dawn after gerenuk or lesser Kudu, both now very rare buck in British East Africa and both, the latter especially, extremely hard to get, always alert and off like the wind at first scent or glimpse of you. Riding up to the crest of high, sandy, rocky ridges, densely covered with thorn and sanseviera, the wild fibre plant, the sort of country these bucks love, lying between N'guraman and the Mau, Outram and I dismounted and for five hours slipped along afoot, closely scanning every opening about us with our glasses.

Everywhere we went the ground was covered with fresh tracks of buck of all sorts, from little dik-dik up to giant eland, and much giraffe and rhino and some buffalo sign, and yet throughout the first five hours' tramp we saw no animals save three herds of beautiful impala, which we carefully avoided disturbing, and a few tribes of tiny monkeys and giant apes, which barked and chattered their surprise and then swung away through the treetops.

Finally, about half-past ten, our quest was rewarded. Suddenly out of his concealment behind a mimosa bush sprang a Kudu bull, about one hundred and fifty yards dead ahead of us, flashed like a meteor across a narrow open glade, seen by me for no more than two seconds, and then, disappearing on our right, headed past us and back along the slope of the ridge we were following.

With little hope of again seeing him, but taking the chance, I sprinted my best about one hundred yards to the next opening in the bush, along the course he was taking, and got there just in time to see him spring out of the tangle into an opening in a field of sanseviera and stop for an instant, head turned and listening, one hundred and fifty yards below me. Knowing I had not a moment to spare, I fired the moment I caught my bead on him, and while I plainly heard the ball hit him heavily, away he bounded, as strong apparently as when I first sighted him.

Running down to take up his spoor, however, I had not gone ten feet before the heavily blood-reddened sanseviera leaves told me I had him. When I reached him he was stone dead, shot through the upper third of the heart by a .35 Mauser soft nose which had passed on clear through and out of him, and yet he had made the marvellous run of one hundred and eighty yards before falling!

His horns were a beautiful pair measuring 31 inches on the outside curve and 15 inches from tip to tip, their perpendicular height being 24 inches, a rare prize in these days when very few African sportsmen's bags include lesser Kudu of any sort.

That night we dined on buffalo tail soup, the liquid thick and strong as beef tea, the meat deliciously sweet and tender, far better flavored than even giraffe tail, and on fried kumbari, followed by roast koorhaan, a bird about the size of and as tender and well flavored as a spring turkey.

The twenty-fourth we moved ten miles up the steeply rising valley of the N'gari Kiti to a camp a thousand feet higher (viz., at 3,000 feet) on a small tributary, the N'gari Nyiro, our first stage on the ascent of the Mau. At this camp we enjoyed a delightfully cool temperature, and it was indeed a great relief from our fortnight in the hot lowlands, where, bar our sleeping hours, we were constantly streaming with sweat. Near the head of this valley dwells a small tribe of Loita Masai, who disown allegiance to Lenani, and who, besides the care of their flocks and herds, and contrary to Masai tradition and habits, till the soil and eat its produce.

Here, high up on the foothills of the Mau, we spent our Christmas Eve, rather a silent one, for me, I know, a very sad one, each filled with longings for those he loved best.

Christmas Day we sent our donkey loads and twenty porters on to the summit, under our headman, ourselves remaining in camp to finish curing our trophies, for heavy rain had fallen the night before and their drying was unfinished, for me a lazy day, the first real rest since the start, spent alternately making diary notes, dozing, and reading the latest New York Heralds (my latest!), of dates from November 1 to 8, which till then I had not had time to open, papers with the first news I had read, other than a three-line Reuter despatch, of the happy results of our elections, and stating that President Roosevelt had delayed his sailing date for Mombasa until March 24. That would bring him here the end of April, still really a month too early, for the big rains usually do not stop before the end of May.

The morning of the twenty-sixth we were off at daylight for the ascent of the Mau, over Outram Pass, the only accessible point known for nearly a hundred miles north of the border. The buttressing foothills and higher slopes of the range that seem to offer easy access to the summit prove on trial only comparatively isolated uplifts, either hopelessly precipitous on the far side or leading to downright impassable cliffs above. While guide to the Imperial Boundary Survey four years before Outram discovered this pass, and there are now in the country only two men besides himself who know it.

By desperate hard work, drenched within by perspiration and without by the sopping wet grass and foliage, we reached the summit at 6,500 feet, being an ascent from our camp of 3,500 feet in three hours. Threefourths of the way the thorn scrub on the mountain side was so dense that progress was only possible afoot up winding rhino trails so steep and shut in by creepers, one could not ride. Then we got up out of the jungle, into a more open, big-timber country of less steep slope, where occasionally we could for a few hundred yards rest our tired legs and bursting lungs. Just here we lost our first donkey, of characteristic tsetse fly sickness, and lucky we were it was so far only one.

Just before arriving at the summit the real key to the pass was reached, a lofty knife-blade ridge scarce eight feet wide, strewn with granite bowlders, which connected the buttress we had ascended with the upper escarpment. On either side this ridge fell away almost perpendicularly for probably 2,500 feet, and along it we rode for the several hundred yards of its length, so fagged we did not mind chances of a mule stumble that might easily toss man and beast over the edge, for often the scattered bowlders compelled riding along its very lip.

Unfortunately, heavy banks of cloud lay 1,500 to 2,000 feet below us on either side, and deprived us of what, on a clear day, must be a most magnificent view to north, south, and east.

The summit reached, we crossed a superb belt of big timber, hardwood trunks five or six feet through, rising sixty to eighty feet straight as a spear shaft and without a limb, and then began a rapid descent through the richest wild grass country I have ever seen, green, sweet, juicy, and such a thick mat one could not walk a halfmile through it without exhaustion. At 5,400 feet we camped on a high bench above the headwaters of the N'gari Kiti, which a few miles away drops to the arid eastern plains through an impassable gorge. We found all too tired to engage in the usual evening shoot.

The twenty-seventh we travelled ten miles west, most of the time within a few thousand yards of the German boundary, over the beautifully grassed, timbered, and watered inter-range region of the Mau, much of it hard going but nothing like the previous day's cruelty. Besides, the air was exquisite, keen and bracing to a degree that, for the first day since our start, made men and animals step out as if they were really alive. We camped early, at 6,100 feet, on a boisterous little mountain stream to hunt eland, the biggest and finest of the antelope family, the larger bulls weighing up to fifteen hundred, now extinct or rare in most parts. Here they are thick, to judge by the trails. But as usual they are hard to see when you want them, especially since they stick pretty close in thorn scrub. We also hoped to bag here in the tall timber of the higher ridges our legal quota of colobus monkeys, the big long-furred black and white chaps, most prized, by sportsmen, of all the monkey tribe. It was a fine shooting country, thick belts of heavy forest alternating with wide, open glades and thorny slopes.

Going out afoot at noon with Judd and our gun bearers, within an hour we sighted several eland, some grazing, others dozing among the mimosa, and stalked the big bull of the lot to within an easy two hundred yards. There I fired and hit him behind the shoulder with the .405 so hard he staggered and nearly fell, but knowing their great vitality and taking no chances, Judd and I gave him two more each, when he stumbled behind a thicket. But upon running up, sure we had him, it was only to see his tail wig-wagging us a farewell as he entered heavy timber four hundred yards away. Through long grass and forest, trailing was slow and difficult, but so Awala and I followed him for nearly four hours, when, with night approaching and camp far behind, we had to give him up.

No colobii did we see going out or back, but I shot two birds of most beautiful plumage, both plantain eaters, blue heads shading into green necks, with red wings and long blue tails, a poor apology for what we went after, but still lovely trophies.

The twenty-eighth missed being our red-letter day by several sizes. Always difficult to keep a marching column of porters in close order, in a trackless, rugged mountain country, where the long grass is lined everywhere with the passing of wandering game, the moment any stragglers lose sight of the advance or rear, there is always a chance of their getting lost. Molo, the burly Kavirondo table boy, had been intrusted with a valuable twelve-bore Purdy and the water bottles, and ordered to stay in reach of my mule's tail. But by mid-forenoon I missed him and halted the advance. A scant hour before I had killed two kongoni for the porters, and he was then present. But when first the quick-marching porters and then the slow-moving donkeys came in, neither porters nor donkey boys remembered seeing him since the last kill. So there was nothing for it but to off-saddle and stop, and send boys out with guns and whistles to try to signal him.

Finally, after four hours, he was brought in, worn out and fagged from a five-mile detour south of our course into German East Africa, all come of sheer stupidity, careless indifference to his morning orders, and loss of touch with the column.

Our luncheon was over and we were ready to resume the march, so immediately he appeared I ordered him stripped of the cartridge bag and gun, his insignia as a tent boy, assigned him the heaviest load in the lot, and told him if he was not in the night camp with the first ten porters he would carry two sixty-pound loads the next day. The result was amusing, for throughout a particularly hard afternoon's march, heavily burdened as he was, he was never one hundred feet behind my mule. But he got in surly and ugly, his great underlip pendent somewhere in the vicinity of his knees.

Indeed, the fact is after all that the African black is nothing but a grown-up child, on whom no punishment short of a corporal drubbing counts. The load penalty I had decreed only left him surly; but when, later, Judd ordered him out with others to fetch firewood and he sat tight by his fire and returned a surly stare, and Judd hurled at him a heavy knobkerrie that landed him a hard smash on the shins, out he flew and did the work of three men, cheerfully singing at his task.

Nor was Molo's getting lost our only mishap, for at 4 P. M. we awakened to the fact that all the donkeys and over half the porters had lost touch with the advance and strayed in the jungle. And by every ill token the lot lost had all our tents, blankets, and the cook's mess kit.

We were then on the higher slopes of Lengijabi Mountain, at a height of 6,800 feet, and the keen evening chill of the high plateau had already driven us into our coats. We built big signal fires of grass and green leaves that sent up tall smoke columns, and searched with our glasses, the lower country we had crossed, but all to no purpose, until, about an hour before sunset, we sighted them crossing a bit of open slope at least five miles away, headed due north instead of west! So plainly there was nothing to do but camp where we were, on a rocky slope steep as a roof and at least four hundred feet above the nearest water, rain pools in the canyon below.

Of course a runner was sent after the stragglers, and about 9 P. M. a few lead porters got in with a part of the mess kit and we had a bit of supper, most conveniently, for no more were we laid down, somewhat sheltered in wind-breaking nooks of the rocks, and wrapped in nothing but our raincoats, before a pelting cold rain came on. It drove us into a huddle about the camp fire for the rest of the night, and caused heavy drafts on our philosophy to concede, what was really the fact, that the boys were little to be blamed for going astray in the frightful tangle of deep gulches and thorn and cactus thicket our afternoon's course had traversed.

However, by sun-up the last of the strayed porters climbed into camp, for they had reached the bottom of the canyon beneath us early in the morning but had found ascent in the dark impossible.

Here, again, we were upon a trek practically impassable to any white man but Outram, for from Duck Creek, our night camp of the twenty-ninth, to the Kibaibai Hills and Springs, a distance of fifty-five miles, there are no streams or springs, not a drop of water except natural rain tanks he found while leading the advance of the Boundary Survey. But, mystery to me though it was, he was able to find them again, and straight to each he marched, unerring, notwithstanding none lay near by any prominent landmark, now plunging down to the bottom of a deep gulch covered with scrub we had to crawl through, again winding up a dry, rocky gorge like as two peas to many others near by, again scrambling to the summit of some lofty crag, undistinguishable by us from its fellows. Only once in the four camps we made on this fifty-five-mile dry belt did Outram fail to score true on the water, and then he fetched it after a two hours' search.

The night of the twenty-ninth, after an easy march over treeless uplands of the eastern slope of the Mau Plateau, we camped about three miles from Mount Ol Albwa, beside one of Outram's clear, cold rain pools and in a thick grove of candelabrum cactus, and took good pains to stoutly boma our mules and donkeys inside a narrow ring formed by our eight tents and camp fires, for three lion were close to our camp the previous night, and thence west they were about every night and might give one a look-in any time. And by eight o'clock we were not sorry we were well bomaed, for two big fellows, big indeed if they were big as their deep voices, were hailing from a distance of a few hundred yards, hailing us with deep guttural grunts which, bar the fierce snarl when attacking from short range, is about the only sound one ever hears from the wild lion. Few men have ever heard him "roar," and only one such case have I heard of where he was not at the time in battle with one of his mates.

For fifteen minutes our serenaders slowly approached us, and then their voices receded; off they were for a prowl in another direction.

Now we were come again into a country alive with game, wooded hills, ravines, and naked plains alike, eland, Wildebeeste, topi, Granti and Thompsoni zebra, buffalo, giraffe, rhino, water buck, all thronged in for fresh range, there made available during the rains, from their dry-season haunts near the springs and small creeks of distant better watered sections of the Mau.

So the next morning I went out with Outram after eland. It was slow, hard work, of necessity afoot, for the eland are few, and since they may be found running with almost any mob of game, every bunch of zebra, Wildebeeste, impala, or other buck one sees, one needs to scan everything carefully with glasses, and then, if no eland are present, slip softly past, without disturbing them, to the next mob.

Shortly after sunrise and when well up on the north slope of Ol Albwa, slipping along through the bush some distance from Outram, seventy-five yards ahead in a little opening I saw a group of, I didn't know what, big black fellows with dull yellow tortoise-like spots, great round ears, upstanding manes, and white-tipped tails, coolly looking me over and snarling in concert. Whatever they were I wanted one of those quadrupedal conundrums, and dropped the biggest I could see, tall as a big setter, with a ball through the shoulder—when off out of sight scampered the eight or ten of his fellows.

When Outram came up and I asked him what it was I had bagged, he replied:

"Wild dog — and you are in luck, for usually when you kill one the pack is on you in a second, and it is up in a tree or down their throats for yours. Why, during the Survey Dr. Chevalier was treed by a pack of about eighty, and notwithstanding he soon killed twenty or thirty, all he had cartridges for, up the tree they held him for five mortal hours."

So clearly I was lucky, for I am none too well built for tree-climbing, and the local variety of thorn tree is amazingly contrived to make desperate tough going for the best climber.

A half-hour later, while crossing a small patch of threefoot grass, out of it a few feet in front of me up stood the wide-hooded, blue-black, hideous head of a seven-foot m'piri or black cobra, poisonous as an adder, an ill-mannered beggar who spits at you and ruins the sight if he hits an eye, so these Africanders say. This chap took a snapshot at me, but if I can't climb trees I am ready to back myself at heavy odds as a snake-dodger. I wanted his skin, but before I could get the shotgun he had slipped into thick bush where none of us cared to follow him.

It was eleven o'clock before we sighted eland, when a herd of eight came over the summit, startled by a shot by Judd on the opposite side of the mountain. We had only an instant's glimpse of them, quite out of safe range, and then they were lost in the bush. But we soon got their trail and for six hours followed it, up and down, through glade and bush, to a three-fourths complete circuit of Ol Albwa's broad flanks. Only once more did we sight them, still out of range.

But while the day yielded nothing tangible but the wild dog and a buck shot for the porters, it was still a day that had one's nerves a-tingle and every sense alert from dawn till dark; for fresh rhino and buffalo sign was everywhere, lion tracks made that same morning were several times encountered on paths we had to follow to hold to our eland spoor, and any turn of a bush might have brought on a scrap that would take quick and straight shooting to win.

The real reason for our stop of a day at Ol Albwa, however, was in order to send back a lot of porters to search for my Kudu head, which had been lost off one of the donkey loads two nights before, when they were astray in the thickets about Lengijabi. And it was delighted I was when, upon reaching camp in the evening, I found the men returned with it. For the Kudu was, so far, my greatest treasure. Any man may have his chance at a rhino or buffalo if he cares to incur the risks of going after them, but few sportsmen have the luck to bag a Kudu.

About Albwa, one of the gulches shows in the wash great quantities of garnets of the sort always found in conjunction with the Kimberley blue clay diamond formation, but we found none of them "in place."

IV. SEEN FROM A RHINO'S BED

THE last day of the old year 1908 we did a hard march of sixteen miles, the first two-thirds over the rolling, billowy, short-grassed Mau Plateau, through almost solid herds of game as ignorant of man, his weapons, and his guile as were the first of their species, game that at first fled madly at sight of us, and then often trotted back, out of sheer curiosity, to near approach. The sight carried me back to our own plains of the early '70's, for in form, in color, and in action, though not in size or in pelt, the Wildebeeste at a few hundred yards so closely resembles the American bison, that any old-timer might easily fancy himself transported back by some happy miracle to the days of his youth and the old buffalo range that now remain no more than a memory to the few still living who once knew them.

During the morning I shot a particularly fine buck, which Judd and Outram agreed was not a true Granti. Unless a Robertsi, it was a hitherto unrecorded species. Smaller of body bulk than the common Granti, its horns had much greater spread and an entirely different curvature. They measured 23 ½ inches in height on the outer curve and 19 inches spread, tip to tip. Clearly the buck was no individual freak, for we saw so many like him that it was perfectly plain he is the characteristic type of southern Mau Granti.

The last third of this day's march was a descent of a thousand feet through a maze of dry gulches and dense thorn scrub that tore everything tearable to tatters, and added a few more gashes to arms and hands that already looked and felt as if they had done active service in a leopard fight.

This night for the first time our hitherto unfaltering guide failed to find readily the water-holes for which he was steering. In fact, for half the afternoon our little column was lost in three separate sections, each from the others, and Outram lost to all of us; and it was not until sunset that, by shooting, yelling, and smoke signalling, Judd and I got the lot once more together, just as Outram stumbled out of the thorns, rent and bleeding by his two hours' prowl through the gulches, with the good news that he had water.

And right where he got the water most others would have sat and died of thirst. But a scant inch of slightly damp clay at the foot of a high overhanging bank, a scant dozen stalks of coarse marsh grass that looked as if it would sell its birthright for a bit of real marsh, cuddling close to the damp clay in the bottom of a sandy, stony gulch, dry as a bone, had been enough to catch the eye of this veteran of the West Australian desert. And after an hour's digging with shovels and crowbars, we got a hole in the sand that we found we could rely on to fill about once an hour, and that full held about two buckets of good water! Little enough for fifty men and thirty beasts, but still enough.

And there that night, walled in by the close-crowding thorn that left scant room for our camp, with less of water within a day's march of us than the champagne gilded youth and guilty age pour out of a New Year's Eve at Rector's, my tired mates and porters turned in. With no sound in my ears but the sough of the night breeze through the ghastly gray branches of the thorn scrub, the yelps of jackals, the howls of marauding hyenas, and the distant grunts of two prowling lion, I sat alone and saw the Old Year out and the New Year in, lost in sequent visions, forming in the bright embers of my camp fire and disappearing in their ashes, of many a merrier New Year's Eve with dearly loved hands in reach and dearly loved lips toasting me the best, visions of such nights at home, at Sherry's and Delmonico's, at old Martin's and new, visions so clear and real that presently the sweet measures of the Monte Cristo Waltz were delighting my ears, voices babbling, glasses tinkling, laughter ringing then, suddenly rousing to a realization of a fire turned all ghostly gray as the shrouding walls of thorn and a night as chill, if not as white, as many a New Year's Eve at home, I rolled up in my blankets.

New Year's Day brought us out of the arid jungles and into a beautiful park-like country, abounding in clear, cold springs and streams. Just above Kibaibai Spring, where we made our night camp, four years before Outram and Leverson Gower had seen ten maneless (bush) lions wrangling like a lot of dogs over a zebra kill, and shot two of them from a near-by ambush.

Hereabouts rhino sign was thick, and about five o'clock I hid myself in a rhino's bed, beneath low-drooping boughs of a bush that completely shut it in, and immediately beside a deep rhino path, full of fresh sign, about a mile from camp, and there stayed till dark. While no rhino came, it was an amusing evening. Tommys, tiny oribi, and graceful impala entered and leisurely grazed or played across the glade, all about me, often within fifty feet. Could I have stirred to make adequate opening in my shelter, I should have gotten some capital photographs, but the crackle of a twig would have sent them off helter-skelter, and so I sat tight, until, at sundown, all wandered off into the bush toward the hills.

And then, just as I was about to leave, with great clatter, chatter, and barking, and a noise of crashing boughs like rhino smashing through bush, out trooped a big tribe of great man apes, old and young, close to a hundred of them, the biggest above four feet high, pappooses holding to the scruff of their mothers' necks and riding comfortably on their backs, and fierce—faced, long-fanged old men in the lead and out on the flanks.

For half an hour they pranced all around me there, youngsters scuffling and capering, elders digging roots or breaking great boughs and tearing bark, apparently taking in the dessert of the evening meal, for just as the brief twilight was fading into night, and when I was beginning to think I would have to shoot my way out to get back to camp, off they ambled into the bush.

We nooned the second of January on the cascades of the Lenderut River, which some day will be visited as a remarkable bit of African scenery. While then no more than a clear, cold, swift-flowing, loud-rippling brook, in the "big rains" the Lenderut is a roaring torrent. Just at our camp the river has cut its way through a great dyke of close-grained gray crystalline granite, with a drop of probably eighty feet in the half-mile, and, through some freak of the combined chemistry of rock and water or some wizard work of physics, along its bottom and its sides up to high-water level were carved out in the hard rock immense round tanks, some twenty feet deep and big enough for a swimming bath. Indeed, one sees here every sort of vessel represented, narrow-mouth vases, tiny cups, and shallow saucers, all smooth and highly polished of interior and lip as porcelain and all brimful of sweet water, come of the recent rains. From a great pool at the foot of the cascade Outram caught some fine eight-pound kumbari, while I caught him and a bit of the gorge with my camera, the first time this world-old cascade has come under snapshot fire.

That night's camp was the most beautiful of any on this safari, beside an ice-cold brook, a tributary of the Lenderut thickly lined with wild date palms and wild figs, about a mile below its source in a dozen great springs which covered nearly a square mile in area.

And that same square mile gave me about the uncanniest and toughest two hours I ever had. Rhino and buffalo tracks were thick about, and at five o'clock I took Awala and a porter, crossed the brook, and strolled up toward the springs on the chance of a shot. On the way up we slipped past several herds of impala and other buck, but it was not until we were near what I supposed to be the source of the brook that anything happened. There was a great crash and smash within the bush a few yards on our right that sounded more like buffalo than rhino. I waited a few minutes, on the chance they would come out, and then crept down into the edge of the thicket opposite the point at which we last heard them. Peering within, the bush looked fairly open,— thickcrowding giant ficus trees and palms, but not much undergrowth or vines. Directly beneath, the bank pitched steeply down to what I then supposed was the single source of the brook, and down it we softly slid and about through the palms we tiptoed, eyes keenly watching for a sight of the bush-smashers. But while the ground was hard trampled all about, rough tree trunks often worn smooth by the rubbing of giant bodies, nothing did we see but baboons.

Presently, when the declining sun warned us it was time to get out, I told Awala to lead out straight across the bush for camp, for our course had bent from east sharply north, and apparently the short-cut would save us a mile or more.

On he led. As we advanced, the game paths became fainter, and finally stopped altogether, bang up against a solid wall of vines and bush, solid looking and as dense a mass in fact as an ivy-clad wall. But through it, scarce thirty yards away it seemed, was the bright light of the open country. So through the vine wall we began cutting our way with our knives, clambering over and through them, up an ascent and down a declivity, only to find ourselves literally swinging on a network of vines fifteen feet above another brook.

The air was stifling; the labor exhausting; we were drenched with sweat. But just beyond us lay another patch of daylight that lured us ahead, and so other gleams of light lured us on over more rises and drops, each drop with a new spring brook at the bottom, whose presence we realized only by the murmur, except once when Awala slipped off his vine perch into one of them, taking a good ten-foot drop and a climb back up a vine, a vine twisted and looking precisely like a half-inch manila rope.

Oh, for the prehensile tail of one of the baboons playing about among the branches above us and grimacing their amusement over the wretched stagger we were making at their pet sort of semi-aërial travel, or for the wings of the great vultures and marabout storks perched in scores aloft on the highest trees, grimly weighing their chances of fat picking against our chance of escape!

While still twilight without, black night was now fallen within the jungle, and further progress ahead had become impossible.

No alternatives remained except to pass the night on any part of the wide vine hammock we liked to stop on, or to attempt to feel our way back along the route we had come, which was not amusing, for we knew there were several points where a slip through the vine floor might mean a broken leg, or worse.

To be sure we were in a measure safe enough on the vines, for nothing short of a leopard could get to us, and I much doubt if even he could, but wringing wet as we were, to stop there without a dry change of clothing or cover meant fever or pneumonia.

So there was nothing for it but to try to back-track ourselves, and back we turned. Sometimes, through small openings in the leafy canopy above us, the young moon helped us a bit, but most of the way it was feel every step of advance with hands and feet. Heads bumped limbs of trees, and leaves and twigs were so constantly jabbing us in the face that, to save our eyes, we crept ahead with closed lids, until finally we reached the open game paths and were lucky enough to win out into the open glades west of the main brook.

It was near nine o'clock when we reached camp, where Judd and Outram had been signalling us with shots and yells we plainly heard but had not answered, no use, for they could no more have gotten to us than we to them.

The afternoon and night of the third we spent in the lovely park-like country at the foot of Kibololet. Here I shot my first topi bull, a beautiful member of the family of larger antelope, unknown anywhere between Mombasa and Uganda, but down there abundant, a bright yellow of shank, a dark glossy brown of thigh, with a shade of chestnut roan on back and ribs that in certain lights glistens like highly burnished bronze.

While stealing close within the shadow of some bush for the shot at this chap, out slowly into the glade in front of me, two hundred yards away, came a great bull giraffe, and then directly along behind him trooped eight of his mates. Their lofty heads and necks much the color of the surrounding bush, above which they towered before entering the open, the impression of their approach was quite as startling as if one were to see the Singer, St. Paul, and Manhattan Life Buildings strolling, Indian file, up Fifth Avenue. And when, after watching them for perhaps twenty minutes browsing off the bush tops, I bowled over the topi, all looked up in surprise at the crack of the rifle, but not one moved until I entered the open, and then they lurched away, at about as graceful a pace as one might expect of the Singer Building out on stilts.

The fourth, the last day of our march to the Mara River, was to see my first serious disappointment and defeat, in fact two of them. We were then entering a section where specially fine specimens of water buck are found, with horns nearly a fourth longer and wider of spread than in most other parts. Before nine o'clock I sighted the biggest water-buck head I had ever seen, stalked him, and gave him a .405 in the shoulder that dropped him in his tracks, but within a half-minute he was up and off. For two hours I trailed him before finally losing him in the bush, sighting him twice, but both times out of range. This was annoying, but I knew there were plenty more like him and I should have other chances.

But a far greater shock was in store. Next to the sable, the roan antelope is far and away the most beautiful and rare of his tribe, and few sportsmen in these days get a chance at one, except by making a special trip to some remote region where they are still found. Outram had never seen or heard of roan thereabouts, north and east of the Mara, but had promised me a sight of them by a three days' trek west of the Mara to the crest of the Isuria Escarpment.

And yet about noon, while Judd and I were well ahead of the safari and within three miles of the river, strolling along a thin fringe of bush eight hundred yards below us was a great buck, strange to me but quickly identified by Judd as a splendid roan. He was all alone, no other game near, and had not seen us, so noting his course angled toward us, down we dropped, flat in the grass, and waited. On he came until within five hundred yards. Then fortune again favored me, a fly bit him, or perhaps a snake gave him a scare, for, suddenly, he swerved from his course straight toward us, and bounded another one hundred yards nearer, before again settling down to graze. Apparently he was a certain gift. Presently, and when within an easy three hundred yards, he again shifted his course and my best chance was come, for thereafter he would be drawing away. My shot knocked him flat, and Judd yelled, "Got him! Got him! You've got your roan!" But in an instant he was up again, and we saw that, firing at him quartering as he turned, I had only broken his left hip. Before he was fairly on his legs I gave him a second, this time fair in the left shoulder, and down he dropped, limp as an empty sack, and lay still. Then we shook hands and I slung my gun strap over my shoulder and we walked toward him when, wonder of wonders, up again he sprang, and before I could again cover him he was out of sight behind the fringe of bush. For five hours we trailed him through glade and bush with a dozen of our best boys, but to no purpose. Twice we sighted him at long range and twice I missed him, flurried and short-winded with the chase.

I was heartbroken, for no such chance for a fine roan was likely ever to come to me again. The next day I had twenty boys out from dawn to dark searching for him, under promise of a tempting reward, but all to no purpose. And then I was sorry indeed any of my shots had reached and torn his beautiful roan sides!

The fact is, the vitality of these African antelope is past belief; their thick hides are such tough shields that only a heart, spine, or head shot drops them to stay. The very next day I knocked two water buck and one topi flat as flounders at two hundred and seventy-five yards with three successive shots. There they lay motionless while the herd of mixed game scampered away, so lay for at least five minutes until my calls for the boys to come and get the meat roused both water buck, and off they bounded. And, come to the topi, I even found the great .405 ball that had passed through his heart had stopped well within the skin of the opposite side, a shot that would have passed clean through an elk.

Outram's little fifteen-pound cross between an Irish and a bull terrier, Pugge, caught up with one of the buck and detained him, but not for long. Pugge's tactics are always practical, if not scientific; disdaining fence for a throat grip, she always goes for the first mouthful she can get, usually fetching up with a leap that fastens her teeth so near an actual tail hold that she hangs well above and clear of reach of the sharp hind hoofs; and so often have I seen her dangle and swing for five to ten minutes till the buck went down. But this old water buck was too strong and artful for her, and after tossing her about for a few minutes, vainly trying to reach her with hoofs and horns, he sidestepped and swung her a smash against a thorn tree that put her out of the day's running.

Then the cunning old buck entered a belt of heavy jungle two or three miles in length and a half-mile broad, impassable to man except on buffalo paths, and along these for two and a half hours Outram and I tracked him, ourselves bent double or on hands and knees, beneath boughs and vines, the buck by turns leaping waterholes, entering the brook, and tramping up or down it, doubling on his own tracks, passing out to the open as if to cross a glade, and then slipping back into the jungle a few yards away, all shrewd tactics to throw us off his track, so shrewd they deserved to win, as at last they did. But the old bravo's escape was not for long. The very next morning about eight o'clock I shot a rather good topi bull, with seventeen-inch horns, cunning as a serpent, that after an hour's painstaking stalk compelled me to shoot at four hundred and fifty yards, a head-on shot that luckily caught him in the centre of the forehead.

While the boys were removing the head and skin I took a circle for bush buck, and within five hundred yards of where we had lost my wounded water buck the day before, found his head, spine, and a few ribs, the carcass eaten the night before by lion, and quarters and shoulders later toted off by hyena. His identity was past question, for one of the ribs showed fracture by the bullet that passed through his lungs. And he was a good one too, horns 27 inches high and 19 inches in spread, the tip of one horn splintered, whether in some battle for mastery of his herd or in his last night's finish fight with lion, I could only guess.

While taking this buck's head, I heard a shot a halfmile away from Judd's .450. Returned to camp at noon, I learned he had sighted a lioness at two hundred and fifty yards in the edge of the bush, perhaps the one that had retrieved my buck, and had wounded her, but had felt it imprudent to follow her into the dense bush she was in until, if badly hit, she had stiffened of her wound.

At 4 P. M. he and I went out with our gun bearers on a prowl for her, he with a .450, I with a twelve-bore and buckshot, the bearers with spare rifles. We easily found where she had passed on into the jungle and for half an hour were able to follow her spoor along buffalo paths. But not a drop of blood could we find. Then we lost all sign and had to give her up. Nor was I, personally, deeply grieved. In the semi-twilight of the bush, never able to see more than thirty feet in any direction, half the time with ducking heads (to avoid entanglement with vines and thorns) that prevented all outlook ahead or about, the situation impressed one as unconducive to longevity.

Returned to camp at dark, another bit of luck developed, Outram had just come in with the head of the second of the two water buck I shot the day before. While no better than twenty-one inches in height and sixteen inches in spread, the horns were much more graceful than the head of No. 1. Curiously, Outram had found the head and close-picked spine within a quarter of a mile of where No. I had been found—so, obviously, two lion had dined well at my expense the night before, to say nothing of the hyenas that wait, snarling, for the lion's leavings, the jackals that wait upon the hyenas, and the vultures and marabout storks that permit the jackals scant time for more than a hasty nibble.

V. FICKLE EQUATORIAL FASHIONS

TWENTY-THREE full days en route from Nairobi to the Mara River, our first week's permanent camp there was a constant delight.

The camp was pitched on a high bluff, forty feet above its margin, beneath the dense shade of its heavily timbered banks, just at the foot of rippling rapids that sang us to sleep at night and greeted us with good cheer at our dawn awakening.

Down to this point the Mara is a hastening, hustling mountain torrent of the sort that gives one the impression of pounding along at its best pace for fear another may steal its logical tributaries; but here, become swollen and opulent of its thrift and push, like Dooley's "Magnate" preparing to "sell out the trust to the trustful," the Mara steadies to a lounging, indifferent gait for a dignified tender of its golden flood to Victoria Nyanza and Nileside commerce.

About us in early morning and late evening the taller trees were alive with monkeys, monkeys blue, gray, black and white, tawny, monkeys tiny as kittens and big as men, the long-haired and the short-furred, the younger apparently out as investigation committees on our intrusion, swinging by their tails as low as they dared in wideeyed, wrinkle-browed study of our doings, the elders usually grouped aloft in solemn conclave, receiving and debating the reports of their committees. Obviously we brought them a lot of shocks, the greatest, the discharge of a gun in or near camp, which sent them barking to cover for hours. But, oddly, our next greatest startler to them was my daylight cold sponge-bath, which always set their teeth clicking and voices madly chattering, whether of sympathetic chills at thought of a cold dip so early, or of superstitious fear of what must have looked in the early dawn like a ghost-white figure disporting itself in the water beneath them, we could only conjecture.

It is a country of wondrous strange contradictions, is Africa. Near the end of the little rains, everywhere about us in the open glades were the loveliest green meadow lands, brilliant with flowers still, but the wild timothy tops browning a bit, the home farmer's hint to oil and sharpen his mower, and the cricket's chirp and the droning chorus of abounding insect life helped to fix the season as a waning home June. And yet cast the eyes aloft to the broad belt of deciduous forest lining the river and they there lingered lovingly on every brilliant hue with which the early frosts of Autumn paint all northern tree life except the pines and firs, while the ground beneath the canvas veranda of my tent boasted a carpet of fallen leaves bright tinted and variegated as any come of a Persian loom.

Thus on the Mara does thrifty Autumn hustle Summer aside and get the first cuddle in the soft lap of Spring. Days never to be forgotten were those first seven on the Mara. Up at 4 A. M. for a cold dip and light breakfast; off as soon as you can see your rifle sights; at five, a faint flush in the east, the usually tipsy-standing Southern Cross then properly perpendicular in the southern sky, while the two "pointers" of the Dipper are straight down, indexing the position of the dear old Polar Star we there never saw, both Dipper and Cross low down on the horizon, almost nestled in the treetops; a well-oiled rifle in your hand; your Somali spare gun bearer trailing behind, and, far behind him, four shenzi porters to carry your day's bag, and your syce and mule; off through dripping dew-bejewelled grass that under the sun's first rays glitters like a sleet-clad northern landscape, slowly slipping along the edge of thickets, thumb on hammer, finger in trigger guard, every sense tense for whatever the next turn of the bush may bring you in arm's length of, lion, rhino, buffalo, or any sort of buck; always working carefully up wind, trying to tread lightly as a cat; out into an animal kingdom virgin of man and his wiles as Adam found the denizens of Eden; out and up, ever rising toward some ridge crest, shapes tiny and of vast bulk springing ghost-like out of the half light, creeping, halting, peering for some trophy that may win you admission to the Valhalla of Rowland Ward's record trophy-elect; stealing in wide detours past the undesirable, to avoid startling them, for set a single beast agog and off presently thunders everything on four legs within a thousand yards of you, notice to the teeming herds near and far that some peril is at hand.

So on and on you go, carefully scanning each new group with your glasses, until presently aloft towers a pair of horns of majestic spread that marks a monarch worthy of best craft, then up for safe range you steal, crouching from bush to tree and tree to rock, crawling belly tight to mother earth through sheltering grass if all other cover lacks, until presently, mind and muscle atuned to perfect concert, your cheek cuddles close to your rifle stock and down goes your quarry of a well-placed shot. Out at once comes the tape and quickly settles your fate. Then on and on you go throughout the livelong day, for a new victory or at least a try for one.

While fine specimens of buck of all sorts fell to our guns, not a single one of the big fellows did either of us see, with the single exception of the lioness sighted by Judd. And yet the grunts of lion were heard about our camp every night. We dropped kills for them at evening, but upon crawling up, behind anthill or bush, for a sight of them at dawn, never found anything but the skeleton wreck of Leo's repast; we found their fresh spoor, often not an hour old, entering jungle paths, but try to follow them as we might, stooping, clambering, on hands and knees among the vines and thorns, we always failed to sight them.

Buffalo sign was thick about, often of mornings in the wet grass so fresh it was almost unexplainable why we had not seen them, and always we found the bush a network of their paths.

All up and down the river hippo paths worn from three to eight feet deep alternated with crocodile slides, and yet, bar one eighteen-foot crocodile shot by Outram, no hippo or crocodile did we see.

Even though these big fellows are all-night prowlers and feeders, lying up in concealment usually by day, out early of mornings and late of nights as we were, poking into their retreats as, none too wisely, we often did, it was miraculous how we managed to miss sighting them, but so miss them we did.

When Outram was last on the Mara it was impassable, booming bank full, but now its waters were fallen to such an extent that we were able to ford the island rapid alongside our camp, and by a day's work of the wapagazi digging cuttings in the perpendicular west bank and hacking bush, to get our saddle mules across. The result well repaid us, for all sorts of game were even more abundant there than north of the river. Working into the hills to the west, we were out no more than three miles before we caught a glimpse of a herd of Masai cattle in the glades below a belt of heavy forest high up on our right. Riding toward them, in half an hour we sighted the Masai village and approached.

It was the usual Masai munyata, a tall and thick zareba of thorn, probably three hundred feet in diameter, the long, low, round-topped thatch-and-wattle huts, thickly plastered, top and sides, with cow dung that, dried, makes them cool by day and tight and warm by night, ranged in a solid circle around the inner wall of the zareba. And every night within this circle of huts their flocks of fat-tailed, piebald sheep and their herds of sleek, square-built, hump-necked cattle are penned, and the one gate of the zareba tightly closed and guarded throughout the night against predatory neighbors.

Nor with the gate rushed and the centre of the village occupied are the Masai at the mercy of a native enemy. Each hut is a tiny castle, of effective protection against arrow and spear. The single doorway of each hut, instead of opening at right angles to the inner wall, opens laterally with it for six or eight feet, when a sharp turn opens to the interior. These entrances are so low and narrow that only one person at a time may enter, crouched almost to hands and knees — thus, if an enemy, offering a hopelessly exposed neck to the short shrift of the Masai short sword, while tiny arrow loopholes command all approaches.

These Masai were once the most powerful race of the eastern plateau, notwithstanding they were far fewer numerically than the Wakikuyu or the Wakamba. Slender, graceful, sinewy men, a light chocolate in color, with regular features, often with thin, straight noses and little of the pendulous negroid lip, probably the offspring of some great ancient Galla raid and trek that lodged itself among its vanquished, the Masai are the gentlemen par excellence of the British East African plateau. Hire to white men as tenders of flocks they sometimes do, but no menial task, no other form of labor will they perform. They plant no crops and in diet subsist entirely upon their flocks and herds, now that game-killing by natives is forbidden and in a measure stopped. Their chief diet is mixed milk and blood, the latter drawn from the necks of their butter-fat bullocks.

Our approach created a sensation. Lads herding sheep and women fetching water from a near-by spring flitted away through the bush like shadows, and we were halted some time a hundred yards from the gate before a group of elder men and young warriors came out, alert, suspicious, nervously clutching their spears. Presently, however, they recalled Outram from old Boundary Survey days of five years before, and, assured we were not Germans, of whom they hold a guilty fear, due to their notoriously frequent raids on natives and settlers in German territory, their suspicion was allayed. Excepting the members of the Survey Commission and one lone professional elephant hunter, no white men had ever before been among them, they told us.

As none of the men with us spoke Masai, we had to send back to camp for an interpreter. Upon his arrival we learned the sultani (chief) of this munyata was young Koydelot, a handsome lad of no more than twenty-two, son of the head witch doctor of a half-dozen neighboring munyatas. Shortly thereafter the elder came with a half-dozen of his headmen, himself habited in a handsome gray monkey-skin cloak, looped over the left shoulder and covering him to the thighs. Gravely seated behind his straight-planted war spear upon a little round six-inch-high stool, carved from a single piece of hardwood, surrounded by the skin-clad group of his bow and spear men, Koydelot was not without a certain crude dignity, which he succeeded in maintaining until one of the party plucked a short blade of grass, rolled it into a pellet, pressed it apparently into the toe of his boot, exhibited empty hands, made upward passes over legs and body, and then plucked it from his mouth. Koydelot rolled off his stool with wonder and shied away. Indeed, shortly thereafter the beginnings of a good entente between us were almost hopelessly ruined when another of the party exhibited to the Masai a lovely full set of teeth, and then, after a seemingly violent wrench at the lower teeth, showed an empty under jaw! Off into the bush some scurried and away from us all withdrew in wide-eyed, gaping wonder and dread of creatures with such uncanny attributes. Nor did we make much further progress with them till a third got out a press-the-spring-and-it-flies-shut tape measure. At first most of them, the women especially, seemed to take it as a pocket edition of some sort of snake, but once we convinced them it had no fangs, each had to have his or her play with it for the next half-hour.

This meeting with the Masai solved for us what had been a serious problem. All the time Judd could spare was expired, and he was then planning an attempt for a short-cut to some station of the Uganda Railway, one hundred and thirty to one hundred and sixty miles north of us. But to the north and northwest intervened the Isuria and Lumbwa ranges, gashed with deep watersheds and clothed with belts of dense forest, while to the northeast lay the mighty uplift of the Mau and unknown dry stretches of alternating lava and jungle of the Kidong Valley. Without a path or guide, either way was sure to be desperately hard and slow going. Four days before we had sent three of our wapagazi into the northwest, hunting for some Masai munyata, and since they were only rationed for three days we had begun to fear the Wanderobo had picked them up. Thus it was a great relief when we found Koydelot could give us two of his elmorani (warriors) who knew a practicable route to the Lumbwa tribe, whence guides could be gotten to Lumbwa station on the Uganda Railway.

When we reached camp late that afternoon, after a fine day's sport that yielded us several good trophies, we found Koydelot and his court awaiting us with a fine fat-tail sheep, the usual native "backsheesh," which we reciprocated to the full of its value in beads and "Americani" (unbleached cotton cloth).

A lot of our beads, however, we found unacceptable, even some of the most brilliant-hued of the lot: they were not in style! It is an absolute fact that in no set of the haute monde the world over is fashion more fickle and transient than among the African savages. Traders of no small means have been ruined, trekking into the interior hundreds of miles with wares that proved unsalable at any price. In the few months of their absence the fancy of the ebony beauties had shifted red or white beads were demanded by those who, previously, would look at none but blue beads, iron wire preferred to copper or brass, popular prints of cotton discarded.

Indeed, no manufacturers have a busier, harder study for attractive new patterns than the English and German printers of cheap cottons for the African trade. But it is a satisfaction to find that in plain, unbleached cotton goods no English or European cotton spinners have been able to compete with our New England mills, whose goods have held first esteem throughout Central Africa since first introduced, through Zanzibar, way back in the '60's, and still fetch better prices than the best European products.

At dawn on January 11, Judd pulled out north with Masai guides, hoping to reach Lumbwa in six or eight days. With him I sent back twenty-three of our porters, reducing our safari to a total of thirty, including Outram and myself. Sorry indeed were we to part with Will Judd, as rollicking, jolly, and able a mate as man ever had.

The day after Judd's departure we were delighted to be assured by one of Koydelot's sons that he could guide us to elephant, three days' march north of west of our camp, within the great basin lying between the Sotik and Kisii country and to the south of the Kisii highlands, delighted because we had been under the impression there were no elephant within much less than a fortnight's march of our Mara camp. Nor had we realized the Kavirondo were so near, a most important fact to us then, as our supply of posho (native grain food, beans, corn, or millet) was nearing total exhaustion, and the Kavirondo grew abundant crops of metama (Egyptian corn).

With a lot of mixed porters, exhaustion of posho is always a most serious thing, no matter how abundant game meat may be. If he can get meat, your Wakamba asks nothing else. Your Wakikuyu will touch no kind of meat, even to a point of impending starvation; indeed when we had already cut the others to half rations of posho—a full ration being one and one-half pounds per day per man—and were giving them all the meat they could eat, our Wakikuyu pathetically pleaded that their fathers had never eaten meat and that they could not, and full posho they had to have. So it was every last one of these aboriginal vegetarians that we rushed back to the railway with Judd. Your Mohammedan Swahili will eat no meat not properly halaled by one of their own faith, the throat cut, and the carcass properly bled before death. Your Somali will touch no form of food but rice and halaled meat. Thus, while none of our porters would dare desert from the Mara camp for fear of being bagged by Wanderobo, we confronted plenty of trouble when the posho gave out.

So we lost no time. At dawn the next morning we were en route in light marching order, leaving Regal in charge of our base camp, all donkeys, and the spare mules. Our course was almost due north, through rolling hills and broad plains sloping up from the main west fork of the Mara to the foot of the Isuria Escarpment, a vast black wall, inaccessible at most points, that stretched out of our ken into the horizon to northeast and southwest.

Five miles out we reached the munyata of Koydelot, senior, who welcomed us with gifts of great gourds of milk, which we received but promptly turned over to the porters at our noon camp, as the Masai practice of cleansing their dairy vessels leaves Masai milk impossible, save when one sees it milked direct into one of his own vessels, when it is found sweet and rich as the milk of the best Jersey cow.

Out of the village we were followed by fifteen or twenty of Koydelot's young elmorani, keen I should shoot them some buck, whose skins they prize as cloaks, the back sinews furnishing their best bow strings. In the next three miles I bowled over several, to the great delight of the young warriors.

Before we parted with this fine lot of young fellows, I got some excellent pictures, the only ones I have ever seen, of a group of Masai bowmen. The youngster in front of the group is Akuna, our guide, a son of Koydelot, pock-marked, but lithe and graceful as a panther, who on trail or elephant spoor for twenty days glided ahead of me silent as a shadow, wise in every form of jungle lore, but in all else simple as a little child, pleased with the skin and sinews of a fresh kill as any woman with a new Worth dress, and going into ecstasies over an empty cigarette tin. On spoor fierce-eyed, intent, tireless, relentless as a leopard, his light cloak wrapped tightly in a narrow roll about his waist, his knob-kerrie and short sword stuck in his girdle, his bow held perpendicularly to protect the bow string from the wet grass, the leather quiver at his back carrying his firesticks and heavy poison-tipped war arrows, Akuna's sinewy figure was a model of an aboriginal militant worthy of the best sculptor.

Shortly before our noon camp we passed yet another munyata, the last below the escarpment, and throughout our nooning its parti-colored flocks and herds, grazing hither and yon about us, appearing and disappearing among the trees, were ever producing effects like a gigantic animated kaleidoscope.

During the afternoon I bagged a fine pair of twenty-seven-inch impala horns and a twenty-two-inch "Tommy."

The ascent of the escarpment late in the afternoon, while no more than 1,300 feet, was so much like scrambling up a bowlder-studded, thorn-clad Gothic roof that it pumped all the wind out of even the hardy Outram and took the last ounce of go out of the loaded porters.

The summit of Isuria we found a lovely rolling country, with wide areas of tender, sweet grass, shoulderhigh, and thick mats of heavy timber, where herds of beautiful topi often stood within a hundred yards, watching us in wide-eyed surprise.

Our tents were up none too soon that evening, for directly we were sheltered a heavy thunderstorm broke. And scarcely had the last hoarse rumbles of the storm died on our ears, about midnight, than they were followed by the deep bass grunts of a lion prowling near, in fact, so very near that all the porters, who were sleeping by fires well sheltered in the dense bush, came hurrying into the centre of the camp and there spent the night, within the narrowest circle of fires we had to build at any time on that safari. All about us old Leo circled, so circled all night long, keen of hunger or wonder, one or the other.

Often one could hear a twig break beneath his stealthy tread, but not once did he pass within the ring of our firelight. Toward dawn he gave us up as a bad—probably too fiery-job and stalked grumblingly away.

And, by the way, it was in a ravine of this escarpment that Outram had a particularly curious experience. Out after buck meat for the porters, beneath a slightly leaning thorn tree he saw writhing about the tall grass tops what he took to be the head and neck of a python, and fired at it. At the shot, a big leopard bounded, snarling, away into the bush. Advancing beneath the tree to see what the leopard had been crouched over, he was surprised to find nothing but a narrow area of trampled grass and much absolutely fresh blood, so sprinkled about that evidently it was not come of the wound he had given the leopard. Suddenly, while standing puzzling over what the leopard's kill could have been that might be made away with so completely, hide, meat, and bone, he became conscious of a steady drip! drip! drip! on his coat sleeve, and, upon lifting his arm, discovered a stream of blood running down it! Glancing aloft, his puzzle was solved. There, in a high fork of the tree at least eighteen feet from the ground, were cleverly wedged, heads to tails, their legs even artfully intertwined to steady them, the carcasses of two freshly killed young topi antelope, weighing forty to fifty pounds each. Obviously the leopard, after a strenuous morning winning and safely stowing his day's repast, had been resting himself beneath the tree and lapping the dripping blood as an appetizer.

About seven o'clock that morning, while riding a short distance ahead of the safari, I sighted four eland, two of them splendid bulls, magnificent great fellows that looked as big as beeves. With no means of stopping the noisy advancing porters without alarming the eland, I had to chance a three-hundred-yard shot at the biggest bull. He staggered, bounded into the air, and hit the ground going at a sharp trot, like that fast gait in the elk which few ponies can overtake until it is broken into a gallop, after his speeding mates. All were out of sight almost in an instant, with no chance for a second shot but a snap at the second bull that, unfortunately, hit him in the hind quarters and did not down him. Hurrying to the turn of bush where they had disappeared, I took up their trail, plain to follow as a wagon road for two miles through the dripping grass, great splashes of blood on the tall grass tops proving a high shoulder shot in the big bull and distinguishing his tracks from the others.

Then the eland passed through a series of glades criss-crossed in every direction that morning by topi and other game that soon had my Somali shikari and myself puzzling, for already the blood sign from the congealing wound had lessened until we could no longer find it at all. At this juncture up came one of my Masai, Habia, from the safari. His spooring, then and thereafter for hours, was masterly, better than I have ever seen done by Indian or cowboy.

Crouched and bent until he was carrying his nose close to ground almost as a hunting hound on cooling scent, at a short distance wholly hidden in the tall grass, he glided about the glade, amidst the network of trails, pausing seldom, for no more than five minutes before he signalled me to him, and plucked and showed me a blade of grass that showed a blood splotch scarcely bigger than a pin head. Then off down the spoor he started and along it held, up hill and down, through tall grass, winding through broad belts of jungle on game trails and off them, along the rocky bottoms of dry ravines, into and through or up or down water, never at fault for an instant except where the bull had taken water, at a pace that kept me blown almost to the point of collapse, for full four hours. Early it became evident that the bull had elected to play a lone hand in the game of losing us, and had cut away free of his mates. Often we heard him a few yards away through the bush, but only once again did I sight him, about noon, at the top of a long, steep ascent that apparently had overtaxed even his energies, where he stood with hanging head, his shoulder wound plainly showing. But before I could free myself of the mesh of bush we were leaving, off again he trotted and I had to content myself with a snapshot that, hitting him in the hip, only served to hasten his pace.

And right there I realized the chase for me was useless. There was no more than another two or three miles' go left in me. Besides, while Habia and Awala could slip through the bush silent as ghosts, do my best I was now and then breaking dry twigs or stumbling on toe-entangling vines, and notwithstanding the two-hundred-and-six-pound handicap with which I had left Nairobi was then reduced to close to one hundred and eighty pounds.

Obviously the only chance was to leave my eland to them, in the hope that Habia might stalk near enough to plant a finishing poisoned arrow — which, freshly prepared, can be relied on to kill in twenty minutes, if it penetrates the flesh at all. So on I sent them and back toward the waiting safari wearily I tramped until I metmy syce and mule, which Outram had thoughtfully sent after me, guided by Akuna.

It was long after dark when my two trailers reached camp that night, empty-handed. Twice had they sighted the bull, but approach him they could not. It was a heavy disappointment, for in these days it is not so many chances a man has for such a superb eland.

Early the next morning our path led us to the first munyata west of the escarpment. After a few words from Akuna, the Masai received us cordially and the women brought us great gourds of milk.

Beneath a wide-spreading thorn tree just without the gate of the village, the chief and a dozen or more of the elders sat about the embers of a fire, working overtime, harder by far than usual, for all seemed to be busy at once lending advice in soft-toned Masai chorus to a youth of eighteen, who, by great effort, was contriving to make one knife-stroke about every five minutes on a stave of wood he was shaping for a bow.

All were skin clad, in so far as they were clad at all, except the chief himself, who sported an antiquated red and yellow laprobe of a pattern I have observed to be popular among the Wakamba, from whom it was probably traded or looted, and an extraordinary bracelet of claws and teeth, flint and obsidian, whether a charm or an insignia of rank I could only guess. Short and lean, bearded, with regular, sharp-cut features, a complexion so light (for even a Masai) that he was almost sallow, and great slumbering, speculative, introspective dark eyes that occasionally lit up with ominous fires, dignified, reserved, quiet, the chief bore a remarkable resemblance to Jay Gould!

Halting at this village for a half-hour's rest of the porters, the youthful bowmaker and his advisory committee of older bowmen prompted me to propose an archery prize competition. At first they failed to catch the idea, but when I stuck a silver rupee (about the diameter of a half-dollar piece) in the end of a split stick planted in the ground at twenty yards from a line I drew, and explained that each might, in turn, have a single shot until the rupee was fairly hit, the hitter to have it, all but the chief skurried within the munyata for their bows and quivers.

And back presently they came on the run, every male armed, from seven-year-old toddlers to seventy-year-old doddlers, and we lined them up for turn shooting.

One wrinkled and palsied old scrap of parchment, palsied in all but his greed, finding himself landed at the extreme foot of the line, promptly squatted with a great sheaf of close upon twenty arrows before him, and began a continuous but shockingly wild flight of them in the general direction of the target. And stop him we could not, short of actual physical violence. Nor did we long try, for it was only too apparent that the target was much safer from him than were we or his lined-up mates; for, seeming himself to realize that nothing but luck and quick work could win for him, he began trying to shoot so fast that at least a third of his arrows flew from his bow string at every angle from the true line of fire but a flat one, flew feebly, to be sure, but still hard enough to put an eye out.

So, with no more notice of him by his competitors than a chorus of indulgent laughs, the match proceeded fairly, none of the others seeking unfair advantage.

The average Masai bow is from five to six feet long, and it takes three fingers and a strong wrist and shoulder to draw the heavy, iron-tipped, thirty-inch war and big game arrows to the head. But for this contest they used the shorter blunt-headed arrows that serve them for bagging birds and rabbits.

Quickly it became evident the prizes must fall to some lad or youth, for all the men shot badly, close, to be sure, but inches out of line or over or below the target. With their ancient best amusement and most profitable occupation of predatory raids on their neighbors largely stopped for several years, and game-shooting forbidden by law and made dangerous for them, no incentive remains for the mature elmorani to keep in practice with the bow.

One youngster no more than eight or ten years old proved a wonder: his first shot grazed the top of the first rupee, his second hit it fairly, his third shot barely missed the second by a hair, and his fourth sent it spinning, hit plumb centre. He was the son of the six-foot-six elmoran who stands at the front of the line in the photograph, to whom, in dancing, shouting glee, he brought and gave his shining trophies and then clung cuddling proudly to one giant paternal leg.

And, after the rupees had been duly examined and admired by all present, none but Old Parchment showing any envy or heartache over his own failure, good sportsmen and true all but him, the trophies were prudently handed over by the father to the boy's mother for safekeeping, and on to the little victor's own youngsters they doubtless will one day be passed.

VI. ALONG UNMAPPED NILE SOURCES

WE descended to and crossed the Maggori River at an altitude of 4,750 feet, there a tumbling, broiling hill torrent thirty feet wide pouring down towards Victoria Nyanza out of the Lumbwa highlands, through broad belts of heavy timber.

A few miles south of the Maggori, rising toward the divide between that stream and the Oyani River, the main southern tributary of the Kuja, our path, bending slightly north again, led us, true to Akuna's promise, into abundant elephant sign. In fact, from 1 P. M. to 5 P. M., when we reached the numerous munyatas of Toroni's Loita Masai, elephant spoor was crossing our path at right angles every few hundred yards, some only a few hours old. Great limbs growing twenty feet from the ground and torn down that very morning, at one point blocked our trail, while here and there in the long grass broad paths were tramped deep and smooth as if made by the marching hosts of all Tammany's most portly. Our food supply was so low we could not then afford to stop on any uncertainty; so, since our trail was bending north to a half-circle of a big basin toward which the elephant tracks headed, I detached Akuna and Habia with orders to try to locate them and to intercept us if they found them.

That night we camped in a high hill basin about the slopes of which were scattered a half-dozen of Toroni's munyatas. We had made about sixty-five miles in our three days out from our Mara camp, heavy marching for loaded porters.

Shortly after dark our trackers came in with word the elephant had moved down into the great long basin to the north and northeast of Toroni's. Hereabouts there was practically no small game and we were wholly out of posho, but having still enough fresh meat for the porters for one day, we decided to have our first try for elephant the next day.

Off at 5 A. M., in twenty minutes we were sopping wet from the alternating belts of dripping grass and jungle that cover that country, jungle and heavy timber along the streams, grass upon the hillslopes.

We started on our saddle mules, but soon had to discard them, notwithstanding they were as sure-footed as the best of their usually safe-going breed. In fact, mine never dumped me but once, and then was thoughtful enough to choose as the occasion a particularly hot day and as the place the middle of a cold stream, so I forgave him.

But that basin, as, indeed, is practically all good elephant country now remaining, was impossible mounted. The shortest grass was a sort of wild timothy five to six feet high, its lower third a thick mat man or beast could scarcely kick his way through, and, what was far worse, the ground beneath on all hillslopes was thickly strewn with hidden bowlders, big and little, going afoot in which meant constant slipping and stumbling that acutely wrenched every muscle in you, while to attempt it mounted meant to court the certainty of a broken leg or arm.

Then here we ran into our first true elephant grass, ten to fifteen feet high, that shuts one in like a wall and that one can scarcely wallow through at all except on elephant paths.

But such paths we soon struck, all with more or less fresh sign, and picked and followed the freshest sign, sometimes going twenty minutes through grass where we could not see two yards in any direction, except straight into the zenith; sometimes along dusky jungle paths, where even the zenith view was shut out from us; sometimes into tall forest, where wide areas were trampled bare of undergrowth and hard and smooth as a floor, vast, dim-lighted, sylvan assembly chambers of the great pachyderms; often across acres of flat marsh-land or spring-sodden hillside where advance was only possible by treading carefully between elephant footprints, a slip into of which meant a plunge to one's waist or neck in cold water, for not even the pig loves mud more than the elephant.

On and on for six hours we by turns slipped, plodded, wallowed, and crawled, lured and buoyed by the almost warm sign, and then, all in, pumped of wind and strength, had to give it up and strike for a short-cut to the Mara trail, which we reached half-way back to the Maggori.

And when that night the two Masai whom we had sent on upon the spoor dropped, dead spent, by our camp fire, it was with disgust we learned that a scant hour after we left them they had sighted two big tuskers.

That morning our porters had no breakfast, but an easy four hours' march brought us down to the villages of the Jalou Nilotic Kavirondo that thickly line the hillslopes of the Oyani and the Kuja for miles, a superb race physically who dwell in easy plenty amid their numerous flocks and herds and broad russet-brown fields of ripening Egyptian corn.

There we counted on abundance, and learning the head Sultani dwelt in a large stone-walled village we could see lying three miles away across the Oyani, hurried Saiba, our headman, and some porters across to buy metama (flour ground from Egyptian millet). But after an hour and a half they returned with startling word from the Sultani that there was no flour in the valley, that all their stock had been sold and delivered the day before to two muzungu (Europeans) recently come up from the lake with a big safari, one a "medicine man," and then camped three miles below us.

Our situation was desperate, and there was nothing for it but an appeal to their generosity, whoever they might be the first white men we had heard of since leaving Nairobi.

So Outram and I jumped on our mules and made our best pace to the camp, which we found on a high hilltop at least a mile from the river. So located, indeed, were all the Kavirondo villages, to our surprise, high and far back from the Oyani, and all looked newly built.

As we approached, we quickly recognized it as a boma of Government officials, by the uniformed Askaris on sentry duty and lolling about their huts.

Come to the two ample tents of the muzungu, we were received by two gentlemen with quiet, "How do you do's," just as if we were fellow clubmen whom they had been having whiskey and soda with daily all their lives, the very hall-mark of that best bred type of Briton who stubbornly refuses to be surprised by anything. Such a startling apparition as visitors in the remote wilds of Texas or Dakota (when they were happy enough to possess such wilds as these) inevitably would have wrung out a startled but wholly genial, "Well, stranger, where in hell did you come from, and who might you be anyway?"

And then, even before we had gotten into a pair of quickly proffered easy chairs, followed that simple but ever welcome ritual of good-fellowship, "Fancy you men could do a drink. Boy! lete (bring) whiskey and soda!"

As soon as I had safely lodged half the bubbling pale amber contents of my glass where it couldn't get away, I introduced Outram and myself by name and got another pair of "How do you do's," but no names.

Then, pressed by the need of our hungry porters, I explained we were on safari from Nairobi, out of posho and trekked over from the Mara to buy some, but had found the Kavirondos' surplus exhausted. This promptly brought a kind offer of enough to do us for the moment, and expression of the opinion we would be unable to buy the fifteen or twenty loads we wanted short of the Government boma at Kisii, three days' journey to the northeast.

Just where we were we had not known, except that we were somewhere on the Oyani River, near its head, we had imagined. So that when, shortly, we learned that the lake port of Karungu was only eight hours distant, we were astonished to realize that we were no more than fifteen miles in an air line from Victoria Nyanza, and well to the west of Port Florence, the western terminus at the lake of the Uganda Railway.

Then when presently one gentleman inadvertently, and I fancy much to his annoyance, revealed half of the carefully guarded secret of the identity of both himself and the other, by referring to his companion as "Dr. Baker," this hint, and the location of camp and native villages far from flowing water, disclosed the whole matter to me. It was a new "Sleeping Sickness Camp," one of the chain of camps the Administrations of the British East and Uganda Protectorates are surrounding the west, north, and east ends of the lake with in a desperate attempt to check the spread within their territory. They also aim to alleviate as far as possible the sufferings of the hundreds of thousands of victims of this dread and most mysterious disease.

Of the cause of the sleeping sickness or of any effective cure or means of prevention of its spread, little more is now known than when, a few years ago, it swept down upon the lake, apparently out of the Congo jungles, the most relentless and the worst of all the physical scourges medical science has had to battle with.

Practically all known of it is that it is carried by a variety of the tsetse fly which is never found beyond a few hundred yards of the lake or rivers; that the tsetse which has not bitten a victim of the disease is harmless; that the tsetse quickly disappears when areas of lake shore or stream side are denuded of all timber, bush, and long grass, and that, therefore, water margins may be made comparatively safe by such denudation over a belt of adequate width; and that the fly may be wholly escaped by removal one to two miles from lake or stream margin. As for the best treatment so far discovered, it is admittedly no more than alleviating.

With these scraps of useful information gained, the Governments are doing their best, concentrating the infected on islands that, like lepers, they are never permitted to leave, or assembling them in isolated hospital camps under the most able medical attendance, and removing the uninfected, en masse, to highlands beyond known fly-infested areas.

Already hundreds of thousands have died of it, nor is its spread anywhere really checked. It is creeping north and east from the lake, down into German and Portuguese territory, invading the boundaries of Rhodesia. Great islands like the Sessi group, and vast strips of the mainland that a few years ago carried a dense population of the intelligent, thrifty, and prosperous Baganda, to-day own no tenants but their dead, while their bountiful banana plantations and cotton fields have reverted to howling jungle.

Indeed, unless means of prevention and cure are found, at any time the sleeping sickness may become a world problem of the toughest. Often the disease does not develop until a year or more after any possibility of infection. And since the scoundrelly little tsetse conveys it, some other depraved type of fly or mosquito indigenous to America, Asia, or Europe may yet acquire a tiny jag of infection from some returned African dweller or traveller, returned apparently well but fallen a victim to the disease, which will serve to establish it abroad.

Thus, undoubtedly, the disease crossed the divide between the Congo and lake watersheds, not in a poison-laden fly but in a victim of the malady.

Of its origin or history in barbarous, pestilential Congo nothing definite is known, except that it has long lurked and worked there, perhaps, certainly quite conceivably, a scourge directly caused by and come as a punishment for generations of the most ruthless and reckless human slaughter, where thousands upon thousands of mutilated dead were left where they fell to foul the steaming jungle air and envenom the myriad local types of tropical insect life. Indeed, that there may be some grain of fact in this ventured fancy is suggested by the coincidence that the advent of the sleeping sickness in Uganda followed close upon the heels of the wave of wholesale slaughter, by revolted Congo Askaris and cannibal Baleka, that swept across several thousands of square miles of densely populated territory to the west of Lake Kivu and nearly adjacent to Ankori, Uganda's southwest Province, where practically all who escaped the barbarous invaders perished of hunger and of diseases bred of the festering corpses with which villages, paths, and fields were thickly strewn.

Early symptoms of sleeping sickness are found in the swelling of glands at the base of the neck, just above the collar bone, followed by enlargment of other glands. Usually the patient lives several years, often five or more, most of the time more or less addled of brain, in the latter stages frequently insane. As the disease progresses, the patient becomes greatly emaciated, notwithstanding an inordinate appetite for meat. The drowsy sleeping stage is one of the late symptoms.

Fortunately in British territory only two white men have fallen victims of the disease, so far as I could learn, although scores of Europeans, officials and missionaries, have been freely exposed to it. Both (one an attending physician of the sick) returned to Europe for treatment, but without avail.

When I remarked that I imagined they were establishing a sleeping sickness camp, we were told they had recently marched up from Karungu for that purpose and would the next day begin the construction of a permanent dispensary, hospital, and administration buildings. Asked if there were many sufferers from the disease in the valley, Dr. Baker replied he had no doubt he could get in for treatment five thousand cases in two days, if he had facilities for handling them. Only one patient was brought in when we were there, a man of powerful frame, securely bound with bark rope, for he was mad as a hatter, with homicidal tendency. Repeatedly he had tried to kill some of his fellow villagers, and was forever screaming for a chance at a muzungu. Ankles and wrists were raw of the restraining ropes that had shackled him for weeks. He was chained in a hut and given an opiate.

The view from the veranda of their tents was lovely, down the broad, steep-sloping valley of the palm-lined Oyani to its junction with the Kuja, on north across the Kuja to the tall blue crags of Mt. Homa, west to the lofty purple crest of the Gwasi range, the highest peak rising immediately above the lake, and to the perfect pyramid of Nundewot, behind which lay Karungu.

It was not until after tea and the pair had consented to stroll over to our tents for a "sundowner," the happy hour and ceremony for which all prudent Africanders thirstily, and often grouchily, wait, for the prudent adjure spirits until sunset, that I learned (and then only by bluntly asking Dr. Baker while we were walking down a winding Kavirondo path) of the second gentleman what his modesty or habits of reserve had concealed—that he was Assistant Deputy Commissioner Northcote, the chief administrative officer of that district of the Province of Kisumu. Though a young man, for years he had been a close student and solver of native and provincial problems, one of the little group of cool-headed, justdealing, quick-acting, hard-hitting Britons who, often isolated among savage thousands many days' march from any outside support, with a staff of not more than one to three whites, never backed by more than a handful of native Askaris, have by their diplomacy and daring won and are holding for the Crown its east and central African Empire.

And, although one of the younger members of the administrative corps, Mr. Northcote is by no means one of the least distinguished. For it was he who, while in charge of the Kisii Boma, himself received a spear stab from a rebellious native that started the recent Kisii revolt, but stubbornly held out till forces arrived adequate to hammer the Kisii into submission.

Finding our camp pitched on a low bench only three hundred yards from the Oyani, Dr. Baker advised us to move at least a mile south of and two hundred feet above the river, for safe escape of flies and mosquitoes, good advice on which we promptly acted.

The next morning the chief of several Kavirondo villages, old Agilo, came to our camp decorously robed in a red blanket and crowned with a tiara of beaded leather, the diadem of this insignia of royalty being a gray stoneware ointment pot, its mouth bound tightly to the centre of his forehead and its body standing straight out from the head, giving him the appearance of a two-legged stub-horned unicorn.

Nor were blanket and tiara all of his gaudy regalia, for on the back of his head he wore a great brown sun helmet that no more was permitted to change its angle than was the tightly bound pot or his stony set features their expression. So tightly did the helmet cling to its fixed angle that we suspected it was attached to the tiara and, thus, an integral part of it.

With Agilo came a dozen or more of his head men, superb great fellows black as ink, several well above six feet, muscled like finely trained athletes, with thirty-three-inch waists and forty-six-inch chests, all naked as they were born save for portieres of grease-sodden ringlets that dangled about necks and faces and innumerable brass and iron wire bangles, covering often the major part of arms and legs.

There came with him a string of totos, perhaps another dozen, just a few of the more recent evidences of his predilection for paternity, boys and girls, most of them so tiny it was a miracle how their slender, wobbly little shanks contrived to tote about their great pot bellies.

There were also a half-dozen matrons and maids carrying baskets of metama flour, the posho we so badly needed, all in the Kavirondo full dress of their station, the maids wearing nothing but their amiable smiles and a slender string of beads about the waist, the matrons each distinguished by a little four-inch tuft of cow-tail hair pendent, aft, from a like string of beads.

Innocent, these ebony beauties and extraordinary beauties of figure many of the young maids and matrons are innocent physically and mentally of costume and all that it means as was Mother Eve herself, not even a decade of contact and acquaintance with the white race resident along the lake, and its highly elevating and refining influences, has served either to induce Kavirondo women to clothe their nakedness or to surrender an integrity to strict virtue no clothed race, red, yellow, black, or white, can boast. To this day few Kavirondo women will have any man except one of their own blood, and him only after due observance of the Kavirondo marriage ritual, a formal surrender of her by her parents for value received in cattle or in sheep.

Posho in sight, Outram quickly got out and attractively displayed our remaining stock of "trade goods." The "Americani" was already exhausted, parted with in return for the "backsheesh," in sheep, milk, and honey, brought by the Sultanis of different Masai munyatas.

But our ten-pound tin of beads still remained nearly intact, big beads and little, strung as bracelets, anklets, and necklaces, beads of glass and of porcelain, red, white, and blue, pink, green, and amber, beads gilt and silvered a glittering store of coveted treasure the first glimpse of which drew from old Agilo a few brief, sharp orders to one and another, spoken in the rolling roar of mouth-pouting, tongue-wobbling, blubbering labials with which Kavirondo communicate confidences, that soon wrought wonders.

Out of this posho-less land, within half an hour naked women, young and old, came ambling into camp with baskets of metama, and active barter began. Some wanted rupees — probably such only as were short of liquid funds to pay their annual hut tax of Rs. 3, but few could resist the temptation of such a rare chance of acquiring stunning new full-dress costumes as was afforded by the heaps of tiny shining gauds piled at Outram's tent door. And such master of native foibles he proved that by night we had acquired twenty loads of metama (one thousand, two hundred pounds) at a cost of about a cent a pound. And in this price figured liberal donations of "backsheesh," to Agilo in coin of the Protectorate and to others in trinkets.

Indeed so pleased were the Kavirondo with their traffic that in the afternoon Agilo's son led to our tents a group of young warriors, all armed and gorgeously decked in war dress, himself mounted bareback on a bridled brindle steer and wearing his father's war bonnet, a two-story mass of superb black ostrich feathers, with a circle of white ostrich feathers sticking out at right angles from the top of the second story, while another wore a gorgeous war bonnet made of grayish yellow monkey skin, tall as a grenadier's busby and shaped much like one.

Up before us they danced, singing a chorus of welcome, occasionally led by His Ostrich Plumes, as often as he could succeed in persuading his long-horned brindle mount to stay anywhere in the vicinity. Then they lined up and gave us a war dance, some of the more striking poses of which are shown in my photographs, fierce charges, individually and in line, stealthy approaches or retreats behind the cover of their enormous shields, with brandishings of spears and grimacings of face calculated to chill the marrow of the boldest enemy.

To this afternoon's festivity Agilo sociably brought as generous a jag of wembe (native spirits, brewed of honey and metama) as his system could hold, and continued to carry it to the end of the day without serious injury to his Sultanic tiara or dignity. And when at our evening parting I risked giving him a modest jorum of gin, which I told him was a sample of the sort of water found in most of the streams in my country, he wolfed it down, coughed and spluttered, and then gurgled to me (through the interpreter) an earnest inquiry as to how many days' march it was to my country, whether the expression of a polite interest in my wandering or of a keen appreciation of American "water" he did not explain.

That night, January 18, I sat down to an unwonted luxury, a perusal of the "latest" news, as contained in one copy each of the London Weekly Times and the London Daily Mail, both of December 18, come a day or two before to Northcote and by him kindly given to me.

Oddly, camped there upon the Oyani, which is the main southern branch of the Kuja, and come recently from the Mara, the two largest tributaries of Victoria Nyanza, the mother of the Nile, a traveller for weeks along and between the Nile's remotest sources, and in territory still plotted as "unknown" upon the most recently published maps, a region a scant dozen white men have ever entered, the very first article to catch my eye in The Times was an account of the Royal Geographical Society's meeting in commemoration of the fiftieth anniversary of Speke's solution of the world-old Nile source mystery by the discovery of Victoria Nyanza, the crowning feat of the many most notable of his African explorations, begun the year I was born, 1856.

The next day we wasted on promises of Agilo to furnish porters he did not produce to carry our posho to the Mara, and for which he was promised a premium for himself of Rs. 1 each. However, the delay gave us opportunity for the pleasure of having Northcote and Baker at luncheon;

and while we had nothing better than chop boxes to serve as table and seats, and a menu I am sure Oscar would have improved, whether our guests enjoyed it or not, I know Outram and I did.

During luncheon Northcote cracked almost to a shatter our hope of elephant, by telling us that while there were probably three to four hundred elephant ranging between the Kisii Highlands and the Maggori, the Masai on the east and the Kavirondo on the west, the big tuskers were largely shot out by poaching ivory hunters from German territory; of course, we might with rare luck strike a good one, but the herds were kept so constantly on the march, by movements of the native population densely crowding around them, and their country was so nearly inaccessible, that it would be sheer luck if we sighted them at all, no matter how hard we worked.

However, despite this discouragement, we decided to give them a good try, and the following day marched back to Toroni's, sending ahead of us three men to fetch on from our Mara camp enough donkeys to carry the posho we left with Northcote.

That morning, ranging ahead and far to the west of the safari in hope of seeing roan, I sighted a topi wearing what looked to me a record pair of horns. The best I could do was to get a three hundred and fifty yard shot, but down of it he tumbled, and, after several ineffectual efforts to rise, lay still. Having learned nothing yet of experience, I turned to call up my syce and mule, only to be nudged by my gun bearer and shown a gleaming russet flank disappearing into the bush.

Quickly Habia picked up the blood-stained trail.

For three hours we followed it, but never once had he laid down, and only once, from a hilltop, did I sight him with my glasses, drooping slowly along in the valley beneath us; but by the time we could climb down he was gone, gone for good, as blood flow had stopped and he had reached a maze of trails made by other buck.

Swinging to bear off toward Toroni's, we had not gone a half-mile before I sighted a real prize, a Lichtenstein hartebeeste bull and a fine big old chap. On this fellow I took no chances, and rained lead into him until he collapsed and lay still, and at that it took five 9 m.m. soft nose Mauser bullets to do the work, notwithstanding the first was in the shoulder and the second a fair centre chest shot. His horns were 19 inches on the outer curve, 7 inches in spread, 10 inches at base, while from tip of nose to tip of horns he measured 30 inches.

But, like many another hard-won, dear-loved treasure the Fates refuse to spare one, my ownership of the Lichtenstein was so brief I scarcely had time to get well acquainted with it. That night the head skin was carefully removed and skull and under jaw cleaned, the skin sheltered from the dew and the jaw and skull and horns placed on top of one of the boys' grass huts, six feet from the ground, within a circle of bush no more than thirty feet in diameter, close about which at least a dozen of us were sleeping, the only gap between huts and tents filled in by the tethered mules, our two dogs lolling among us.

During the night nothing unusual happened, except that my boy, Salem, sleeping near the mess fire and next the hut that held the trophies, awakened toward morning, heard near at hand a soft leopard purr, and, looking about, saw a pair of glowing eyes taking in the camp; but the two or three firebrands he threw at it sent it scampering away, and shortly he dozed off again.

But when morning came the Lichtenstein skull and horns were gone! Gone for good, notwithstanding all my porters and a lot of Toroni's Masai were out all day searching grass and bush for them, gone in spite of the fact that the skull was stripped clean of meat except tiny clinging fragments that, altogether, would scarcely surfeit a mouse, apparently filched by the leopard out of sheer devilment, for about the boys' fires were many sticks loaded with cooking meat of the day's kill or perhaps he had tasted their cooking and disapproved it. That it was the leopard was certain, for no tracks but his were found near camp.

Thus I still remain the possessor of a fine Lichtenstein under jaw and head skin, but fear I shall always lack a skull and pair of horns to fit it.

Indeed in the African bush one cannot be too careful of anything he values, else he is sure sooner or later to fall a victim of one or another of the night marauders of the jungle. While most of the night prowlers are after meat, alive or dead, to the hyena all is fish that enters his net: boots, leggings, or gun cases, are to him attractive types of entrees, while bridles, saddles, or curing hides are pièces de résistance he appears to adore. Really, after learning, on wholly trustworthy authority, of an incident of the joint Anglo-German Boundary Survey four years ago, I am puzzled to fancy what can be safe against mighty hyena jaws.

One evening Herr Hauptmann Schlobach, the Imperial German Commissioner, had some meat cut up on the lid of a fifty-pound chop box that stood immediately before the door of his tent. In the morning the box was gone, but search soon discovered deeply imprinted hyena tracks which, followed, led to the missing chop box lying full eighty yards outside the camp, its lid licked clean, deep teeth marks at one corner showing how it had been lifted and carried!

VII. SURROUNDED BY WILD ELEPHANT

OUR two Masai and several of Toroni's were sent out at daylight on a prowl for fresh elephant tracks, but returned after dark, worn to a frazzle by their fourteen hours' plod through grass and bush, with news that all the sign was several days old and showed movement south and east toward the Maggori River.

In the afternoon Toroni paid us a visit, accompanied by a score of his headmen and followed by a small delegation of his wives and children, seventeen of the wives and more of the children than I took time to count, the women and children chanting a chorus of welcome to the accompaniment of the jingle, as they danced up to us, of beautifully made iron and brass wire chains, necklaces, and stomachers. The central figures in the photograph are Toroni, his youngest and pet wife, and the Heiress Apparent, a type of Ethiopian beauty not easy to beat.

At first I took their coming as a visit of state, but was soon made to realize that their real purpose was to seek medical attendance.

Whoever had preceded us there I do not know, but it must have been some amiable white man who fed them sugar or chocolate as medicine. For, although about as sturdy and sound looking a lot, from old to young, as could be picked from any people, all were sufferers of something and in a desperate bad way of it, according to their story: all must have dawa (medicine) and get it quick to be safe of living the day out.

With a medicine chest that held nothing but permanganate of potash, bandages, quinine, calomel and salts, and little indeed of these, I was up a stump. But, since something must be done, I launched boldly out upon the to me uncharted sea of diagnosis, all the time racking my brains for schemes to husband our precious little store of medicines.

The first prescription I ventured on, a dose of salts, gave me a hint the patient made a shocking wry face over it. So to the next two I gave quinine and made them bite and chew the pills, and to the third, a wrinkled old boy with a slight bark off the shin, I applied an extra strong solution of permanganate that made him howl and at the same time served to relieve me of further demands for dawa.

After another forenoon out, the twenty-second of January, our Masai reported again all elephant trekked toward the Maggori, so in the afternoon we marched about ten miles southeast, camping on a little stream the Masai called "Looseandgiddy," as near as we could understand them, two miles from its junction with the Maggori.

Before starting we paid Toroni a farewell visit, in hope of a chance to buy some swords, bows, coats, snuff boxes, spears, etc. But not a thing did we get, except a photograph of the interior of the munyata, Toroni lording it in the centre of the picture. Neither among the Kavirondo nor at Toroni's were we able to get even a price set on a single curio, much less to buy one: tight to their weapons, war panoply, and personal trinkets both lots stuck.

When we arrived at the munyata we found practically all the men and youths out tending their flocks and herds, while the ladies of the village were divided about equally into three busy groups.

At the time it was quite the height of the local dry season, so that there was no rain whatever except a torrential all-night downpour every third night, with heavy thunder and lightning, and on each two intervening nights two to three hour showers that would make a stranger yell for a life preserver, all which was not especially conservative of the Masai architecture.

Thus the first of the three groups of Masai ladies we encountered were engaged in gathering handfuls of fresh cow dung and plastering damaged roofs with it; the second group, seated beneath trees near the gate, was engaged in braiding rush mats; while the third lolled in the shade, alternatingly dozing and watching Groups One and Two, these latter, probably, the Sultani's favorites.

Inquiring for Toroni, we were pointed to a lone tree on a hill two hundred yards away, where we found him stretched on a lion skin, frayed and worn of years as was he himself, sleeping off what must have been an extra heavy overnight jag of "bang" or tembo, for the hour of our call was near noon. Indeed it was with some difficulty we roused sufficient energy in him to get him to toddle back to the munyata and stand long enough to be photographed.

About our "Looseandgiddy" camp elephant sign from one to three days old was thick everywhere; individual tracks, roads beaten smooth thirty feet wide, many trees one to two feet thick and thirty to forty feet high uprooted, wallows, tall giant tree trunks rubbed bare of bark and stained or plastered with mud ten feet from the ground, elephant "rub-downs" after a mud bath. One such tree stood immediately before my tent door, bare of bark and mud-stained ten feet from its base, and with a heavy limb extending at right angles from the trunk eleven feet from the ground whose underside was also barked and mud-stained, proving there was at least one worthy old giant tusker left living thereabouts.

And yet for three days we ranged the country round about from dawn to dark, south to the Maggori and north toward the Kisii, without sighting anything but a few buck.

The morning of the fourth day, disgusted by fruitless prowls,

Outram and I lay in camp, when at ten o'clock one of our two Masai came panting in with word he had a big bull marked down two hours to the north, having left his mate on watch. And off we were trekking in five minutes at the best pace we could make through grass, bowlders, and bush.

Sharp at twelve the watching Masai stopped us. Below his hillside post lay the heavily timbered valley of a tributary of the Oyani, and down into the timber he pointed.

While light, the wind was wrong for an approach from that side, so we made a wide detour to the south and wormed our way through the half-mile of timber to the west side, only to find the wind had shifted. Then we made another wide circle, recrossed to the east side of the valley, and, finding the wind held fair, swung round to a point where we could plainly hear what we took to be our bull-for the boys had seen only one alternately smashing bush and splashing water.

Here Akuna and Habia stripped themselves of skin wraps, sandals, neck chains, and ear rings, of every thing but a bow and three poisoned arrows each, and crept into the wall of vine and foliage. Outram and I, followed by our two gun bearers, ourselves stripped of everything that could catch, scratch, or rattle, crept in after them. By all ill luck there were no elephant or other game paths where we entered, making progress doubly difficult.

While midday with a blazing sun outside, within the forest was dark as a heavily curtained room. Our progress was like swimming through breakers, waves of vines and foliage engulfing us at nearly every step. Sometimes we could not see an arm's length about us, usually no more than ten feet; and when not corkscrewing ourselves through vines and creepers, we were clambering up the one side and glissading down the other of mosscovered and slippery fallen forest giants.

About a hundred yards in we reached the muddy stream, and there encountered redoubled difficulties. Flowing in a straight or steep-banked channel ten to twenty feet deep and thirty to forty feet wide, it did its best toward boxing the compass every thirty yards, serpentine as the vines that dangle above it or the python that twine in ambush upon its overhanging boughs.

At the first crossing Awala, my gun bearer, slipped and fell splashing into the creek fifteen feet below, but luckily at the same instant the tusker had hold of a bough he wanted in his business and was making racket enough to drown any noise short of a shot.

All the time we were drawing nearer our quarry, pushing deeper toward the centre of the bush, working carefully up wind, there so light one could scarce feel it, the two naked Masai gliding ahead of us keen as hounds and silent and sinuous of movement as snakes.

Not a sound had we heard save from the one point, apparently all made by one elephant; therefore we felt assured we were in luck and had before us a really big old tusker, for such usually flock by their lonesomes or in pairs.

After three crossings of the brook, we were able to work along it perhaps eighty yards, to a place where we had to stop. Immediately in front of us, not ten feet away it seemed and we later found it was actually twenty feet, behind a solid wall of foliage was our elephant.

And no sooner were we stopped than, as if as a concerted tip to us that they had us where they wanted us, all about us rose sounds of elephant—a smashing branch here, a mighty sigh of surfeit there, a splash in the stream, the suck of a great foot pulled from mud! We had innocently meandered into the middle of a feeding herd!

They were even behind us, and absolutely the only direction in which we could see thirty feet was immediately to our left, where a fallen log bridged the creek from bank to bank twenty feet above the water, and that happened to be the only point from which we did not hear them.

If we had tried we could scarcely have put ourselves in a more foolish or dangerous position; for no matter how heavy the ivory he sights, no experienced elephant hunter shoots in the middle of a herd he has unwittingly pushed into; whichever way they start they go, and like as not it will be the hunter's way; while if a wounded bull doesn't hunt you down as relentlessly as a fiend, it is an even bet some pet lady of his harem will.

Neither Outram nor I had ever seen wild elephant, much less hunted them, and what to do was a puzzle to us the more so that questions and answers must needs be limited to silent signs. Of course we might have slipped away to probable safety across the fallen tree trunk, but that was not precisely what we had been doing a fortnight's marching and scouting for.

So there we stood, still as statues, eyes roving aloft, ahead, to right and aft, not daring even to cock a gun (I had a Winchester .405 in my hands with a Mauser 9 m.m. in reserve) before catching a glimpse of a head, expecting every instant to see a giant trunk reaching down for us.

Of course every move they made sounded as if they were coming; not once by any happy chance did we hear any sound that suggested a recessional.

And so expectantly we stood, I myself, I frankly admit, gripping my teeth together till they ached to help hold my nerves steady; and so round us they fed and amused themselves full twenty minutes, they in as blissful ignorance of our presence as we of what was going to happen, or how hard it would happen when it got well started.

After a number of minutes, anywhere from twenty to thirty probably, the two Masai tiptoed across the fallen tree and slipped a few feet up stream, where both crouched and gestured violently to us to come at once.

They were at precisely a point to see behind the screen in front of me and have in view the elephant they had located as the big bull they had seen and reported, provided he was not also screened from the east.

At the moment there was a tremendous racket all about us, and I thought I would chance it.

The log was level half the way, and then rose in a steep five-foot bend to its lodgement on the farther bank, green with loose-clinging wet moss; and, by all contraries in this maze of tangle, not a single vine or branch within reach of it.

Out I started, with gun transversed as a balancing pole, and steadied, I suppose, by our dilemma, over it I safely got, notwithstanding groans and yieldings of the rotten trunk that I thought surely would dump me twenty feet to the stream beneath. Indeed, I had to go so gingerly that the more active Outram shinned down a vine, waded the creek, and hand-over-handed up another vine to a close finish, both in time and silence, with my crossing.

Crept up to the Masai, to our disgust we found no more was there to be seen than from our previous stand, though we could see fifty yards on our left, useful if the elephant moved that way, and on that they had summoned us.

But scarcely had we taken in our new position before a very hell of torment broke loose on our front,— trees crashing as if they were being levelled by a cyclone, trumpetings shrill and blood-chilling as the storm's angriest voices, the dull thud of bumping colossi and the sharp almost metallic clash of ivory tusks grinding in the mad stampede, like the rasp of giant swords in deadly play.

For a half-second, or minute, or hour, I give it up which, the outer lot raced straight in on the chap in front of us, and therefore straight at us, while there was nothing for us to do but stand fast, ready to pump lead into the faces of the first-comers on the off chance of turning them.

Beside us, steady as rocks, stayed the two little Masai, each with a slender, puny arrow half-drawn to the head, safe enough in time to kill but powerless to stop. Indeed, I recall a flying wish I might be excused long enough from the more urgent duties of the moment to snapshot them—with every muscle of their lithe, graceful bodies tense, left foot advanced, knees slightly bent, and sinewy fingers tugging at bow strings, they were for an artist an ideal pose of flint-age warriors.

Of course the creek lay between us, which might seem measurable protection, but it was not, for elephant go up and down declivities, almost in their stride, that would balk almost anything less agile than an ape.

But, come directly up to "our" elephant, of his fancy or theirs, all whirled and thundered straight away from us, angling to our right. And back across logs and creek, through vines and scrub, we hurdled as best we could for chance of a sight of them.

But scarcely were we a hundred feet beyond the creek, before directly back upon their tracks they came at as mad a pace as their start, and back to our original stand by the stream side we dashed.

These were the most trying seconds of the lot, for it seemed certain we had to face a straight onrush and turn them or take whatever was coming to us.

It proved to be our day to learn a lot of the elephant's whims and of the downright stark miraculous things he can do when he likes.

Stock-still they stopped ten yards from us (as we afterwards proved), but hidden from us as before, and this time bunched to perhaps a half-circle about us. Stopped, and for probably ten minutes there was utter silence in the forest, save for the barking of monkeys querulous of all the row, and then the beggars started feeding and amusing themselves as before. This continued for perhaps fifteen minutes, when absolutely all sound again ceased and the wood was still of them as if they had all dropped dead which in fact, in our ignorance we fancied they had, dead asleep.

And there we sat for the larger part of an hour, wondering what length of afternoon siesta is approved in well-regulated elephant families, in constant expectation of renewed movement by some of the herd, and in hope of a show for a shot at a bull worth while. That they were still within the toss of a biscuit of us we would have sworn.

But when, presently, a slight stir among the leaves directly before Outram made us throw up our rifles, out stepped Akuna, who had raced out of our sight in pursuit of the first stampede to track its route and had been cut off from us by their sudden return, with the incredible intelligence that the elephant were gone out of the bush and trekking away into the north.

Was the Masai mad or were we? Or was it all just a dream? Or had we been drunk of the excitement of a real experience?

Magic! No prestidigitator could touch this vanishing act, from under our very noses, of tons and tons of ambulant weight in country where we pigmies could scarce stir without causing noise, where nothing short of a legitimate spook or a handily manipulated "materializing spirit" could circulate without twig-snapping and leaf-rustling!

And yet it proved to be true. Gone were they all, by what miracles of stealth I doubt if the oldest elephant hunter knows: one has them before him, almost within gun-barrel touch, and then they are gone! That is all.

And yet in our case the spoor of their leaving showed that, besides the obstacles of the forest growth, they had within fifty feet of us crossed a wide area of mud into which their great bulk had stamped footprints eighteen inches deep (one measuring twenty-two inches from toe to heel), and then passed down into and across the gravelly stream bed, that crunched to our lightest tread.

How many were there? Quien sabe? Massed in the onrush of mad flight, it sounded like two thousand in fact, as well as we could judge from the tracks merging outside the bush into a great, broad, improvised road, there were between twenty and forty.

If seeing alone were believing, there were no elephant, for not the smallest glimpse of one did any of our party get. But there all about lay bark-stripped boughs, the wreck of their luncheon, there on the sturdier tree trunks within a few yards of our position was the wet mud of their "rub-down."

On their spoor we followed until we realized it was useless to go farther-off they were, as usual in such cases, for a twenty to forty mile constitutional, bearing toward the Kisii Highlands.

So we headed for camp, reaching there long after dark just as tired as if we had really done something.

One more day we lay at the "Looseandgiddy" camp, circling the country again carefully as far as we could reach until convinced all the sign of elephant thereabouts had been made by the departed herd. While profitless of game, the day was interesting and amusing. I was ranging to the south, alone with Habia, incidentally looking for a Lichtenstein bull which I had wounded late the previous evening near camp, and which had trekked off that way. A country where tracking an individual buck was impossible, my only guide to his retreat was the birds, the vultures or marabouts. These carrion feeders must certainly be gifted with eyesight of high telescopic power. Drop a kill without a bird in sight, and before you get the skin off, usually, the ill-favored tribe are all about you in a thick flight or glaring hungrily down from perch in neighboring treetops. Rarely does a wounded buck travel a mile before he is spied by some winged scout soaring so high in the blue he is an almost indistinguishable speck, and then it is only a matter of an instant when, by some weird signal code none but the birds themselves will ever know, a merciless crew is cruising near above him from which there is for him no escape if he once goes down, for, by some cruelly cunning felon instinct, their first assault is upon his dimming eyes. Nor, though strong enough to keep his feet for hours or fight off attack if down, may he reckon on escape — all day long they hover above him, all night long perch about any bushy nook in which he may be vainly seeking rest.

It is bad enough to shoot and kill any harmless beast, only explainable as an irrepressible survival of aboriginal instincts, bred into some of us past eradication by generations of ancestral skin-wearing, two-legged carnivora, but it is absolutely wicked to wound such and leave them, and I never leave a wounded beast so long as chance remains of reaching and finishing him.

The Lichtenstein, however, proved too strong for both man and bird. Early, within two miles of camp, a slowsoaring, circling crew of birds marked him down for us on a high hillslope, covered with grass, rocks, and bush one could not get through without so much noise that approach was impossible. Off he would go each time at such a pace, shown by the fast-shifting birds, that after two hours we saw that further pursuit must be useless.

Then we swung across the top of the high hill we had been following, and I got a superb view of the great valley of the Maggori River and its wide watershed, far south into German territory, the distant hills showing a line of smoke columns that told of dense native settlement.

Descending toward the river, suddenly my Masai stopped and bent and listened. We were in good elephant country, sign all about, on our immediate right a deep, heavily timbered gorge, and I, too, paused to listen, but all I could hear was the peculiar twitter-twitter of a flitting flock of tiny birds, strange to me.

Presently off down hill darted Habia, faster than I could follow over such bad going, out of my sight in a half-dozen jumps. Whatever had started him or whatever he was after I could not fancy, but on I followed.

Shortly I found him, at the turn of a bush, bent over gathering wisps of dry and green grass and twining and pressing them into a tight round wad. This finished to suit him, he ran to me with it and signed he wanted a match, quicker a bit but no surer than his own fire sticks.

Puzzled, but powerless to question him, I gave him matches, when he ran to a big bowlder almost hidden in the long grass, bent and parted the tangle at one corner of its base, crouched, lighted his wad of grass, and close against the bottom of the rock laid it, bending his face close down above the smoking grass and tightly hooding head and smoke with his skin coat.

'Hello," thought I, "here's a new cure for influenza," for he had been snuffling and coughing from a cold for a day or two. I started to approach, the better to watch him, when out and all about me roared a colony of mad bees, wild for revenge upon the looter of their hard-won honey. And, as usual, the real looter got off far the lightest, how I don't know for he was in a crowd of them for several minutes while I was tumbling down hill at my best pace and keeping ahead of all but their fastest sprinters, too. In fact, just for once even Habia could not catch me—until I had safely outfooted the last of my other pursuers. Nor did I feel at all adequately compensated when he came panting up to me with four great cakes of beautiful amber honey, each about twelve inches by five inches in size, three tucked under the arm that held his bow and knob-kerrie, the full half of the fourth down his throat, and the other half following as fast as he could ram it down without quite choking to death, as also followed down the same insatiable little maw within the next half-hour practically all of the three other great slabs; a nibble or two did for me, for that particular lot was of indifferent flavor. But, flavor or no flavor, with that little savage honey was honey and stood no more show of prolonged existence than a smuggled box of chocolate caramels in a girls' boarding school.

Lower down the slope I sighted with my glasses a herd of water buck far away across the Maggori, two fine heads in the lot. Supposing the river little more there than the broiling, overgrown brook we had crossed a few miles higher up, I hurried down toward it, in spite of a torrent of b'r'ring, clucking, sputtering Masai that was plainly a stagger at protest. Pushing through the wide belt of thorn and palm that lined the stream, I soon learned the reason: before me stretched a broad yellow flood, over a hundred feet wide and looking deep enough to float a cruiser and mean enough to harbor crocodiles. That was quite too large an order. But directly the murmur of distant rapids caught my ear. A half-mile down stream we found them, the river cascading down a sharp descent among a lot of big white bowlders—bowlders so thickly strewn in the roaring, plunging current I thought I could negotiate them. To mid-stream I did get, but there the next jump was hopelessly long from a wet and slippery take-off, and I had to give it up. Nor did I get back ashore any too easily, for where, coming, I had picked rough surfaces and edges to alight on, returning, reverse sides offered no better than smooth slopes that kept me moving quickly once I started; for, once tumbled into it, no man could have made shore out of that turmoil.

However, I did not regret the detour when I got a lovely photograph of the head of the boiling rapid and the palms that crown it. And I regretted it less when, ten minutes later, taking shelter in bush from a heavy shower, I found a wild cherry tree loaded with delicious fruit half ripe, golden and crimson; ripe, their fat sides reflecting all the richer, duskier ruby lights a decanter of port flashes back at the candles.

Sweet were those cherries of flavor as they were beautiful of favor; and there we stayed so long eating them that, what with that delay, and, tipped by another twitter of honey birds, the scenting, robbing, and consumption of another bee treasure store by Habia (this time found in a hollow tree), night fell upon us so far from camp that none but an aboriginal's instincts for location and direction could have brought us in.

That day our donkeys arrived from the Mara and were pushed on to Mr. Northcote's boma for the posho we had left with him.

The next two days we travelled east toward the Mara, camping at noon of the second day on the wide reaches of low, rolling tableland that form the crest of the Isuria Escarpment, and near its eastern brink, where it drops almost sheer twelve hundred feet to the valley of the Mara.

Burned the year before of its tangle of old grass, then carpeted with a short two-foot growth of juicy blue grass, its tops already seeded and browning, stirred by the breezes into ever shifting patterns, reflecting sunlight on its crests and shadowed in its hollows, dotted here and there with wild olives and mats of bush, it looked like a vast field of richly embossed Spanish leather tinged with every hue of russet and of green.

Quick is Dame Nature's scene-shifting in Equatorial Africa. A fortnight earlier rain was pouring nightly; vivid greens were everywhere, ponds in every hollow, the birds blithely twittering their merriest spring songs, the sun blazing out of a vault of cobalt blue.

Returned, with the rain stopped no more than four days—as we could plainly see from our "Looseandgiddy" camp—we found busy, pulsing Spring had made a one-bound leap into the restful lap of "Indian Summer"; birds indolent, slow of flight, and little prone to song; the sharp, high-keyed metallic ring of the African crickets' chirp mellowed to lower, lazier notes; the drone of myriad insects; flights of grasshoppers rising as one walked, in white clouds that looked like an inverted, uprising snow storm; a heavy haze over all the land that completely hid the outlook down upon and across the valley of the Mara until, standing upon the edge of the escarpment, it seemed as if one had stepped out upon some bold headland and was gazing off across a fog-hid sea.

Out at 3 P. M. Outram and I strolled, in different directions, on the chance of roan or eland and to kill meat for the camp, of which we had had little for many days while in the Maggori-Oyani country.

Tiny thirty-pound oribi were thick almost as the grasshoppers, and about as hard to shoot. Usually you never saw them until they rose out of the grass at your feet and dodged away at express speed, with low-bent heads all hidden from your sight in the grass, rising occasionally in mighty leaps six or eight feet above the grass tops for a glimpse of whatever might be going on around them. Occasionally you had a glimpse of two little ears or a slender pair of four-inch, straight upstanding horns, and caught through the grass tops the gleam of great liquid eyes fixed upon you in wondering inquiry, and then a graceful, fourteen-carat golden-yellow body went alternately gliding and rocketing past you. They take shooting, do these little oribi, for while sometimes you can get a standing shot at from seventy-five to one hundred and fifty yards, usually all you see is the little head and neck, and it's a guess for the position of the body.

While I saw no roan or eland, that was rather a banner evening for me in shooting. My bag included one fine water buck with twenty-six-inch horns, three Coke's hartebeeste bulls, and two oribi, each killed with a single shot except the big four-hundred-pound water buck, which needed a second to down him.

And never have I seen such extraordinary evidence of the amazing vitality of African game, big and little, as there. The first of the two oribi bounded away as if not hit, although I knew I must have struck it.

Following the line of its flight, and leaving my gun bearer to try to follow its actual trail, at the turn of a bush I saw an oribi standing that I took to be mine, but before I could shoot, off he bounded, and several more rose from the grass and followed him. Then off a long way on my left I spied another lone oribi and began stalking. Presently it trotted ahead, and I saw that it was followed by what I took to be its toto (kid), nuzzling eagerly for dinner. Then down lay the "doe" and into its belly dove a little yellow head, apparently not longer to be denied a suckle.

Surprised, wondering if antelope really suckle their young while recumbent, I stole closer and closer, until directly I was astounded to find that the pair were the wounded oribi buck and my blood-thirsty little Irish bull terrier Pugge, who, unknown to me, had rushed across from Outram at the sound of my shot and found and tackled the wounded quarry.

This buck there lay full seven hundred yards from where he had received my full shot! And how much farther he might have gone without Pugge's intervention I can only conjecture.

Outram played in better luck, for he sighted roan and brought in the only one he contrived to get a shot at, a fine young buck but with immature horns.

That night our camp looked like a well-stocked butcher's shop, with its one thousand, five hundred pounds of hanging meat; and from dark to dawn our crowd of shenzi porters sat noisily gorging themselves, like a bunch of Indians after a big buffalo kill, and cutting into strips and smoke-curing the meat they could not stow inside them. Nor were they the only hungry ones about, for repeatedly a tribe of laughing hyena tried to rush the meat, and were only kept off by the firebrands the jealous porters kept throwing at them.

One more try we had for roan and eland from that camp, but without success, travelling ten miles southeast along the escarpment to the skeleton of a triangulation beacon, built there on a high promontory five years before by Outram for the Boundary Survey. After we had abandoned hope of getting better game that day, I mortally wounded a big wart-hog, but he showed a lot of fight and got three more shots.

Groggy, but not down, Outram called to the porter leading her to loose Pugge. Stupidly released with the leading chain still fast to her collar, the plucky little terrier bounded to the attack, and hot and heavy she and the pig had it for ten minutes.

But the porter's blunder nearly cost us Pugge's life, for midway of the fight the pig fell and lay upon the chain, and then, shaking her loose from her pet hold aft, swung and caught her by the throat, slitting it to ribbons but luckily not puncturing the jugular. It all happened so quickly that before Outram got in a finishing shot Pugge had wrested free of the boar's sharp tusks and was herself tackling again as furiously as ever.

Early in the afternoon we parted, Outram swinging to the west and I to the east. Just at sundown I shot a good Chandler reed buck in one of the favorite haunts of its kind, among the crags along the edge of the escarpment. Night fell before the buck was skinned, and although the moon was well on in its first quarter I should never have made the six miles to camp, winding among endless isolated clumps of timber and belts of heavy forest, but for the brute instinct of Habia, my little Wanderobo-bred Masai, who always brought me in on air lines, no matter how dark the night was.

VIII. "CLOSE THING, THAT, RIGHT-OH!"

THE next morning, January 30, we received a message from our Engabai (Masai name for Mara) camp to the effect that a mysterious lone muzungu was there awaiting us, whom Outram was not long in placing as a sort of cross between a trader and a raider, whose camp in German territory had been seized recently and his arms, goods, and cattle confiscated or destroyed by German Askaris, one of the fast-disappearing class of ivory hunters and traders who a few years ago were winning fortunes at their dangerous game.

Indeed, I have met men who have cleared as high as $75,000 off their ivory taken on a six months' expedition, some traded from the natives but most of it fallen to their own guns. Then came the game laws, the game rangers to enforce them, and heavy penalties for infringement, making contraband all ivory but the insignificant lots shot under a sportsman's license. Not a few rebelled against these laws, the hardy, independent lot, many gentlemen bred, who for years had endured every hardship and taken their lives in their hands every morning they went out into forest or long grass after tuskers, every hour they spent in the fever-breeding jungles, elephants' haunt, lured by the love of adventure and the chance of gains adequate to afford them every last luxury of civilization for the half-year they spent out of the bush. But while elephants and other game had to be protected to save them from extinction, it was a misfortune for the country that it should have become necessary to legislate this class out of the field. Expressed official opinions to the contrary notwithstanding, these latterday ivory hunters and traders, come in on the heels of the departing Arabs, were pacifiers of the natives, working usually as individuals, all alone, or at best in pairs, without armed escorts, with none but native attendants and porters, their prosperity and indeed their very existence dependent upon just, fair dealing with all natives with whom they came in contact.

What with diplomacy and sheer bluff, these men often settled tribal turbulence, and even succeeded in making peace between tribes that, previously, had never ceased warring with and raiding each other. Sometimes, to be sure, they won peace at cost of blood, but peace they always strove for as most conducive to their own success.

Indeed, several of these men often wielded more actual influence and power over thousands of natives than that inspired by all the authority and armed force of the established Government as when John Boies went among the hostile Kikuyu alone and brought in food supplies that saved from impending famine hundreds of Swahilis and East Indians employed in building the Uganda Railway, followed this stroke by pacifying and amalgamating thirty-five hostile factions of the Kikuyu, and so firmly held the rein on them that five thousand Kikuyu warriors were equally ready to make war or till their shambas at his command, ruled them with such undisputed sway that he was actually made king of the Kikuyu; or as when John Alfred Jordan went alone into the Setik and brought into Kericho chiefs that had refused to come on Government summons, and whom the Government felt they had no force adequate to fetch, chiefs who had never before entered a British post or camp.

And it was one of these men, no other than John Alfred Jordan himself, we found at our Engabai camp when we trekked down there January 31.

Above six feet in height, high-browed, with keen, brightly intellectual face lighted by big, brown, dreamy eyes that glint dangerous lights when lit by a spirit of devilment or fury, beardless save for a wisp of dark moustache and two little chin tufts that served to accentuate a set of lean, square jaws, with the long, slender, delicate hands of an artist belied by a great reach of arm and Fitzsimmons shoulders, usually slow and indolent of motion but a cat in activity and a whirlwind in force when roused, Jordan silent about the camp fire, meditative, in repose bore a remarkable resemblance to Robert Louis Stevenson.

A native-born Englishman, of experience in our own Far West, a trooper in the Cape Mounted Police through the Transvaal War, when I met him Jordan had been ivory hunting and trading all the way from the Boran and Turkana country along the southern border of Abyssinia away south far into German territory, and never, I will stake my head, a wrong-doer at anything save in venturing his life on long, lonely exiles far from all other white men in territory which the Government had seen fit to leave in its raw state of black occupation and to declare "closed" alike to traders, travellers, and sportsmen, except under special license, like mine and not easy to get, never a wrong-doer except as he may have engaged in just a bit of ivory poaching or in gathering wild rubber in "closed" districts, for which he has fallen under official ban.

The chance meeting was fortunate alike to Jordan and to us. To us he meant the best expert advice on where to find elephant and how best to attack them; to him we meant a source of much-needed supplies, for which he never hinted a want but which we soon saw he lacked and were glad to be able to make him take.

Himself a trespasser within the "closed" territory I was then in by courtesy of Lieutenant-Governor Jackson, we found Jordan accompanied by three warriors, superb big fellows, and a boy, all Lumbwa; with no better shelter than a grass hut of the sort natives soon throw together for a night's camp; with absolutely no food supply but native posho and a slender flock of sheep and goats he had saved from the German raid of his camp; unarmed save with two cartridges and an old, worn-out .303 rifle, dangerous to none but him who fired it; with no wardrobe but the brown cord shooting coat and frayed khaki shorts and puttees he stood in; with his right leg from ankle to knee raw of eczema (then and for months previously) for lack of proper dressing and of which he suffered unintermitting tortures without a murmur (most luckily I had with me some oxynol which soon gave him relief and had him nearly cured of eczema when we parted),⊠ nevertheless this man was richer far in happiness and in perfect content with his environment and lot, desperate hard as it might seem to others, than all the princes of finance put together, happiest, doubtless, for that the fine fibre of his mentality obviously held not even the most fragile film of greed or envy.

So soon as he learned I was keen for elephant, lion, and a bigger rhino than the N'gari Kiti kill, he volunteered his own services and that of his Lumbwa and Wanderobo subjects in locating them for me. Nor did he want nor would he accept any recompense; instead, had I let him, within the first week he would have stripped himself of his one available asset, his pathetically small flock of fat-tailed sheep and goats killing them for our table and trading them to natives for spears, shields, swords, and rare rhino horn knob-kerries, curios he knew I sought. Chided for his prodigality and improvidence, quick came the chap's philosophy.

"Well, you see anything else would not be playing my game. As you find me here, I am living my life, the life that suits me. Here, somewhere, in a quiet nook of the African forest, I shall probably finish.

"Money? It means nothing to me. I've made money, lots of it, in the past, and had no more good of it I found real value in than I get here.

"I've been among the first in a dozen of the great African mining camps, but never once pegged a claim. Why? Not my game. I'm only a hunter and native trader. Enough! A bit short of trade goods now, as you see; not a scrap of 'Americani' or a single 'Buda' bead left, thanks to the Germans, but I'll get on, rightoh! no fear.

"Towns? More than a day or two of any of them is hateful to me; 'doddering hermit,' I dare say some fools might call me, but I love my kind well as any other your kind, fellows with the nerve to cut loose and go it alone down here where even the thriftiest official has never yet ventured to lead his Askaris after hut tax.

"Come along with me and I'll show you such shooting as you never dreamed of, elephant, rhino, lion, buffalo. Trek with me four or five days northwest into the Rongana River country, and I'll summon my Wanderobo and Lumbwa friends to mark them down for us. I'll show them to you, right enough—then it's up to you to get them."

Travelling for weeks along and through forests we knew to be haunts of the Wanderobo; always compelled to be watchful for their dangerous pitfall game-traps; occasionally stumbling across their temporary hut villages, the only approach to a town these shifty, wandering hunters ever build, but never seeing one of them; knowing that travellers who have needed forest guides and have succeeded in surprising, capturing, and binding any of them, saw the awesome spectacle of creatures in man's image fighting as furiously for liberty as madmen, frothing mouths gnawing at their bonds like wild beasts; primitive creatures whose only earthly fixed assets are their bows and iron-tipped arrows, their rudely fashioned iron short swords and narrow-bladed hatchets, and their two fire sticks; their only food besides wild honey the wild game whose own supreme cunning and stealth they are compelled to surpass to enable them to make a kill with their short-range weapons; roving dwellers in chill high altitudes where their women and children go cold and a-hunger when they fail to fetch in skins and meat, I expressed surprise and gratification that he could command the services of these matchless trackers.

"Wanderobo?" he replied. "Command them? Rather! Why, man, I've lived alone and hunted with them for months at a time-gone hungry with them when sudden shifts of the game occurred and their most dreaded spectre, famine, brooded over every hut; set their broken bones, dressed their wounds. Come to me? Just watch them in a run. Only it may bother me a lot to hold them when they find two strange muzungu with me, for the Wanderobo are still wild and suspicious as a buffalo.

"Of course, what with the pushing out of white settlements, shooting safaris, and consequent thinning out of the game, their forest life is growing harder and harder every year, notwithstanding in one season only six or seven years ago the Wanderobo of the upper Maggori traded the ivory of no less than four hundred elephant in Karungu and in German territory to Greek traders.

"Indeed, that little band, Labusoni's lot, are, so far as I know, the only group of the real Wanderobo elephant hunters still left. Many have already amalgamated with the Masai and are living in munyatas, among them even a son of Labusoni, the old medicine chief.

"About eight years ago the most profitable industry of Mataia, chief of the warlike Lumbwa, was capturing Wanderobo and holding them for ransom in ivory and raiding the Southern Masai for cattle and women, until finally he had burned all the munyatas along and to the west of the Engabai and the Masai were all speared or scattered.

"Old Koydelot, chief witch doctor of the Masai, was one of the few who escaped to asylum among the Wanderobo. There his 'medicine' was soon found to be so strong he was able to win over a lot of Wanderobo, whom later he amalgamated with a few Masai fugitives and built the little group of munyatas between the Engabaiand the escarpment, their flocks and herds chiefly the fruit of raids of German natives.

"Only the old hard-shells, dyed-in-the-wools like Labusoni, have clung to the old forest life.

"Labusoni? Eighty now, if he is a day, but every sunrise sees him off into the bush with bow and arrows, like the meanest of his followers, ears keen for the twitter of a honey-bird or the whirr of a bee swarm, shrewd old eyes scanning bush and grass for buck. Twice when nearly starved he has gone with his family to his son, at Koydelot's, but the monotony of munyata shepherd life was too slow for him, and as soon as he was fattened up a bit, back into the bush he trekked.

"My word, but one of Labusoni's old-fashioned elephant round-ups was a sight!

"Of nights before such hunts he assembled all his men about a small fire apart from the huts, after all the women and children had gone to sleep.

"Then Labusoni began to chant the elephant song, the Wanderobo war song, recounting the glories of the chase the craft and bravery of the boldest, the big kills they had made, the need of their women and children, the riches in beads and trinkets the ivory spoils would bring, the stout bow strings their great back sinews would furnish, the matchless shields and enduring sandals their thick hides, the capacious pouches their great bladders, the vast stores of fat with which Wanderobo love to smear the outer as well as the inner man.

"On and on Labusoni would sing, voice rising shriller and shriller, until his wild henchmen were wrought up to a madness of which all eyes at the same time gleamed savage fury and streamed tears, limbs trembled like wind-shaken reeds, nervous fingers snatched sword blades from their sheaths, and the grim shadows brooding about the camp fire were set all brightly alight with the shimmer of brandishing blades.

"Then, dropping his voice to quiet tones, Labusoni personally addressed each in turn:

"Coboli! your father was no coward; in my youth he loved to dodge under the bellies of the Big Ones and stab them from beneath. If you are afraid, stay in your hut with your women!

"Njunge! your father got none but sons; if you are turned woman, go stalking little buck!

"Minyatuke! if the thought of the thunder of the Big Ones rushing when they get your wind makes you tremble, go follow the honey-birds!

"Sibibi! if the shrill screams of rage of the arrowhit weaken your finger tug at the bow string, stay fleshing and dressing skins with the women!

"Weana! if the crash of falling forest to the charge of a maddened herd quickens your heart beat, give your women and children to a real man and go stab yourself for a cur!

""Surbube! for you it should be enough to remember you are son of Labusoni, who has missed no chance of a kill of the Big Ones since his youth, and who will be following them until his old carcass is tossed to the fisi (hyena), the common end of all our people!

"The effects of song and personal appeal were so deeply stirring of every savage instinct, that usually by the time Labusoni was finished several of his men were so stark frenzied mad, they were actually amuck, frothing at the mouth, slashing right and left with their weapons, and often many had to be seized and bound.

"Morning come, cooled from the night's excitement, steady nerved of the past week's complete abstinence from honey beer and women always practised as preparation for an elephant hunt, the band stole out of the forest in single file, silent as ghosts, led by Labusoni, to a camp three or four miles from the position of a located herd. At dawn of the following day, two scouts made a thorough reconnaissance and reported. If all conditions were favorable, Labusoni handed to each bits of 'medicine,' herbs and roots potential to stouten their hearts, built a rude arch of green boughs and then led his men beneath it to the chase, every ear strained for the first note of Ol Toilo, the luck bird: if heard behind them, a guaranty of safety for all; if to the right, or ahead, or unheard, a sign of a good kill, but with casualties; if on the left, such a certainty of a poor kill and heavy losses of men that the chase was for the day abandoned.

"Unless Ol Toilo forbade, on the column moved to near approach of the herd, when it was halted and Labusoni disposed his forces for the attack, the old men holding the position they then occupied, the lione (uncircumcised youths) being sent to the right of the herd, the elmorani (young warriors) to the left and the farther side.

"In long grass the Wanderobo never attack elephant, escape from attack by the wounded is too nearly impossible. When found so placed, the herd was frightened into a dash for the nearest forest by the yells and skin-coat shaking of the outer flankers, while within the wood their mates awaited the onrush, seventy-two-inch bows bent, thirty-six-inch arrows drawn to their poisoned tips.

"So, with keen-biting, empoisoned arrow flights and frantic yells and skin shaking, for a time the herd was turned hither and yon, from one line of flankers to another, sometimes was so held for as much as an hour within an area no more than a half-mile square, with individual duels here and there between the wounded and one or another of their enemies whom they had sighted and whom they pursued with such fury and cunning of attack that naught but a Wanderobo's wind and dexterity at dodging and tree climbing left the pigmy assailant any chance at all of escape.

"Ultimately, of course, the herd broke through the attacking lines, and then the search for the dead began, and runners were sent to fetch up the women and children; and thereabout, upon and literally inside their kills, the tribe camped until every last fragment of meat was eaten, every bone cracked, and its sweet, fat contents sucked.

"As high as thirty elephant have fallen in such a hunt within an hour to one attacking party numbering no more than forty men."

February 1 was for me a day of remarkably mixed luck in the matter of shooting, for, after beginning with six clean misses of a splendid water buck I much wanted, at ranges from one hundred and twenty-five to one hundred and seventy-five yards, I finished by killing a gray Wildebeeste bull at six hundred yards and three kongoni at three hundred to four hundred yards, each dropping to a single shot. Two of the kongoni were left as lion bait, but with small hopes, for there game was too plenty to leave it likely they would touch a cold kill.

All that night lion were heard about camp, two in the direction the kills lay; but when I went out to them at dawn I found one kongoni eaten by leopard, and a mixed breakfast party of hyena, jackals, vultures, and marabout storks on and about the other, with lion tracks fresh in the blood but no sign he had touched the carcass.

Wanting a better Wildebeeste than that killed the day before, after breakfast Jordan and I rode away across the level plain to a low range of hills south of us, and there in those hills we saw such a sight as I never shall see again.

Come to the slightly rolling hillcrest and into a bit of open meadow perhaps two hundred yards square, to the east of us extended far as one could see an area of open scrub one could see into perhaps one hundred and fifty yards, apparently empty of game save for two Wildebeeste bulls that stood near its edge, one a fine one that later, when I got to him, proved to have a pair of twenty-four-inch horns, with a seventeen-inch spread.

At the first echo of my shot, hell broke loose behind him, and out of the seemingly empty scrub poured a wild stampede of game in thousands, Wildebeeste, topi, kongoni, zebra, Granti, Thompsoni, impala, wart-hogs, giraffe, water buck, oribi—all racing in mad terror at top speed and in an unbroken column twenty to one hundred beasts in width and solid as a charging squadron, a column that was ten to fifteen minutes passing us, first and last, that left our ears deafened with its thunder and that we estimated at anywhere from ten thousand to fifteen thousand head.

Plunging northwest across our little clearing, their sleek skins flashing back to the early morning sun every bright hue Nature had clad them in, muscles heaving and rippling beneath their shining hides, it was the sight of a lifetime, and looked as if an all-comers' Marathon was on and the entire animal kingdom started in it.

But, suddenly, while we stood in dumb wonder at the stupendous spectacle, marvelling whether the racing procession would ever end, some scare or freak of the leaders turned them back south out of the bush into which they had disappeared, back into our clearing and straight down upon Jordan and me as if they were fiends hunting us to the death instead of mere fear-maddened beasts, probably unconscious of our presence.

With neither time nor room to shift out of their path, there was nothing to do but stand and shoot into the leaders. And while only a matter of seconds, it seemed a lifetime before we had knocked over three Wildebeeste and five zebras and had turned the thundering tide slightly west of us.

Then we caught our breath and stood another seven or eight minutes in silent awe of their numbers, their beauty, their grace and speed, their terror-fixed eyes, their heaving flanks and shrilling nostrils, as they pounded past us, their nearer line never more than ten to twenty yards from us, golden impala leaping high into the air, only to disappear back into the angry animal wave beneath them like porpoise dropping back into a stormtossed sea, zebra galloping low and swift, kongoni bounding now and then as if something had bitten them, grayish black masses of Wildebeeste shouldering everything out of the way, giraffe awkwardly side-wheeling along in giant strides and towering above the heaving mass like ambulant watch towers, pigs humping along as best they could and ripping viciously with shining tusks when too close crowded.

It was not until the tail of the tide had swept quite out of sight into the south that either spoke, and then the imperturbable Jordan remarked:

"Jolly close thing, that, right-oh! Looked like you and me for pulp! Wonder if there's another flood on and these beggars have heard Noah the Second's 'all aboard' whistle?"

Then he strolled away to finish two of the wounded and I over to the stiffening Wildebeeste bull, whose life had bought us this incomparable spectacle, heart-broken that I could not have had Radclyffe Dugmere beside me with his camera.

IX. A HIDEOUS OLD HAUNTER

TO avoid the terrific heat, after the rains stopped in the lower valleys, which began blazing down upon the Engabai plains shortly after dawn, we broke camp at 3 A. M., February 3, reaching the summit of Isuria at 8 A. M., and finding our donkeys safely arrived there with the posho we had bought in Kavirondo. Then we marched on to permanent camp at one of Jordan's old bomas, where he had spent a year along with his Wanderobo and Lumbwa, his cows, sheep, and fowls, trading a bit, shooting a bit, idling and musing a lot, chief of the native chiefs, happy as a king until down upon him descended a collector and party of Askaris on a raiding search for ivory they fancied he had but never found, when in disgust he slipped away to another forest nook, and lodged himself anew.

Dawn found us out after eland or roan, but by noon we were back empty-handed — apparently the game had shifted, for there was little sign about to the west of us.

In camp we found Mataia, chief of the Manga Lumbwa, the stoutest vassal chief of Jordan's overlordship, with Arab Tumo, his foremost warrior, and two young elmorani, all come at Jordan's summons from their country, a full day's journey north.

Jordan, Mataia seemed to worship no other could bear his gun or do him service, while with his own kind I soon learned no ruler was ever more despotic or cruel.

Obedience to Mataia's command was instant or some ghastly punishment was administered.

In Mataia's domestic relations, discipline was carried to a highly effective if not a refined art.

If one of his wives brought him a great sufuria (cooking pot) heaped with food that did not suit him, he made her sit down and gorge the lot, followed by water in quarts until she was sufficiently near bursting to give him some confidence she might remember the next day how he liked his victuals cooked. If another stitched his new monkey-skin cloak badly, the least hint of her carelessness she could expect would be a warm application on the naked stomach in the form of Mataia's heated sword blade; while if one were suspected of too deep interest in any predatory swain of the tribe, a slash from Mataia's razor-edged sword blade, landed wherever his large experience and fertile fancy taught him it was likely to hurt most, usually served to protect the imperilled family honor, at least temporarily.

At 2 P.M. we went out again after game, led by Mataia, Arab Tumo, Arab Barta, and Mosoni as scouts and trackers. At 5 P. M., having seen nothing but topi and oribi, we were headed back toward camp, when Mosoni sighted a lone roan antelope.

Instantly all of us dropped out of sight in the grass, and Mosoni and I began circling for the wind. What with the grass and thickly scattered mats of bush, stalking was easy, so that we were soon well up within seventy-five yards of the roan. With its head down and back to us, I could not tell whether it was cow or bull, and therefore I crouched awaiting a better view, well under cover from it. But just then out of the tail of my eye I caught sight of two splendid roan bulls off on our right to which, not having previously seen, we were uncovered and which were trotting up to their mate, who at the instant caught the alarm and with them bounded behind bush, all out of sight before I even got my gun to my shoulder.

Then, while I was engaged in invoking backhanded blessings on this my second failure at a good chance of a roan trophy, out from behind a bush bounded a great roan beauty bigger than a water buck, and stopped broadside for a second's glimpse of us on a little anthill one hundred and seventy-five yards away, nose up and head turned to us, graceful horns sweeping back almost to its long sorrel mane, its red roan body glistening in the evening sun like burnished copper. Scarcely was he stopped, before I had a bead on his shoulder this time, and at the shot he went off at the buck-jump that usually spells a safe hit. A dozen bounds and he was out of sight, but, taking his trail, we found him down and stone dead one hundred and fifty yards from where he was hit. While the horns were disappointing, only twenty inches on the outer curve and six inches from tip to tip, it was a beautiful head, and I had my roan.

Our camp near the old Jordan boma was one of the loveliest on the entire trip. Wanderobo-colored a bit in thought and habit, Jordan camped us in dense forest, near a cold mountain brook, forest so thick one might have passed within a few yards without seeing us, so thick of foliage that it shut out the heavy night dews and the burning midday sun, where it was warm of nights and delightfully cool by day, the bush about us alive with monkeys and forest guinea fowl, darker blue of plumage and better eating by far than the sort found on the plains

After the experience of that camp, I never again pitched our tents outside a forest when one was at hand to shelter us.

Nights about the camp fires with Jordan were never dull. Some incident of the day or turn of the talk always served to start him on some stirring tale of weird bush happenings. That night he was particularly interesting, notwithstanding a heavy electrical storm was on and we were tightly shut in my tent, with no light but the dull flicker of our pipes.

"Wonder how long it will be before the last of all the strange animal and reptilian types native to Africa have been taken and classified?" he mused.

"What do you mean?" I asked. "Are there many types left which have been seen but remain untaken?"

"God only knows how many," he replied. "Why, it is only four years ago I killed my bongo and got the first perfect bongo skin ever taken. Before that Deputy Commissioner Isaac had gotten a piece of a bongo hide from the Wanderobo and had sent it to the British Museum, but mine was the first whole skin ever seen by a white man, and not so very many have been shot since.

"My word, but they are beauties! — bright red as an impala, white of jaw, with nine white stripes over sides, back, and quarters, short of leg but heavier of body than a roan, with horns curved and shaped like a bush buck's but tipped white as ivory. Mine was a corker, nine feet, six inches from nose to tail tip, with twenty-nine and one-half-inch horns. And it's hard to get, the beggars are; never see them outside the heaviest forest or afoot except at nights or at dawn or in the dusk. Indeed, I only got mine after putting out a lot of Wanderobo for days and days to beat up the forest.

"What did I do with him? Nothing, just nothing. Helpful Government did it all for me. A new species unincluded in the game license, when I got to the Eldama Ravine Boma, Collector Foaker seized skin and head, under instructions from Provincial Commissioner Hobley, and they were sold at public auction at Mombasa for £50, a little later reselling at £250.

"Odd ones! Why, there's the okapi, sort of a cross between a giraffe and a, I don't know what, perhaps a 'what is it.' Hyde Baker killed two in the Congo country less than three years ago, and one or two Germans have taken them; that's all.

"Then there's that infernal horror of a reptilian 'bounder' that comes up the Maggori River out of the lake the Lumbwa have christened Dingonek. And it's real prize money that beauty would fetch, five or ten thousand quid at least, and you bet I've got my Wanderobo and Lumbwa always on the lookout for one when the Maggori is in flood.

"Ever see one? Did I? Rather! Mataia, the boy there, and Mosoni were with me. It was only about a year ago. Mataia vows he has seen two since; can't tell whether he really saw them or dreamed he did — like as not the latter, for I know Dingonek were trying to crawl into my blankets for weeks after we saw that 'bounder.'

"How was it? Well, we were on the march approaching the Maggori, and I had stayed back with the porters and sheep and had sent the Lumbwa ahead to look for a drift we could cross river was up and booming and chances poor. Presently I heard the bush smashing and up raced my Lumbwa, wide-eyed and gray as their black skins could get, with the yarn that they had seen a frightful strange beast on the river bank, which at sight of them had plunged into the water as they described it, some sort of cross between a sea serpent, a leopard, and a whale. Thinking they had gone crazy or were pulling my leg, I told them I'd believe them if they could show me, but not before. After a long shauri [palaver] among themselves, back they finally ventured, returning in half an hour to say that it lay full length exposed on the water in midstream.

"Down to the Maggori I hurried, and there their 'bounder' lay, right-oh!

'Holy saints, but he was a sight—fourteen or fifteen feet long, head big as that of a lioness but shaped and marked like a leopard, two long white fangs sticking down straight out of his upper jaw, back broad as a hippo, scaled like an armadillo, but colored and marked like a leopard, and a broad fin tail, with slow, lazy swishes of which he was easily holding himself level in the swift current, headed up stream.

Gad! but he was a hideous old haunter of a nightmare, was that beast-fish, that made you want an aëroplane to feel safe of him; for while he lay up stream of me, I had been brought down to the river bank precisely where he had taken water, and there all about me in the soft mud and loam were the imprints of feet wide of diameter as a hippo's but clawed like a reptile's, feet you knew could carry him ashore and claws you could be bally well sure no man could ever get loose from once they had nipped him.

"Blast that blighter's fangs, but they looked long enough to go clean through a man.

"He had not seen or heard me, and how long I stood and watched him I don't know. Anyway, when I began to fear he would shift or turn and see me, I gave him a .303 hard-nose behind his leopard ear and then hell split for fair!

"Straight up out of the water he sprang, straight as if standing on his blooming tail — must have jumped off it, I fancy.

"Me? Well, I never quit sprinting until I was atop of the bank and deep in the bush-fancier burst of speed than any wounded bull elephant ever got out of me, my word for that!

"That was one time when my presence of mind didn't succeed in getting away with me from the starting post, and when, finally, it overtook me, and I bunched nerve enough to stop and listen, the bush ahead of me was still smashing with flying Lumbwa, but all was silent astern.

"His legs? What were they like? Blest if I know! The same second that he stood up on his tail, I got too busy with my own legs to study his.

"Gory wonder, was that fellow; a .303, where placed, should have killed anything, for he was less than ten yards from me when I shot, but though we watched waters and shores over a range of several miles for two days, no sight did we get of him or his tracks.

'Ask Mataia, Mosoni, or the lad there what they saw.' I did so, through my own interpreter, Salem, and got from each a voluble description of beast and incident differing in no essential details from Jordan's description.

Moreover, were it necessary, which I do not myself regard it, the strongest corroboration is obtainable of the existence in Victoria Nyanza of a reptile or serpent of huge size, untaken and unclassed.

While in Uganda with ex-Collector James Martin in November last, he told me it was a well-known fact that at intervals in the past, usually long intervals, a great water serpent or reptile was seen on or near the north shore of the lake, which was worshipped by the natives, who believed its coming a harbinger of heavy crops and large increase of their flocks and herds.

Again, in December, while dining with the Senior Deputy Commissioner, C. W. Hobley, C. M. G., at his residence in Nairobi, the very night before starting on this safari, in speaking of the origin of the sleeping sickness Mr. Hobley told me that the Baganda, Wasoga, and Kavirondo of the north shore of the lake had from time immemorial sacrificed burnt offerings of cattle and sheep to a lake reptile of great size and terrible appearance they called Luquata, which occasionally appeared along or near the shore; that since the last coming of Luquata was just shortly before the first outbreak of the sleeping sickness, the natives firmly believe that the muzungu have killed Luquata with the purpose and as the means of making them victims of the dread plague. Of the existence in the lake of such an unclassed reptile, Mr. Hobley considered there was no question.

The next morning found Jordan and three of my porters down with bad attacks of fever. Butterenjonie, chief of the pure Masai on the Amala River, had arrived early on a summons from Jordan, and he and Mataia were sent to the northeast into the forest to try to locate the Wanderobo, while Outram and I went out on a search for eland, and three parties were started off twenty-five miles south to buy fowls and eggs from Korkosch, chief of the Mongorrori—a longish jaunt to market, to be sure, but still the nearest the country afforded where such luxuries were obtainable. But the day proved a bad one all round. Outram and I came in with clean guns and Butterenjonie and Mataia returned without any Wanderobo.

By the sixth all the invalids were able to travel again, and we made a short four-hour march northwest, camping on the edge of a great forest from which the Wanderobo were seldom long absent, and again sent out searchers for them. Here we were well within the great basin representing the watershed of the upper Maggori.

On the seventh we crossed the Maggori, climbed a high divide, and stopped on the Rongana, a tributary of the Maggori, at a point Jordan had chosen for our permanent elephant camp.

Toward noon Mataia returned bringing four Wanderobo, stalwart, wild-eyed fellows, sturdier than the Masai but less massive than the Lumbwa, all armed with heavy six-foot bows, knob-kerries, and swords shorter of blade and broader of point than the Masai, all carrying large leather pouches filled with honey, then their principal food, and clad in skin cloaks of Masai mode. About our fire they stood for two or three hours, shifty-eyed, alert for wonders and against surprise, answering only in monosyllables.

There was no unbending or evidence of moderating mistrust, notwithstanding Jordan's assurance my presence meant no harm, until I had given an empty cigarette tin to one, an empty whiskey bottle to another, a sardine tin to the third, a pickle jar to the fourth, and to each a fistful of native tobacco and several pinches of black pepper, to them munificence unparalleled that first cracked and then, finally, broke the thick ice of their reserve.

Indeed, we were getting on fairly until I stupidly let them listen to the ticking of my watch. This nearly smashed our improving entente, for we failed entirely to convince them the watch did not hold a muungu (god) no Wanderobo had business with, nor were they again put at ease until they saw it safely shut out of sight in my steel clothes box and a saddle stacked atop of the box.

I was particularly keen to have one of their camps moved over near ours, in order to get photographs of Wanderobo on an elephant kill, if we were lucky enough to make one—Labusoni's group if possible, but he, they told us, was then a long day's journey away. So during the evening Jordan held a big shauri with the four.

To bringing their women and children they were slow to consent, but at last agreed, three to go to fetch them, one to stay. Then again came a rub; the man picked to stay with us objected that he had a lot of honey marked that his family needed; we would give them posho in its stead; basi (enough), and he had to concur. Then he was reminded that he had at home a new toto he must go fetch, as his wife would have all she could carry in the shape of family gods and goods; we would send a porter to carry the baby; basi, and he gave it up.

That night, to my regret, I had to decree corporal punishment. In fact, no man can run an African safari and maintain order and obedience among his men without an occasional flogging with the kiboko, a heavy, flexible whip three to four feet long, cut from a single strip of rhino or hippo hide.

Kindness the African native mistakes for fear of him.

Gratitude he is innocent of perhaps because generations of Arab dominion, tyranny, and cruelty, which must have served largely to mould his character, never afforded him anything to be grateful for. If bred of a warrior race, he is apt to stick beside you in the face of a lion, elephant, rhino, or buffalo charge, but only because to run would stamp him among his fellows as a coward, unworthy to bear arms. But pull one, drowning, from a river at risk of your own life, or nurse him of wounds or through a threatened mortal sickness though you may, such are always among the first to shirk or desert you in time of need. Flog one soundly for his derelictions and you have an industrious, cheerfully obedient servant.

With us that far bluff and threats had largely served, for I was reluctant to resort to whipping where it could be avoided, but at last I found my threats had worn threadbare.

The day's march was a very short one, and as early as 8 A. M. we had left our donkeys at the Maggori, no more than three miles back from our new permanent camp, and had put our headman with them to hasten forward the head donkey man, Mafuta, and his charges, for the day threatened rain and that serious injury to the posho and to several uncured head skins the donkeys carried.

Two natives serving as headmen I had already deposed for failure to keep our marching column safely closed up, and the then incumbent was Marini, a six-foot-two Menyamwezi giant.

Hours passed, but no donkeys came. Three times during the day I sent messengers to hasten them, the first two returning with word they were unloaded and resting at the Maggori. Late in the afternoon the third message reached Marini and Mafuta, that if they did not bring their men and animals on at once I would come back and kufa (kill) the pair. This served to the extent of fetching them into camp nearly two hours after dark with every load drenched, for meantime a heavy thunder storm had broken over us.

There were no questions, for apology or excuse was impossible; the donkeys were fat and underloaded, men and beasts fresh of several days' rest, the morning's march to the Maggori only two hours, and yet both Marini and Mafuta came in sulky, glowering, rebellious, their men grinning over "doing" a muzungu out of a day's loafing as they liked.

About the alternately blazing and spluttering fire, for the foliage above our forest camp was still dripping of the rain, sat a grim group of Wanderobo and Lumbwa, the fire glinting brightly from their ivory-white teeth as from the long blades of their straight-planted spears, slicing huge mouthfuls of meat from the roasting sticks before them with their sharp sword blades, and wolfing down the meat like beasts, apathetic spectators of and a fitting frame for the savage punishment necessary to prevent a general revolt.

"Mafuta, strip and chine (down)," my interpreter called.

For an instant Mafuta glowered rebellion, and then sullenly stripped himself of the tatterdemalion wreck of a brown cord coat that began and ended his costume, and dropped to the ground beside the fire, prone upon his face.

"Marini, give him ten!" was the next order.

Fancying himself well out of it, Marini handed Mafuta ten beauties, administered with absolute impartiality, five on either half of the buttocks, under which the culprit winced and writhed but uttered no plaint.

Marini stepped back and Mafuta bounded to his feet, drew himself up, and saluted me with one hand while rubbing with the other whichever place still hurt most, a smile on his face, and a cheerful "Thanks, bwana (master)" he really meant, an ugly rebel converted to a lot better opinion of his employer. Off he started, but only to be stopped.

"Engoja (wait), Mafuta! Chine, Marini! Mafuta, give Marini ten of the best!"

A shot would have startled the giant less, but down he lay and at him Mafuta flew, with a vigor that could have left no doubt in Marini's mind that Mafuta had become a wholehearted and sincere convert to the beautiful theory so few are willing to practise, that it is more blessed to give than to receive!

Now come within fifty or sixty miles of Kericho, the nearest Government police post and mail and telegraph station, Outram started on the eighth on another try to get my mail, with nine porters to fetch new supplies, and followed by little yellow Pugge. Later in the day we missed Rollo, the big setter, and concluded he had followed Outram's safari.

Outram off, Jordan hurried away the three Wanderobo to bring up their village and sent three Lumbwa, Arab Tumo, Arab Barta, and Arab Sendow, out on a scout to locate elephant. Then he, Mataia, Mosoni, and I started out on a search for rhino, which there are found with horns up to thirty-four inches in length and would therefore make my N'gari Kiti twenty-three and one-half inches kill look like a toto.

For two hours we skirted the edge of forest, looking for the track of a big fellow returning from the night's feeding to his customary morning nap in the bush; but, finding no spoor except of some of moderate size, we spent another two hours within the forest, on the chance of sighting or hearing one worth while.

And it is downright breath-holding work, nothing less, I believe, for even the coldest blooded man, poking along forest paths strewn with fresh rhino and buffalo sign, always in dusk like late twilight, sometimes along low, winding tunnels through tangles of vines, sometimes along high-arched aisles, always surrounded on all sides by an eight-foot, broad-leaved bush suggesting the rhododendron and carrying great clusters of pale golden fruit that look like bunches of lemon-yellow grapes, whose dense green mass seldom opens you a view of more than five or ten yards' distance and makes most awkward going when one has to side-step a charge. There was a fascination in it I could not resist, and yet whenever I stepped out of the threat-holding shadows of the wood, back, half-blinded, into the light and warmth of the sun, I always found myself feeling much as I fancy a man must feel who might have the luck to find himself climbing out of his own grave. Perhaps older hands get used to it, but I know I never did. And even Arab Tumo, who for four hours stalked ahead of me silent as a graven image, himself the vanquisher, with no aid but that of his own good spear, of sixty rhino, I noted approached every pathturn crouched and muscle taut for an instant shift.

Now and again the paths were widened into broad bed chambers shaped by the big fellows, always in the lowest, densest roofed bush where the floor was softly strewn with bits of broken twigs, again dropped steeply down to deep, clear, cold pools, richly tapestried round about with the pale green of their moss-covered rock walls, the baths rhino and buffalo love to cool themselves in after a strenuous night afoot.

The first hour our only real sensation was a crashing. stampede of buffalo that caught our wind before we sighted them—and evidently didn't like it, for off to the left through the timber they raced.

The second hour we struck the fresh spoor of two very big male lion and followed it from one path to another until finally they left the paths and bore away into thickets where we lost all trace of them.

Then we quit for the day and jogged back to camp and a late luncheon, where we found the fourth Wanderobo had slipped away unseen, whether for his honey or his toto we could only guess.

With no word come of our elephant scouts, we spent the next forenoon on the fresh spoor of two rhino, one a splendid big bull by his footprints, the other a cow. it was an everlasting lot of sweet things the pair must have had to tell each other. For five hours we kept after them, rarely along paths, breaking through patches of bush or corners of virgin wood only to wind away at random through long grass, for all the world like two lovers blind to all but each other and seeking seclusion from their kind. Three times we heard them near ahead of us in the rhododendrons, but before we could finish a safe stalk they had moved on, and on and on they so outfooted us until Arab Tumo decided they were moving range to the Cabanoa Hills, and that it was useless to follow them longer.

X. IN THE TALL GRASS TUSKERS LOVE

SHORTLY after we got into camp at 3 P. M., February 10, at the end of an eight hours' tramp, five hours on rhino spoor and three hours returning from where we had abandoned it, our three elephant scouts came in with the good news they had located a herd of thirty to forty head on the Sambi River, west of the Cabanoa Hills and about twenty miles from our camp, probably ten miles south of the Government Boma of Kisii. They had seen only two big bulls, both good tuskers, but had heard the tree-smashing of a considerable herd they estimated as stated.

So far, good; but the rest of their news was disappointing. The elephant were in the worst possible country, scarcely any forest except a few very narrow belts in the valleys, and everywhere else, on bottom lands, hillslopes, and summits, elephant grass and dry, brittle weeds twelve to eighteen feet high that enshroud one like a mist and make close stalking well-nigh impossible, and even more difficult to wallow through, and more exhausting, than snowdrifts.

Then, for me, more bad news; none of the Wanderobo had come into my great disappointment and Jordan's bitter disgust. Even the prospect of a possible elephant kill and feast had not served to tempt the tribe from its forest retreat, whether from fear I was some sort of Government official come to clip their liberty, or from the deep-seated suspicion these wild-wood rovers hold of all white men, we knew not.

That evening I found myself rechristened by Mataia. Since his coming to camp I had observed him watching my every movement, following me about, intently studying my most trivial doings; why, I was at a loss to understand. But, plainly, in one way or another I was a most perplexing puzzle to him.

At first his manner rather hinted disapproval, but after a three days' run of particularly good shooting luck, whereby I had killed several buck, all the camp needed, each with a single first shot and two at rather long ranges, he seemed to melt a bit. Then had come the two wearing days on rhino trails, fruitless, but persistently followed wherever they led.

That evening I noted him having a long shauri with Jordan, the substance of which was later communicated to me.

"Mapengo" (Jordan's native name, meaning "false teeth"), Mataia began, "do all the very old white-haired men like Kimèrije work as hard to get meat in their own country as he does here?"

"Who the devil is Kimèrije? What do you mean?" Jordan asked.

"Why, the Bwana Mkubwa [great master], of course. His camp

is full of food, and yet he hunts all the time for meat like a starving Wanderobo for honey. Was he a great elmoran [warrior] among his people when he was young?"

"I'm sure I don't know," Jordan answered.

"Well, I know," Mataia resumed; "he must have been. Why, most all old men won't do anything but sit about and eat and drink wembe, play with their women and children, and watch their sheep and cows. It is only the gray-heads who have in their time been big elmorani, terrors to their neighbors and sackers of big loot, who can't long content themselves about their huts and herds, but always must be slipping off into the bush with their spears, wandering prowlers to the end like old Labusoni.

"Yes, that's it not a doubt. Why, didn't you see him laughing to himself when the buffalo were smashing past us, and then again, after we heard the blow of that old rutting rhino bull and were slipping up on him? Yes, yes; that's the right name I 've given him, Kimèrije." "Kimèrije?" Jordan questioned. "Whatever does that mean in Lumbwa?"

"Kimèrije?" Mataia answered. "Why it means the elmoran who always laughs, that 's Bwana Mkubwa."

Mataia may have been right; perhaps I did laugh in the forest at the stampede of buffalo and at the rhino snorts, but if I did I now apologize to both buffalo and rhino, for so far as my memory serves to recall my most vivid impressions on those two occasions, irrepressible merriment was not one of them.

Sunrise of February 11 found us already trekking toward the elephant herd reported the night before by our Lumbwa scouts. With us Jordan and I took a tent fly, our guns and blankets, a six days' supply of food, my boy Salem as cook, Mataia and six of his elmorani as scouts, and eight porters, more or less of whom we hoped to bring back loaded with ivory.

Our course was northwest, crossing the deep valley of the Rongana River at the salt springs, an hour later fording the N'garoyo, thence through a corner of the Cabanoa Forest, full of rhino and buffalo that kept us dodging to avoid encounters which would compel us to shoot and might alarm elephant, for our entire day's march was through country which always holds more or less elephant and which is swarming with them during the big rains.

Altogether we were probably two hours in a forest none but natives could have wormed us through without using pangas (bush knives), leaving which Mataia led us up the slopes of the Cabanoa Hills, toward their crest, always in grass above our heads, in vines or bush, clambering through the reeds or slipping into the muck of swamps, sometimes for half an hour across dry, level stretches so trampled by elephant during the rains that we had to pick every footstep to avoid a broken leg, likely to come of slipping into some grass-hidden hole eighteen to thirty-six inches deep, stamped by huge pachyderm feet. And hot? Well, rather! It was then the height of the dryest and hottest season of that region, less than a month before the big rains were due to begin, and from dawn to dark the sun poured down its hottest furnace rays out of a sky that pitilessly denied one the temporary shelter of a cloud, burning rays never tempered even measurably save occasionally by the smoke of great grass fires then burning all about us, the work of reckless Wanderobo and other native honey hunters. So that, while starting from an altitude of 5,500 feet at our Rongana camp and climbing more or less steadily toward the 7,000-foot crest of the Cabanoas, and while it was delightfully cool, almost chill, anywhere in the forest or even beneath tree shade in the open, one could not walk ten minutes in the sun before every stitch of clothing was as sopping wet as if he had come out of a plunge in water; and after an hour or two in the open, toiling across the heart-breaking, heavy going that ever beset us, the crown of one's head felt as if the sun were persistently boring a hole in it that must be nearly through the skull, for it hurt cruelly, and nothing relieved it but frequent liftings of the hemlet.

For me, sound in wind and limb, it was bad enough, but for Jordan every step must have been torture. Indeed, throughout this hunt the man was a superb object lesson in patient, unwincing fortitude and iron will power. In his condition, I myself should have been hunting a hospital or an undertaker in quick preference to an elephant or any other game.

Scarce two months before up from a long siege of black-water fever (his fifth attack, and most men do not survive the third), down twice within a fortnight of a heavy go of the plain garden variety of malarial fever few there escape, thin and weak in all but will, his bandaged right leg improving but still more or less raw of eczema from instep to knee, on he plodded or raced from day to day with never a murmur, save an occasional whole-souled curse of a stumble or a thorn.

Asked how he was getting on, always quickly came back a cheerful "Right-oh, old chap! Never better!"

Fortitude! A fortitude that would have made me utterly ashamed to complain in his presence of any bodily suffering short of a broken neck, and I fancy one wouldn't have time to say much about that.

Inflexible, indomitable, mandatory will, acting on fever-weakened joints, shrunken muscles, aching nerve centres, that was all that drove the man along.

But then, if there are elephant in whatever realm Jordan's death-released spirit finds ultimate lodgment, out somewhere in the forest or the tall grass the big tuskers love will be the most likely place to look for it.

About three hours out, Arab Tumo and Arab Barta were ordered to scout ahead, and bounding through the grass like scared impala, were lost to our sight after a half-dozen jumps. Any movement of the herd from their position of the day before must be noted, and it was not at all improbable the elephant might have crossed the crest of Cabanoas and be in our immediate front. Then complete silence was required of the little close-moving column, and on we moved as quietly as we could, climbing, ever climbing, slowly, for though the slope was low it was still enough to keep one's bellows busy.

At length, after eight hours' marching, during which we had covered no more than a scant ten miles, ourselves worn to a frazzle, Mataia camped us in a thicket beside a tiny brook well up toward the top of the Cabanoas, beside a brook so newly born in the bush just above us that it had not yet found voice, its water clear as crystal and cold as ice.

Down to and across the brook we had followed a deep-worn buffalo path, full of sign made that morning, and our camp was pitched literally within a big buffalo dormitory, where by long use they had worn out wide, smooth-floored chambers dimly lighted at midday by a few of the more curious sun rays that contrived to peep through the thick-roofing jungle.

To tell the truth, had I been less tired, it is more than likely I should have tried to seek lodgings more conducive to sound, uninterrupted sleep—where less likely, as a trespasser, to have a dispossession notice poked at me in the form of a pair of forty-inch buffalo horns. But, really, there was "nowhere to go but out" out into the pet lodgings of one sort or another of the Big Fellows, so we were about as well off there as anywhere.

Not until nightfall did our scouts return — with word the main herd had not moved from its previous day's range along the Sambi, but that four big fellows, probably the big bull scouts of the herd, were half-way up the farther hillslope, headed toward a pass whose trails led across our brook a few yards above us, apparently the lead of a trek of the lot back to the Rongana salt springs they never long leave.

It was a beautiful pickle we were in, a regular cul-desac, camped as we were virtually athwart the main elephant highway between the Sambi and their dearly loved salt springs, any move in darkness of our camp and its slender equipment utterly impossible without the probability of neck-breaking or eye-blinding, and no moon till near morning!

But there we were and there we had to stay.

Chill, almost bitter, though the night was, none but the tiniest twig fires were permitted, just enough to fry our meat and to boil our coffee and the men's poshoheaped sufurias.

Absolute silence among the noisy porters was easily obtained by placing among them a Lumbwa elmoran, with orders to smash with his rungu (knob-kerrie) the first noisy mouth, orders he would have been delighted to execute on the first offender.

Then, dead fagged of the tough day, and having arranged a night watch of the camp, with orders to rouse us quickly at the first sound of elephant, buffalo, or rhino, Jordan and I turned in, and never opened an eye till called by Salem at dawn, the buffalo having, obviously, lodged elsewhere, and the tuskers stopped somewhere en route.

Before sun-up, Arab Tumo and Arab Barta were off ahead of us. Shortly thereafter, coffee and a snack gobbled down, Jordan and I followed. The wind barring us from the pass, we were forced to climb straight for the summit, two miles west of the pass, a smooth enough climb, for large areas thereabouts had recently been burned, but so steep it made tough, slow going.

While we were still a hundred feet below the summit, our two scouts appeared upon it, stopping and resting upon their spears, silhouetted against the clear blue sky, still as ebony statues. Evidently their task was finished they had the elephant marked down.

Come to them, they silently pointed far down below and off to the south of us, where for a time I could see nothing but the landscape. Presently, however, my eyes caught glints of sunlight off ivory, but that was all; the huge bodies were indistinguishable in the high grass and weeds about them.

And yet, looking down from our lofty perch on Cabanoas' crest, to right, left, and front of us rolled wave on wave of what looked like gently undulating short-grassed meadow land, the grass seeded and browning, slashed here and there with the rich dark green of the narrow strips of reeds and bush fringing marsh and watercourse, showing few trees and no bush outside the timber. And there at our feet lay a country so terrible that I could wish my bitterest enemy no worse fate than to be compelled to tramp five miles a day across it throughout eternity.

From us the elephant were there about two miles distant, on the southern slope of the pass we had feared they might bring the herd through the night before, perhaps four miles from our camp. To get the wind of them properly for safe stalking, we must swing a good mile to the west of them.

Down we started, down the steep, fire-blackened slope, as fast as we could go.

For a mile, while crossing the "burn," we had open going, but then we plunged into elephant grass and weeds twice our height, into which everywhere Dame Nature, in one of her less kindly moods, had artfully interwoven a slender bush, half of whose stalks stood honestly upright and bore great clusters of lilac-hued flowers, while the other misbegotten half were bent and looped in the grass at every angle best calculated to catch a boot-toe and toss one a header or to enmesh a foot and wrench or break a leg. And once in it, one instantly lost the free control of all his functions but one, which happily was stimulated to abnormal capacity viz., the ability to tell the infernal stuff what he thought of it, and to tell it all.

Just before we left the burnt area, the elephant shifted their position slightly and I had my first good view of them, three huge brown backs, one towering above his mates to magnificent height, evidently one of the rare prizes in these late day hard to find east of the Congo.

The steep slope of the mountain ended in the narrow valley of the Sambi, there timberless, in places marshy and full of tall reeds and cat-tails, elsewhere dry save for great pools trampled all about by the Big Ones, pools where they love to pump up hogsheads of water in their trunks and shower themselves.

Crossing the valley, we climbed its steep southern slope until, off an anthill, we again got a glimpse of the three, finding that they were near their first position and that we then fairly had the wind of them, though it was dangerously light and shifty. Then straight toward them we walked, due east, another half-hour until we reached the descent into a ravine on the eastern slope of which they stood, perhaps sixty yards from its bottom and one hundred and fifty yards from us. From our elevated position the backs of the two larger ones were plainly to be seen, with now and then a glimpse of the smaller one. The big one was indeed a giant. Once his biggest mate moved behind him and disappeared, while No. 3 easily hid behind No. 2. At intervals we had in turn first three, then two, and then only one elephant before us!

There we stood on the hillside, in plain sight of them but beyond their short eye-range, for probably fifteen minutes, watching the great ears lazily swing back and forth, like idle sails flapping in light air, and listened to their rolling stomach rumbles that told of comfortable surfeit, advising under our breath whether to attack or wait till they made into the shade they were sure soon to be seeking, finally deciding to advance. It was a chance we could not afford to lose, for before us were three splendid bulls, the smallest one good enough to satisfy most men.

After the first few steps of the descent we again lost sight of them.

At the bottom of the ravine we passed a lone tree at least sixty feet in height, and then began a slow and the most silent possible stalk up the hill straight to them. But before we had gone twenty yards we realized that successful direct approach was utterly impossible — get through the frightful tangle of grass and shrubs we could not without swishings and cracklings of the dry weeds their keen ears would be sure to hear before we could hope to sight them and get a shot, and the instant they heard us there would be a rush down to investigate the intruders or away to lose them.

So back down the hill we crept to the tree and there stopped, puzzled what to do, until twigs dropping on our heads attracted our attention aloft, and there, perched on a high limb forty feet from the ground, sat old Mataia, gesturing violently that he had the elephant in full view and beckoning us up.

"Up! up!" whispered Jordan. "Up quick, it's your only chance of a shot."

It was twelve feet to the lowest limb and the main trunk was nearly three feet in diameter, but off from the main trunk, waist-high above the ground, grew a twin trunk slightly inclining away from its mate. But what then?

"Can't do it, old chap," I answered.

"You can; you can-off with your boots!" came back at me.

And such is the power of suggestion that in no time I had leggings and boots off, slung my .405 rifle over my back, and managed to swarm up to a painful three-toehold in the close V-shaped crotch. And there I am sure I should have been stalled had not Mataia come to the lower limb and reached me down his great black hand. That, however, served me well, and getting a firm grip of it I managed to wriggle my toes loose, when, with a joint tug, I was swung up to a good grip of the limb, and with Mataia still tugging, contrived to get on it.

There I expected to see the elephant, but they were still invisible. So up another story I swarmed, that stretch easily ten feet, but with the same result.

Meantime Mataia had slipped up to his first perch, still another twenty feet, the last twelve feet up a smooth, slender, perpendicular trunk I probably should never have negotiated without the aid of Mataia, but with his powerful grip in mine, after a couple of swings entirely free from the tree (Jordan later assured me, although I did not realize it at the time) he hitched me up to where I was able to get a grip with my left hand and help myself up to the place he had been occupying.

There at last, forty feet above the ground and balancing myself with my feet on two wide-spread limbs none too strong for my weight, I found myself at last slightly higher than the elephant, sufficiently to have a clear view of the upper fourth of their great brown sides and a glimpse of their gleaming ivory.

Meantime, Jordan, my gun bearer, Awala, and all the natives had swarmed up into the tree, Jordan stopping on the lower limb.

My second gun, a 9 m.m. Mauser, was passed up to Mataia, within arm's length beneath me. Jordan had my double which I should have preferred to use but that its sight was so fine I could not see it well when compelled to shoot into the sun or within the shadows of overhanging foliage.

Just then the elephant moved directly toward us, very slowly, the big one in the lead, stopping thirty yards away and offering a perfect brain shot. Keen to get the pair I hissed down to Jordan, "Up, quick, and help make sure of both."

"Blight it, I can't! Never could stand it up a tree! Fool to come here! Wish I was down!" he hissed back. "Well, well," I persisted, "can't you see them now—can't you shoot from where you are?"

"Just d-d well can't, old chap," Jordan whispered. "Sorry! But this cannon of a .450 would kick me clean over into the Sambi. My word, but it's hard enough sticking here now!"

And then, just as I was advancing my gun for a bead on No. 1's head, off they started again, and in two or three steps were beyond the range of view through the narrow opening in the tree foliage before me, completely hidden from sight; and before I could make shift to another opening and get them again in range, No. 1 was about eighty to one hundred yards off, angling away from us, but moving at a slow walk.

Upon receiving my hard nose .405 behind his left shoulder, a useful shot ranging forward, No. 1 trumpeted pain and rage, stopped an instant, swayed, and then broke into whatever the elephant's pace is, faster than a walk, offering me a fair broadside.

Frequently before my .405 had jammed in the magazine, the second or third cartridge not coming up level with the chamber, a dangerous freak I failed to fathom or correct; and I should have discarded it long before but for its superior accuracy over any other gun and its hard hitting. For a fortnight it had been working like an angel and dropping in its tracks nearly everything I pulled on, and therefore I had elected to trust it that morning.

But by every ill token, tight and fast it jammed at the first shot, compelling me to pass it down to Mataia and get the lighter Mauser, and losing me invaluable time. However, I was lucky enough to get another shot into No. I and one into No. 2 before they got out of range, up wind.

Meantime Jordan had dropped off his limb and was tumbling through the grass, trying for an elevation where he could get a shot. Then, just as I was scrambling down, one of the Lumbwa pointed out two of the elephant on our left, evidently circling west for the wind of whatever had pinked them, three hundred yards from my tree but only about one hundred and fifty from Jordan. There we each got two more shots, turning them back east again, out of our sight.

Rapidly as I could I swung and slid to the ground to find that Mosoni, the Lumbwa elmoran who took my boots when I pulled them off, had followed Jordan and stupidly carried my footgear along. But just in the nick of time to save me from going quite insane with rage, Mataia called down and beckoned me to come up aloft again. Sure they must be returning, and having discovered, to my infinite surprise, that I had my climbing clothes on that day, up again I went faster than before, just in time to get in three good shots on a tremendous big fellow who was circling past about sixty yards south of us, swinging along at a fast pace, trunk up, sniffing for our wind. The last shot badly hurt and stopped him for a few minutes behind some bush, and then he was off over a hill again, turned west.

And scarcely was this chap disappeared before bowling along came another and smaller one, closely following the trail of his mate. By this time, Jordan having gotten back south of the tree and atop of the anthill from which we had had our first good view of them, we each landed two shots in him, when he, too, passed on west out of our sight.

By the time I had gotten to the ground and resumed the boots Jordan had sent back to me, I found myself alone with my gun bearer, Mataia, and Arab Barta, all of whom insisted that No. 1, the giant I first hit, had not returned and must be down or badly sick to the east of us, holding that the two which had just passed us were the two smaller of the trio. However, preferring myself to follow the trail of those I knew to be hard hit, I sent Awala and Barta on a circle to the east for sign of the missing elephant, and with Mataia hurried over to the trail.

There was their spoor plain enough, both heavily blood-marked, bearing west for a mile and then swinging south, still side by side for another half-mile, when one turned west and the other continued on.

Which to follow was a puzzle, for so far, through the long grass and over hard ground, I had found no foot mark to tell which was the large one, nor did I know what had become of Jordan. My choice was unfortunate, for after continuing on south another hour the trail crossed a marsh where I soon saw the footprints could not be those of the big fellow. So leaving Mataia to follow this trail, I struck off southwest to try to cut the other, wallowing through the grass, never with view of anything but sky and hillcrests.

At length, when fagged to a finish by exhaustion and thirst, drenched with perspiration, not another mile of go left in me, just ahead I heard two quick shots from the big .450.

Revived a bit and hurrying on, a couple of hundred yards brought me to Jordan and a dead monster, the man reclining limp aloft upon the beast's high-bulging side and looking nearly as bereft of breath as was the quarry, so dead beat that I thought he was going to roll off in a faint.

Presently, however, he regained his wind and I got his story. At the parting of the trails he had chosen this one and pounded along it as fast as he could, passing two places where the elephant had stopped and bled heavily; at length, come just there near to but unseen in his approach, the beast caught his wind and charged him straight, but luckily landing the best possible turning shot midway of its sensitive trunk—he was given the chance of a shoulder shot that pierced the heart, of which the elephant crashed to the ground and never again rose. The monster was so enormous I never questioned he was No. 1 of the three, until Jordan panted angrily,

"Just look at him, the infernal blankety-blank blighter. Only one tusk, curse him!"

And upon pulling away the grass in which the lower half of his head lay and finding the startling statement true, I cried,

"Well, I am out of luck, then, for he 's no elephant of mine the three had full sets of ivory. Wherever did he come from?"

"But he is yours, all the same," Jordan answered; "he has four of your small 9 m.m. and your .405 in him, two in the lungs, one near the spine, one through his tummy, and another that must have tickled his liver. Look for yourself; they are all here. Beggar would have been down in another hour at the most, for good was groggy when he came for me.

"His ivory beats me, too, for I'd have sworn all three had full sets; thought at first he might have broken it off to spite us, but you'll see the stump shows an old break, six inches from the lip. Hope it hurt the old bounder a lot! Just fancy! The infernal wasteful idiot! D-n his eyes, anyway! Old enough to know better! Twelve or fifteen hundred nice juicy rupees stuck in his face, and he has to go and lose half of them!"

But, disappointing as he was from the commercial point of view of an old professional ivory hunter, he was nevertheless such a gorgeous trophy as I had never dared hope for.

His good tusk was 6 feet, 4 inches in length and 17 inches in circumference at the lip, weighing 62 pounds, and clean kutch (prime) ivory at that, while the stump weighed 21 pounds, a total of 83 pounds, light enough to be sure, but in height at the withers (measuring perpendicularly and not along body curves) he stood 11 feet, 4 inches, while his length from tip of trunk to tip of tail was 27 feet, 8 inches, his girth about the middle 19 feet, the circumference of his front foot 60 inches, and length of ear from base to tip 41 inches.

And precisely in these measurements lies a record the oldest trekker across African veldt and highlands would be bound to feel proud of; for on my return to Juja and an opportunity to consult Rowland Ward's "Records of Big Game," I found that my old Monarch of the Cabanoas is no less than the third largest elephant ever shot; only two have equalled him, and they beat him—one shot in Abyssinia measuring 11 feet, 8 inches in height, one shot near Wadelai measuring 11 feet, 6 inches, while only two are recorded of larger foot measurement than his of 60 inches. Thus, while modest in ivory, he takes third place in the record of the giants of his kind.

Whether or not he was actually the real giant, No. 1, for certain, we never learned, but surely he must have been. Awala and Barta returned late that evening and reported they had found nothing but the two blood spoors we had followed, while Mataia came in long after dark and reported that he had followed the spoor of the smaller elephant until from congealing, blood flow ceased, and shortly thereafter had lost it in a maze of other tracks.

Lying about our fire that evening waiting for the safari, for which we had sent Mosoni, to come up, when I expressed my mortification at having to go on record as having shot my first (and perhaps my last) elephant from the security of a treetop, Jordan growled,

"Well, you can just stow all your worry about that, old chap. Security? Hell!"

"Why?" I asked, in real surprise.

"Why? Why, blight me, but I'd rather face the straight charge of the maddest old tusker than try to swarm up that tree where you were! That's one 'why.' Another you 'd have found quick enough if this bounder had got our wind—he'd have caught the tree trunk aloft there where it's slender and shaken you to a fall that would have finished you without further trouble on his part.

"And me, look at me for a beauty of an intellectual wonder-knowing blighting well I can't climb, and getting up there and having to stop just an easy reach for him to get a good grip of me to pelt you with! And like as not he'd have tried it if he'd gotten to us—they're cunning enough for it, my word for that."

Our camp that night was a tough one, the worst of the entire safari, beside a swamp that provided the only water, a few yards above a big pool that was a regular watering of the main herd; but we lacked energy to seek a better.

All our natives were ranging the next day until midafternoon, some on a search for the wounded, others trying to locate the main herd, but none were successful. Both Jordan and myself were still too tired and sore to do more than struggle to the crest of a high hill, about two miles from camp and to the west of the Sambi, for a look about with the glasses—which proved as fruitless as did the work of our men. On all sides of us almost as far as the eye could reach rolled tall, sunlit billows and dim, shadowy hollows of elephant grass that may have held hundreds of elephant but to us showed none.

Far to the west across the russet sea of browning grass tops, a broad belt of dark green represented the dense forest area where Outram and I had made our débût in pachyderm society a month earlier; and more likely than not the giant trophy that now lay powerless beside our camp was the same magnificent bull we were stalking when, all unwitting, we worked our way quite into the middle of his leafy harem and into two hours of rather unusual anxiety.

On a few miles to the west rose the lofty heights of Toroni's rocky aerie, and nestling near the foot of its northern flank lay the new sleeping sickness boma and hospital we had found Deputy Commissioner North-cote building on the Oyani, while away in the south undulated the blue ridges that separated our "Looseandgiddy" camp from the lower valley of the Maggori River.

We returned to our Sambi camp about three o'clock to find still unfinished the task of removing the elephant's four feet and cleaning them of all bone and flesh, and the cutting out of a four-foot square of hide from his ribs. In fact, the extreme difficulty of incising the tough hide anywhere with ordinary skinning knives was such as to leave it hard to realize how Carl Aikley, of the Field Columbian Museum, and R. I. Cunningham, working by themselves with no better implements, had succeeded at all in completely skinning an elephant in one continuous performance; harder still to credit-what is nevertheless the fact that they finished the work in eighteen hours.

Immediately upon return from their day's scouting, our Lumbwa began a savage, wolfing feast upon the titbits of the carcass that lasted throughout the night. The huge, marrowless, but porous and fat-exuding leg bones were soon hacked out by the heavy short swords and sucked dry of their sweet oily contents, the rich stores of fat stowed fore and aft of the high bony central dome of the skull sacked and consumed, great hunks of meat slashed out and in a few minutes gobbled down, raw hunks of a size, whole, that one would swear must choke even the widest and most elastic python throat or surfeit the emptiest lion.

Ivory-white teeth, set in jaws powerful as a hyena's, tore and disintegrated the tough, raw flesh as easily as civilized incisors and grinders consume the most tender fillet.

And when, shortly before sunset, an abdominal incision was made to reach the great masses of fat about the kidneys, an opportunity was given me for a photograph never before taken and a sight probably never before seen, unless by a professional elephant hunter. The moment the abdominal wall was punctured, high up on the elephant's side up out of the opening rose an intertwining, writhing mass of colossal intestines, each at least eighteen inches in diameter, all tightly distended with the gases of dissolution until, beneath the bright rays of the declining sun, they reflected every brilliant and soft neutral tint of an opal, rose up and up, six feet or more above the carcass, ever slowly gliding and writhing, as if one had before his eyes a gigantic Medusa head crowned with a mass of close-knotted, tortured python—a sight so weirdly ghastly it by turns impelled one to fly from it and held one entranced by its sinuous, serpentine movements and more than serpent radiance of brilliant variegated color.

Nor, night come — instantly the hurrying equatorial sun had dropped, like a lump of lead, below the horizon — was more than the mere tough edge of their voracious animal appetite dulled; for directly the Lumbwa had staggered into camp, each with shoulders laden with the last pound of the coarse-grained red meat he could carry, live coals were filched from beneath Salem's bubbling pots, fires started, long sticks cut, and countless yards of flesh set smoking, drying, roasting. And there about their little fires throughout the livelong night crouched these gorging Bantu gluttons,- creatures risen above the stoneage men that lurk like rude, hideous, hateful caricatures of humanity in the dim dawn of history, only the one short step gained by stumbling on the knowledge that bits of iron-stone reddened in fire may be beaten into blades trustier to kill than any wrought of obsidian or flint. There about their fires they lolled, ever stuffing meat away inside them, God alone knows where, and yarning of past kills of the Big Ones and like luxurious feasts that had served to mark the reddest red-letter days of their hungering, perpetually hungering lives; for the African savage knows no want save hunger for food he may not always easily satisfy.

The next morning found us still half crippled, Jordan with his poor game leg rawer than ever, I with arms and shoulders still so sore of my tree climbing that it was agony to try to level a rifle. But move we had to, for fires started by reckless Wanderobo and Kisii honey hunters were sending up great smoke columns all about us that, unless we hurried, might force us into wide detours from a direct return to our Rongana camp. Luckily the elephant tusks had by that tine loosened to an extent that enabled our men to get them out, after three hours' sharp work.

About 8 A. M. I started Jordan and the safari for the Rongana, and then went off myself with two natives on another four hours' circle of the Sambi basin in hope of finding some trace of our wounded, which it seemed possible might be driven back upon us, if they were still able to travel, by the fires.

But this scout proved as fruitless as its predecessors, and so, shortly after noon, I climbed the Cabanoas and began the descent toward the Rongana.

It was a terrible day, the heat of the sun heightened by that of the fires we often had to skirt closely, the air suffocating with smoke and falling cinders that kept eyes streaming and throats parched and half strangled.

About mid-afternoon, in a forest I chanced on a section of our safari which had been cut off from the others by a fire that had swept down upon them and cut the column in two, forcing the rear lot into a wide circle to the south to escape the advancing flames. In fact, had a high wind risen that day we should never have won through without more or less serious casualties.

It was long after dark when I stumbled into the Rongana camp, black of the smoke as any Bantu, returned to the supreme luxury of a chance to take boots and clothes off and have a bath; for during the four nights of our absence the Big Ones, elephant, rhino, and buffalo, were so thick about us, and there was so much likelihood of a stampede through or a charge of our camp by some of them, that we had not ventured even to remove our boots.

For Jordan these four days across the Cabanoas were near being his finish. I found him, arrived a scant hour ahead of me, flighty of a burning fever and gasping for breath from what seemed to be an acute attack of pneumonia, that took four days of close nursing and about all the quinine, brandy, and mustard our scanty stores afforded to knock out of him.

XI. A MIGHTY SPEAR THRUST

WHILE awaiting Jordan's recovery from the illness we brought on by our elephant hunt on the Sambi River, Nabrisi, brother of the Wanderobo chief, Labusoni, and Bélé, another of his men, came into my Rongana camp and brought me a lot of fine honey and Jordan a batch of lame excuses why the Wanderobo camp had not joined us as promised. Summed up, it was plain these shy forest folk were distrustful of the stranger.

Nabrisi was such a smiling, gentle, kindly faced soul that, despite his black skin, semi-nakedness, primitive arms, and reputation as a reckless elephant hunter, it was hard to think of him except as a most amiable and courteous old gentleman. Bélé, on the contrary, was an ideal type of the Wanderobo elmoran, middle-aged, severely dour of visage, gashed across the forehead with the scar of a sword cut deep enough to lay one's finger in—a wound no white man could have survived; and never once during the week they were with us did I see the flicker of a smile on his face, never once to my knowledge when he was near did I escape a continual, suspicious scrutiny of my every movement from great eyes wide, unblinking, and glaring as those of a buffalo at bay. Round the camp fire at the door of my tent they lolled all day, he and Nabrisi, and beside it they slept at night, on beds primitive as the nuptial couch of Adam and Eve. Each scraped a shallow saucer-shaped area in the soft loam, cleared it of sticks and stones, gathered slender branches of a broad-leaved tree and stuck the butts horizontally into the earth rims about the saucer in concentric rings, until the centre held a thick mat of leaves upon which each stretched himself naked, with feet to the fire and monkey skin cloak rolled up for a pillow, with no cover from the chill morning breezes that for two hours before dawn always in those altitudes made me glad to pull up over me an extra pair of blankets.

At Jordan's orders Nabrisi and Bélé made a three days' circle through Cabanoa Forest and the N'gararu Hills for fresh elephant sign, but on their return they reported the country afire everywhere and the elephant moved west and north into the loftier Kisii Highlands.

February 20, as soon as Jordan was able to ride, I marched the safari twelve miles west to a camp on Soiat Hill, near Mataia's house; and there Outram joined us shortly after our arrival, after a hard eleven days' march to Kericho and back, with a great mass of mail, the accumulation of the last eleven weeks, and with New York papers of as recent date as January 9. The round trip this mail had cost was a trifle under two hundred and fifty miles, a longish jaunt to the post, but still our nearest.

Nor was it altogether a welcome mail that came, for, while much remained undone which I had hoped to do before leaving Africa, it brought advices that left me no alternative but to cut short my safari and book for an early sailing from Mombasa for New York. Otherwise it had been my hope to swing north from Kericho to Eldama Ravine, down Molo River to Lake Baringo for greater Kudu, thence east down the Guaso Narok River past Rumuruti Boma, thence round the north and east flanks of Mt. Kenya, and back through Ft. Hall to Nairobi, a circle on which I should have been pretty sure to get the two more elephant to which I was entitled under my license.

And the abandonment of the trip around Kenya became to me all the more regrettable when, the following evening, porters returned from a trip back to our old Rongana camp to fetch up several loads we had been compelled to leave behind (safely walled up, I had believed, in Mataia's tall and stoutly built cattle boma) with advice that hyena had scented out and stolen two of my elephant feet. Since three of the porters were men we had been compelled to chine under the kiboko a few days before, I did not believe them, but fancied they had thrown away the feet out of revenge. So the same night I forced them to march back under guard of Arab Miner and Mosoni, two of the Lumbwa spearmen, with orders to give them no rest until the feet or proofs of their destruction were found. Late the next afternoon the two Lumbwa came back, spear-prodding ahead of them the sullen porters, bringing me a double handful of fragments of the great horny elephant toe nails, plainly showing marks of hyena teeth. The feet had been completely cleaned of all bone and meat, "cured" by filling them with ashes to absorb and neutralize the fats, until nothing remained but the hard dry leg hide, flinty soles, and horny nails; and yet, incredible as it may seem, every scrap had been eaten by these insatiable scavengers except the fragments brought me. Most fortunately, however, they had taken one front and one hind foot and thus had spared me one of his superb front sixty-inchers.

Noon of the twenty-second found us fourteen miles north of Soiat, after a hard six hours' march toward Kericho over timberless long-grass country so steeply, deeply rolling that every two or three miles included a seven hundred to eight hundred sharp ascent and descent. There we were met by Arab Tumo, who had left us a few days earlier, with word there were great herds of elephant within a mile of his house and only four miles from our camp, but in long-grass country where it would be almost impossible to get at them. And no more had we gotten the news than down upon our stream-side camp from the southwest marched a big safari which we soon learned was that of Lady Colville and her son. Approached, young Colville and his safari leader inquired if we had seen elephant, to which we diplomatically replied that we had men out hunting them. Then they told us they had been out for three months, first in the Laikipia country to the north and later hereabouts, but had seen no elephant, and then were marching for Limirick Plains in the eastern Sotik country for work on a general bag. However, since they camped a scant mile beyond us, we fancied they were as foxy as we were—had news of the herds Tumo had reported and were figuring to strike them before we could, which of course set us plotting to get in ahead of them. Toward mid-afternoon our chance came, when a heavy grass fire swept between our camp and theirs, its thick smoke clouds drifting south before a strong north wind.

Quickly loading a few men with food and blankets and leaving all our tents standing, we slipped away in the shrouding smoke and got well across the first tall summit before the smoke lifted. Later we learned our precautions had been entirely unnecessary, for we were told by the Sotik boma chief that the same morning the other safari had sighted the main herd, and had then retired because, they claimed, they saw none but small tuskers.

That night we camped on a steep hillslope near Tumo's and within a few hundred yards of where the elephant had been feeding earlier in the day. There we were about midway between the Sotik and Kisii bomas and in the extreme northeast corner of the range of the big Kisii herd.

It was an elephant-grass country everywhere, but even worse to work in than the Sambi, for the hills were much more precipitous, there were absolutely no trees to climb for a look about, and every valley was a broad, boggy, reedy swamp trampled by elephant into pit holes until nearly impassable to us.

At dawn we were off. In the first swamp we struck we jumped two rhinos, but they scurried away through the reeds. Two hours later, from an obligingly placed anthill upon a tall summit, upon a lower shoulder of the same hill about a half-mile below us we caught a glimpse of fourteen elephant, while across a deep valley and swamp and on a hillside probably two miles away, appearing and disappearing brown patches and glints of ivory showed us a great herd of anywhere from one hundred to two hundred head.

Had the day been clear the sight would have been superb, well worth the entire trip from Nairobi, but the air was so hazy with smoke the elephant looked like dim spectral shapes rising from the slope of a mighty billow of a faintly moonlit sea.

Already the sun was getting very hot, for neither clouds nor smoke seemed materially to lessen the intensity of the equatorial sun rays—and both herds were on the move for cool quarters for their midday nap, headed, one lot north and the other south toward a broad swamp that lay eight hundred feet below them in a valley trending west toward the Kuja.

They actually seemed a gift, did those elephant or rather a chance at one or two fine bulls of the herd seemed a certainty; for while we could not follow directly on the spoor of the nearer herd without giving them our wind, a leisurely wide circle to the west and descent to the swamp, and a careful stalk up it through its tall rushes or along the slopes that dropped steeply to its margin, seemed sure to bring us to close range of the united herds, floundering about among the lily pads and reeds, showering themselves with their trunks or boring into the dark green masses of the high, dank marsh growths for shelter from the sun.

So off the anthill we stepped and down the precipitous hillslope started, heading northwest, the tall, wiry Lumbwa, Arab Tumo the rhino slayer, in the lead, I next, and the rest trailing along behind. Of course, the moment we descended from the anthill the ghastly gray leaves and stalks of the tall elephant grass closed about each tight as a winding sheet, and shut out view of everything except the patches of sky that now and then appeared through the rustling russet roof above our heads. Each step was like passing from one tight-shut chamber to another, tight-shut as a sodded grave, for the gray stalks were ever springing up behind one with a sinister, malicious suddenness and vigor and with rasping swishes that sounded in my ears like a hoarse, gloating, truculent whisper, "You are ours, ours, OURS! Forever are you ours!"

Indeed, the fevered imagination of the worst dying sinner could never people the dusky shades of Hades with more terrible shapes than the horrors and perils one knows must always be crowding close about him while plunged into that worst of all terrestrial infernos, a region of elephant grass. They are there all about you, scores of the predatory, with any of whom a chance meeting means your death or theirs. At your very feet a poisonous cobra or mamba may be coiling to give you a coup-demorte; within reach of your rifle muzzle a great python may be suppling his mighty folds for the toss of a crushing hitch about your neck; rhino, buffalo, lion, or elephant love and always haunt such convenient ambush, and may at any instant catch your wind and be literally upon you before you have time to throw your rifle to shoulder.

Indeed, no form of duel to the death, fought out in utter darkness, could hold more terrors to try the stoutest heart than a man adrift in a sea of elephant grass finds himself a prey to.

Nor were we that day to be without our bit of experience of the hostile activities of its dangerous denizens.

While modest and refusing to talk at all of his own exploits, the chief Mataia and other Lumbwa repeatedly assured me that no less than sixty rhino had fallen to Arab Tumo's spear thrusts, each killed by him alone in single combat. While the story appeared incredible, large color of truth was lent it by an incident of the morning.

While about half way down from the summit to the swamp, with

Arab Tumo marching ahead of me, and, although no more than six feet in advance, quite out of my sight, suddenly I heard just beyond him the swish and crashing of some mighty body, and jumped forward to Arab Tumo just in time to see a giant rhino, which had been crossing our line of march directly in his front, start to swing for a charge up our line, great head shaking with rage, little pig eyes glaring fury.

It was all over in a second, for when I reached Tumo they were in arm's length of each other, he crouched with spear shortened, and, in the very second of the rhino's swing to charge, with one bound and mighty thrust he drove his great three foot six inch spear blade to entry behind the left shoulder, ranging diagonally through the rhino's vitals towards his right hip, and burying it to the very haft!

Followed instantly a shrill scream of pain, a gush of foam-flecked blood that told of a deadly lung wound, and then the monster wheeled and lurched out of our sight down hill at right angles to our course, Tumo's spear still transfixing him.

So suddenly sprung and so fascinating was the scene, so like a single-handed duel of the old Roman arena between two raw savage monsters of the African jungle, biped against quadruped, that it never occurred to me to shoot, although I might have chanced a snapshot over Tumo's shoulder.

And there Arab Tumo stood quietly smiling, his pulse apparently unquickened by a single beat, signing for permission to follow and recover his spear!

About an hour later, just as we were about to enter the swamp, he rejoined us with the fragments of his spear, the blade broken free of its long-pointed iron butt, which was bent nearly double by some wrench in the ground the rhino had contrived to give it to free his vitals of the gnawing blade! And, once free of the spear, on he had gone Tumo had not seen him again.

Of the elephant we had heard nothing, and, of course, had seen nothing since leaving the mountain top. But if they had held their course, as we felt sure they had, we should there have been about a half-mile below them. So we began a cautious stalk up swamp, silent as we could make it, for they might be moving toward us.

Most of the way we had to wade along the edge of the swamp, sometimes jumping, sometimes slipping into pot holes up to the middle, for everywhere the Big Ones had been trampling. Nor did the water matter, for in elephant grass one never gets a breath of breeze and when we had reached the swamp we were as wet as if we had rolled in it. Both to north and south we found the swamp lined with heavy thorn bush that did not show above the heavy grass tops, but with stems thick as one's wrist, utterly impenetrable except along an elephant path or where occasionally they had trampled it into a tangled springy mattress over which we could occasionally pick our way, bobbing up and down as if on a spring board, five or six feet above the ground.

On we toiled and yet on, expecting every step to sight the gleam of ivory or a flapping ear, to hear a "tummy" rumble or a trumpet, on, for three weary hours, until we had thoroughly scouted the swamp to its head, only to find that by some ill chance both herds had swerved elsewhere, probably northeast; either that or they had doubled in behind us as we descended the mountain.

It was absolutely heartbreaking, but there was nothing to do but drag ourselves to the crest of the nearly perpendicular hill that rose seven or eight hundred feet to the northeast above the top of the swamp, in hope of cutting their spoor or sighting them from the summit.

It was like swarming up a giant Gothic roof, first battling for a bit of opening in the grass and bushes and then grasping grass and weeds and pulling ourselves up into it, labor so exhausting and taxing on our lungs we were over two hours making the ascent. And, once come there, we soon found our work had been for naught; neither on the summit nor on the slopes could we find an anthill; nothing could we see but the sky and the hell of weeds that shut us in. Nor was there another ounce of energy left in us, for it was then at least an hour past midday and we had been marching and stalking since dawn, eight hours or more, through the most laborious going, I believe, the entire world affords.

Then to make our situation worse, our water bottles were empty; in our keenness to get to the elephant we had forgotten to fill them before leaving the swamp. So, after sending three Lumbwa off to try to find the elephant and two more to fetch up our camp to the margin of a swamp we knew must lie at the bottom of the valley to the east of us, we cut with our knives little chambers among the grass roots and into them crawled, and there lay sheltered from the direct rays of the sun for three hours, until our Lumbwa returned with word the elephant were gathered in a swamp three miles northeast of us, from which they might be moving back toward evening past or across a big open "burn" that lay a mile below us.

About 5 P. M. we got down to this "burn," and shortly thereafter our safari reached us and we there pitched camp, among some anthills, from which we could get a bit of a view about. But nothing did we see, until, just at dusk, our watch reported two big bulls about a thousand yards away, heading straight for our camp. Too late to gain anything by trying to go out after them in the gathering darkness, our fires were extinguished, Outram stopped in camp, Jordan took stand two hundred yards to the east, and I the same distance west of camp on the chance the bulls might come smashing along within range.

And there on his post in the moonless, murky night and down among the soft, gray-black ash of the newly burned herbage, each crouched with ready gun till near midnight, when, having heard nothing, I stumbled into camp, called in Jordan, and we had the fires rekindled and rolled up in our blankets.

Such is the luck of the game. Although they should not have gotten our wind, perhaps they did. Anyway, off they had turned, a scant three hundred yards from camp, off into the southwest, had those two bulls, and after them had softly trailed the mighty herd, we soon the next morning learned, two hundred or more strong. And along the broad track they had trampled we followed until, near noon, come to a great "burn" across which we could see for five or six miles, I realized they were settled down to a longer trek than I had time left to follow them on, for the next day at the latest I must press forward on the march through Kericho Boma to Lumbwa Station on the Uganda Railway.

Thus and there, in the Kisii Highlands, virtually ended my safari and shooting "In Closed Territory."

A hard six days' march got us across the Sessi and Isogu Rivers, two mountain torrents that within a fortnight the "big rains" would make impassable, by any means, for weeks, and into Lumbwa Station. It was a toilsome week over steep, rolling, lofty mountain contours, relieved only by a most delightful night at Kericho Boma, where, in my host at a most capital dinner, Deputy Commissioner L. A. F. Jones, I met a man who knew so many of my home club mates it almost seemed as if I were dining before an open window overlooking Madison Square of a softly sibilant May night when the birds are love-making in the scant shelter of the young leaves. In stalwart Angus Madden, commanding the Boma Askaris, I found a ripping Irishman with a heart his big body must have vast trouble holding and a brogue almost as rich as the wit it adorns; and in Bryan Brooke I came to know a giant, brawny young Scot, in whom generations of the gentlest breeding have contrived to engraft the simpatia and imagination of a poet upon a warring, adventurous spirit that no influences can serve to long hold away from the wilds.

Then came Lumbwa—the railway after a total safari trek, what with marching and shooting, that covered something over twelve hundred miles; the entraining of my trophies and myself for Nairobi, and the leaving dear old Outram (quite the best camp mate of all the many I have known, and that's saying a bit, for the trials and vicissitudes of camp life soon show dissonant any human chords not atuned true) to march the safari back to Juja.

XII. POTTING A PYTHON

FOR the American press in general, Theodore Roosevelt's shooting trip in East Africa has served chiefly as a convenient subject of more or less broad jest. Few at home outside the circle of his own family and closer friends have taken it seriously, except the more zealous members of the Society for the Prevention of Cruelty to Animals, who, to the number of some thousands, have joined in petitioning him to look but not to touch-to abstain from slaughter of their cherished (and usually rightly enough cherished) wards. Not one in a million has the faintest conception of what his undertaking really means or of the actual perils inseparable from it.

Compared to a wounded Cape buffalo, lion, leopard, rhino, or elephant, a stricken moose or even a maddened grizzly is child's play. Of infinitely stronger vitality, harder to kill, and possessed of an infernal cunning and a speed of attack and persistence in pursuit, are these African Big Ones, that make them far and away the most dangerous game in the world, with the single exception of the Asiatic tiger.

From the hour Mr. Roosevelt starts on safari and goes under canvas on the Kapiti Plains until, in his descent of the Nile, he has passed the temptation of a final run up the Sobat River, he literally carries his life in his hands, a pawn easy of annexation to any of the many predatory types of beasts and reptiles that swarm in jungle and in plain.

Nor is it his wounded he alone has to be alert for. The struggle for existence in the often densely overcrowded animal kingdom of Central Africa has taught many types the strategical value of instant attack the moment an enemy is sighted—and all are their enemies they fancy they can make their prey.

Rarely does a lone buffalo bull lose a chance at a man, and he makes a straight, furious charge if he thinks he is sighted, or, if unseen, a wide detour to close ambush along one's path and a dash at short range it is extremely difficult to stop or escape.

Most often the rhino charges the moment he scents a man, usually, I believe, from primary motives of curiosity, in fact charges about any and every thing except elephant, from which he flies in mortal fear; but it is none the less necessary to do some straight shooting or to execute a series of amazingly quick sidesteps.

At any moment a man traversing long grass or bush may come upon a lioness and cubs, at no more than arm's length, and lucky indeed he if she is not instantly upon him.

Any night his tent may be invaded by a hungry maneater who

has stolen past drowsing Askari camp sentries, and his spine be crushed under its favorite neck grip before even the approach of peril is suspected, it has happened often enough in the past and often will so happen again.

Out of any bunch of longish grass the wide-hooded head of a black (blue-black) cobra may rise threatening him, and that's no good place to stay; or a sluggish puff adder may lazily await until he is in easy reach of its favorite backward stroke; or a python may toss a halfhitch of its giant coils his way that few get free of once it has enfolded them.

And then there are the fevers so many fall victim to, from plain malarial to "tick fever" (spirillum) and "black water," that one is often years getting wholly rid of-where they don't begin by ridding the earth of him,—and the awful spectre of the sleeping sickness that is now claiming white victims with growing frequency.

Overdrawn? Exaggerations, these? No; not by a hair's breadth; just types of common incident of the sort that, sooner or later, are reasonably certain to be handed, in a more or less mixed job lot, to invaders of the open veldt and bush of Central Africa.

It is a country and a life in which a man untrained in taking care of himself against any and all comers, uninured to confronting deadly peril with steady nerves, is sure to have more frights than fun.

Indeed, any man who is not a quick, cool-headed, and accurate rifle shot is a fool to go after African big game. To be sure not a few such dilettanti sportsmen have so gone, and have returned not only unscathed but with handsome bags of trophies; but alike for their own personal safety and for the major part of their fine collections of big game specimens they remain indebted to the straight shooting of one or another of the splendid little group of professional safari leaders, highly trained expert hunters, like Cunninghame, Will Judd, or Tarlton. The two former men for years made their rifles win them handsome tribute in ivory and in skins, who, accustomed daily to stake their lives upon the accuracy of their aim, one might fancy possessed of iron nerves capable of meeting any situation without a materially quickened heart-heat. But the fact is they know the game so well they are ever keenly alive to its hazards. Within ten yards of a wounded rhino bull in thick bush, I have myself seen Will Judd's cheeks go livid white as the palor of death, but that it was a fighting palor his blazing, red-brown eyes and gripping jaws left no doubt of, palor còme of every nerve and muscle held under such high tension for instant action that the veins were made to pour their ruby blood back into deep arterial streams.

And Theodore Roosevelt himself knows so well what he is going out against must so know it as an intimate of Sir Harry Johnston, F. C. Selous, and others justly famous for the last quarter-century for their work and sport in Central Africa — that the American public can be quite sure he goes from a sheer love and lust of battling that even the perpetual bitter contests against almost overwhelming odds that in history will serve to most strongly mark and distinguish his administration of the nation's affairs, has left unsatisfied.

Seven of the last ten months it has been my privilege to pass in Central Africa I have spent on safari in British and German East Africa and in Uganda, shooting. In that time I have covered most of the country Mr. Roosevelt will shoot over, excepting Mount Kenya and the sections of his homebound journey between the Victoria Nyanza port of Entebbe and the Nile port of Gondokoro, and much of the "closed territory" along the German border which he is not likely to visit.

As guest of Wm. Northrup McMillan, who will be the principal host of Mr. Roosevelt during his stay in Africa, it has been my very great privilege to have at my command the services of his highly trained staff of Somali shikaris, cooks, syces, and mess boys, men who have been with Mr. McMillan six to eight years, on all his expeditions through Abyssinia, along the Blue Nile and the Sobat and in Somaliland, and all of whom have been placed at the disposal of Mr. Roosevelt.

While doubtless in time an equally able staff might be assembled, no other such capable, organized group of native hunters and camp servants exists in Africa to-day. And warrior bred are they all, even down to the mess "boys," men trained in their youth on the sandy, arid plains of Ogadan, to run elephant on ponies and hamstring them with their swords, and to receive charging lion on their spears; fanatic Mohammedans, blood brothers to the Mahdist swordsmen who fell in windrows under the machine-gun fire of the British square at Omdurman, and kinsmen of the men who for eight years have held the frontier of British authority and influence in Somaliland against the Mad Mullah's still more fanatical raiding hordes,—the Mullah who now is giving Britain the most serious native war problem she has had to confront since the Mahdi's downfall.

Regal Wassama, the chef-a chef Sherry would be glad to own is a veteran bearing the scars of three Soudan campaigns.

Djama Aout, the head shikari (gun bearer) is the man who thrust a pistol down the throat of a wounded lion, to save the life of Charles Bulpett, who lay beneath the lion, and there held the pistol till he had fired its six loads, while, meantime, the lion was crunching his arm.

Hassan Yusuf, the second shikari, was a sergeant of Italian horse at the battle of Adowa, and is as steady a man as one could ask to have behind him in any trouble.

Awala Nuer, the third shikari, gets a bit excited in the presence of big game and sometimes does the wrong thing, but never learned to run from anything.

Hadji Ali, the headman, and Abullahi, Adam Robley, Osman, Derria, and Adam Elmy, and the matchless Swahili, Salem bin Juma, are men who can make safari life as comfortable and even luxurious for Mr.

Roosevelt as ever he found the White House, if he finally elects to take them.

But, while I understand he has accepted the offer of their services, I know that his chosen safari leader, R. J. Cunninghame, objects strongly to the use of Somalis, for so he told me at dinner the night before I left Nairobi. In their stead, even as gun bearers, he prefers to use Swahilis, who, when they do wrong, may be given the only corrective that has the slightest useful effect with an African native, viz., anywhere from ten to twenty-five strokes across the buttocks with the kiboko, a flexible but stiff, straight whip four or five feet long and a halfinch thick in the middle, cut out of hippo or rhino hide, that, when it does not draw blood, raises welts double its own diameter.

The kiboko, or even a blow or kick, no Somali will stand; any man who so handles them is pretty certainto find a knife sticking in his ribs, a little sooner or latter, unless he has established extraordinary authority and influence over them as a master they both respect and fear, and even then he is none too safe.

It's a whole lot of diplomacy one needs to successfully and safely handle Somalis, and I believe Cunninghame is quite right that they are a disturbing element in any safari under any man less absolutely their master than Mr. McMillan. Personally I thoroughly liked them, and, thanks to the fact that Mr. McMillan had temporarily transferred to me the mantle of his authority of every sort over them, with right of punishment or dismissal, had comparatively little trouble with them. Once I just had to smash one of the shikaris in the nose for handing me one rifle and passing me the cartridges of another of different calibre in rather a tight corner-but he only drew himself up and gravely said: "You are my bwana (master) and my father; good!" Just how "good" I did not feel any too safe of, however, until my train was pulling out of Nairobi.

Approve it though he of course will not, Mr. Roosevelt will have to close his eyes or accustom himself to occasional severe floggings of the wapagazi (porters), for without it no safari could he held together a fortnight; discipline would soon disappear and that quickly be followed by open revolt or desertion. To the lazy porter a flogging merely serves as a temporary spur to better work, but, oddly, the insolent and rebellious are by it almost invariably transformed into the most respectful, zealous, and efficient men of your command. Nor as a rule do any of the East African tribesmen who serve as porters bear a grudge for a flogging, they just take it as a matter of course, accustomed as they have been to receive far worse in the way of discipline at the hands of their own chiefs.

Indeed, it must be remembered that the black is of a far coarser fibre than the white man, and, therefore, endures and recovers from punishment and wounds no white man could survive.

Ordered to chine (lie prone upon his face), down he goes without a murmur, so lies, unheld and uncomplaining, until the flogging is finished, and then often springs to his feet, draws himself up and salutes his bwana, with a smile.

In the matter of safari leader, Mr. Roosevelt has been well advised. Other African hunters there are, perhaps, in many ways as capable as Mr. R. J. Cunninghame; a few, but none are quite his equal. A man of broad education and a close student of natural history, throughout his seventeen years in the open veldt and bush veldt, the rifle his exclusive trade and capital, the elephant has always meant more to him than ivory and buck more than meat and skins. All the time he has been studying, until to-day he possesses a more comprehensive and accurate knowledge of African game, big and little, the local habitat and habits of each species, than any man living, with the single possible exception of F. C. Selous.

Now about forty years of age, full-bearded and deepwrinkled of face as an Arab, wrinkles all soon get who long dwell in the shimmering glare of the equatorial sun, Mr. Cunninghame's short stature and otherwise slender frame are burdened with a pair of shoulders so massive in depth and breadth as to incline any one to feel sorry for his legs who does not know how tirelessly they carry him from dawn to dark through the heaviest going in elephant grass or bush.

Absolutely in his prime, both in experience and strength, if the organization and routing of the safari are left exclusively to Cunninghame, it is safe to say Mr. Roosevelt will return with such a bag as few, if any, have ever equalled; if there is much interference, he, easily enough, may not return with such a bag, for even with species that are in certain sections absolutely abundant, it is often hard to find them and harder still to locate, stalk, and kill individual fine specimens.

On March 18 Cunninghame and I lunched and dined together in Nairobi. He then told me he was still unable to make any definite plans as to the routing of the safari. He had a tall stack of letters from the White House, each new one conflicting in one feature or another with the advices contained in its predecessor—obviously the result of the mass of suggestions and advice sought from or volunteered by men who had shot in Africa and were presumed to know the game, and all of whom, naturally enough, held more or less differing views.

About all then clear to him was that Mr. Roosevelt would arrive in Mombasa April 22 on the Admiral of the German East African Line, accompanied by his son, Kermit, by F. C. Selous, who was to join him at Naples, and by three representatives of the Smithsonian Institution.

This meant a party of seven white men, including himself, and was giving Cunninghame no little concern, as most of the best shooting is in remote sections where no food is obtainable, even for one's porters, other than meat, and Swahili porters, the best obtainable and the sort engaged by Cunninghame, are Mohammedans who will eat no meat not properly halaled, the throat cut by one of their own faith before the beast is dead. Thus a party of more than two or three men makes a big, unwieldy caravan, naturally difficult to handle, and often desperately hard to provide for.

The last mail, however, brought him advice that the ex-President and his son would not come directly through to Nairobi, but would leave the Uganda Railway at Kapiti Plains, two hundred and eighty-eight miles from Mombasa and thirty-nine miles short of Nairobi, the nearest station to Sir Alfred Pease's Kilima Theki Farm, where he intended stopping for a fortnight for lion, after which he purposed trekking north twenty-five miles across the Athi Plains, to Mr. McMillan's Juja Farm for a stay of two or three weeks. In the meantime, Cunninghame was instructed, he would be expected to take the three Smithsonian scientists on a short safari, wherever they could best get busy accumulating specimens of the smaller mammals and birds. The Juja visit finished, then the party was to be reunited and the big safari start — in such direction as might be later agreed on.

"And it's a jolly heavy load that letter takes off my mind," Cunninghame commented.

'Why?" I asked.

"Why?" he answered; "just because from the first I have by no means enjoyed the gravity of the responsibility I must assume in taking a man of Mr. Roosevelt's high position out after lion. Indeed, I have enjoyed it less since he wrote me that he is a bad shot—'useless with a shotgun and rusty with a rifle,' though this statement, I fancy, from all I have heard of his fine work in your own Far West, will turn out to be overcolored by modesty. But you well know a charging lion doesn't give a man much time nothing but a mortal brain shot can be sure of stopping him—and I myself can miss a shot at times, like anybody else. So if he gets his lion over about Theki⊠and surely at that season the Hills will be able to show him lion there leaving me free to give lion the go-by and proceed with the general bag, it's pleased as Punch I'll be."

"But don't you consider elephant quite as dangerous as lion?" I asked.

"Far more dangerous," he replied, "under certain conditions; less in others. But you don't suppose I'd be infernal fool enough to take Mr. Roosevelt into the long elephant grass and dense forest of the Kisii country where you got your big eleven-footer, do you? There it's so thick a man's just got to go it alone, win or lose. None of that sort of country for me where I've got a life like his on my hands. Never! I'll take him where he can shoot his elephant like a gentleman, in open forest where one can see what's about him and where, if anything goes wrong, one can lend a bit of help. That's the sort of place he'll get his elephant in.

"Where? Oh, probably on the slopes of Mount Kenya, when, during the rains, the elephant have worked down out of the dense bamboo forest of the higher altitudes into open wood, and where they stay till the heat of the dry season drives them back up into the bamboos."

Returned to Juja early in March from three months on safari west along the German border and back through the Kavirondo, Kisii, Sotik, and Lumbwa countries, I had finished a bag that included all the specially desirable species on the Big Game License except lion and bongo. With my passage home booked for March 28, no chance remained for a final try for either of these lacking treasures, except lion. But for them there was yet a possibility.

Lion shift range a lot, following the game. During the thirty days between June and October that I had occupied exclusively (but unsuccessfully) in hunting lion along the Athi, the Ruwero, and the N'durugo, the three boundary rivers of the Juja estate, lion were as a rule heard about the camps every night, though not as thick as usual. But in December they had again drifted back in large numbers, and throughout the winter were seen almost daily by one or another of the Juja employees. On New Year's Day, William Marlow, the superintendent of Mr. McMillan's Long Juju Farm on the N'durugo, four miles from Juja, killed a superb big black-mane, almost a record in those parts, within a mile of his house; and a month later John Destro, the Juja storekeeper, killed a fine lioness a half-mile below the same house, first sighted and shot her in thick thorn at scant ten feet distance, luckily placing a mortal shot that dropped her in her tracks.

Then in February Mr. George, a guest of our Donya Sabuk neighbors Penton and Bunbury, a young man of but comparatively little field experience, with only three days of his stay remaining, camped down near the Caves of a Hundred Lion on the Athi, three miles from Juja. The second evening, sitting under cover atop of the cliffs whose base and crest are honeycombed with openings to caves the lions haunt when hunting thereabouts, he had the unforgivable luck to sight six lion stalking back to their bed chambers, and to kill four of the six, precisely where I had spent a whole fortnight and several sleepless nights trying, vainly, to sight one. Such is the luck of the game.

Even ladies there could then sight lion, for a little later in February Miss Kipp, a guest of Miss Lucas of Donya Sabuk (whose brother was killed by a lion on the Athi three years before), while riding from Juja to the Lucas farm with only one native spearman as attendant, was followed half a mile by a big lioness.

So, encouraged by these stories of recent experiences, the moment I got back I started out and scattered Masai scouts in all directions—but never a bit of fresh sign could they find; apparently the lion had trekked away.

Then on the tenth, Captain A. B. Duirs, the manager of Juja, and I went out on a four days' circle of Komo Rock and Ostrich Hill to the east of the Athi, but while the trip yielded me a superb eland bull, and also a great water python seventeen feet, four inches long, killed in short reeds about a small water-hole four miles from the river, no lion did we find.

The photographs of the eland, of the python, and of the big Boer gharri used on short safari about Juja give some idea of the vast and comparatively level stretches of the Athi Plains, where Mr. Roosevelt will find many sorts of game as thick as he ever saw cattle on the most overcrowded range-hartebeeste, zebra, Granti and Thompsoni (gazelle), impala, water buck, reed buck, giraffe, ostrich, bush buck, duyker, dik-dik, wart-hog, hyena; while the deep pools of its rivers are full of hippo and crocodiles and the thorn thickets and cliffs lining the streams are always full of monkeys, from little blue chaps no bigger than kittens up to great man apes nearly four feet tall. There, too, among the thorns and rocks are favorite lurking places for lion and leopard, as offering convenient ambush for a short dash on buck stringing down to water; and seven miles west on Kamiti Farm, whose shooting will be placed at Mr. Roosevelt's disposal by its owner, Mr. Hugh H. Heatley, the papyrus swamps along the Kamiti are so full of buffalo that every few days Heatley's Boer farmer, Hammond, has to sprint for his life from his ploughing to his house, and the neighbors are predicting it is not likely to be long before the buffalo get him.

Notwithstanding the abundance of the game on the Athi Plains, I fancy Mr. Roosevelt will find it rather the most difficult shooting he will have out here, for seldom does one get a shot at buck there at any he specially wants under three hundred to five hundred yards. Often for miles the plain offers no more cover than a billiard table. As one advances the vast herds part, moving ahead to right and left, frequently in such dense mass it looks as if the entire plain itself had gone adrift. Sometimes rolling ground or bits of bush offer possible stalking on a fine specimen you have picked, but rarely or never when there are not scores or hundreds of other buck near from which you can't hide yourself and which are always off and passing the alarm to your specimen buck before you are within easy range.

For instance, the getting of my eland bull was a typical incident. He was one of twelve, dozing comfortably, some lying and some standing, midway of a low, smooth hillslope. No other buck were at the time within a half-mile of the eland. To get the wind, I had to circle far south of them, and got by without rousing them. But on my return toward them, while still a fourth of a mile from them, Grant and Tommy bounding about ahead of me passed them the tip of coming trouble, so that when I got to the hillcrest it was to see my eland a half-mile below me, moving north with a mass of other game.

Altogether I was four hours playing about those eland, trying for a possible shot at the big bull of the herd followed them five miles to the eastern foot of Donya Sabuk, where, late in the afternoon, I had to content myself with a shot at seven hundred yards that, most luckily, gave him a bad wound in the hind quarter that enabled Duirs to run him on Long Tom and cut and turn him from the herd within easy range of me.

The accompanying photographs, by the way, show Djama Aout and Hassan Yusef, the two Somali shikaris who will serve Mr. Roosevelt while he is shooting about Juja and later on his safari, if he overrides Mr. Cunninghame's prejudice against them, Djama holding the python's head, Hassan his tail. They also show Long Tom and Walleye, the two best Juja shooting ponies, one or both of which will carry Mr. Roosevelt. Walleye, the smaller of the two, a Somali pony, stands still as a statue for a shot from the saddle, and is probably the best lion pony in British East Africa. Long Tom, an East Indian country bred, is less tractable but faster.

His eland Mr. Roosevelt will only get by accepting a special license from the Governor, which, of course, will be given him if he wishes it, for under the new Game Law which went into effect April 1, eland are declared royal game and shooting them is forbidden, under penalty of a heavy fine or imprisonment, or both. Thus my bull will remain one of the very last ever to be killed in British East Africa. Well it is the eland should be saved, in a country in which both horses and mules are easy and frequent prey to several types of fatal horse sicknesses, for they are easily domesticated, and it is hoped their vast bulk of weight and muscle may yet prove of economic value for heavy draft purposes.

Moreover, as Mr. Roosevelt is more likely to shoot and kill than to heed their petitions that he should not shoot, it may interest the members of the Society for the Prevention of Cruelty to Animals to know that the Administration of British East Africa has been compelled to recognize in the new Game Law the loud cries of settlers for protection against the depredations of wild game. Indeed, the game in B. E. A. must be thinned, if not exterminated, before farmers may enjoy the avails of their land holdings. Thus the new law permits proprietors to allow any one holding a game license to shoot all the game he likes on their estates, and practically removes all restrictions against the killing of game on one's own land.

The sheer "vermin" so declared by the law, predatory beasts against which no life is safe, biped or quadruped lion, leopard, hyena, crocodile, etc. (while the "protected" buffalo and rhino are just as dangerous to human life)—the most rabid member of the Society for the Prevention of Cruelty to Animals would not long live neighbor to before unlimbering his guns.

For example, a few days before I left Juja news came from the manager of one of Mr. McMillan's farms that his next neighbor, a young

German named Loder, had been killed by leopard. Swift and Rutherfoord, farmers a day's journey north of Juja, have in the last three years killed sixteen lion had to do it to save their domestic stock from extermination.

The two following items are clipped from The East African Standard of March 27:

THREE LIONS FOUR MILES FROM MOMBASA: A CHANCE FOR MOMBASA SPORTSMEN

The natives of M'tongwe have seriously appealed to European sportsmen in Mombasa for protection. During Monday night three lions took away a cow from a native's boma and on Tuesday night terrified the inhabitants by roaring round their huts seeking food.

On Tuesday afternoon the spoors of the lions were seen clearly marked in the neighborhood of the hole where Makalinga buried the body of the late Mr. London. The natives fear that the spirits of the recently hanged murderers have entered the bodies of the lions and are visiting the village to exact penalties.

A MAN-EATER KILLED

For some time past Messrs. Newland and Tarlton have been receiving reports of the existence of man-eating lions near Lake Magadi. It was reported that several natives lost their lives through them.

Last week Mr. Tarlton sent Mr. Stanton, an employee of the firm, out to ascertain facts and if possible dispose of the danger. On Thursday Mr. Stanton came across a huge lioness and wounded her severely. Following her up, he again hit her, this time through the eye. The shot was not fatal, however, and the enraged animal immediately charged, knocking Mr. Stanton over and stunning him. His gun bearer could not shoot, for fear of hitting Mr. Stanton. As soon as Mr. Stanton rose the brute struck him again. She then made off, and on being followed up by the party she was found crouching behind a bowlder. The gun bearer hit her with a .450 in the jaw, completely smashing it, and then struck her in the side, making a huge gash. Thinking she was quite dead, Mr. Stanton, who was still very dazed, moved up, when he was again attacked; but before he was down the gun bearer finished the matter by firing pointblank.

We have seen the skin and skull which testify to the fight. Strange to say, Mr. Stanton was struck each time by the pads of the beast's feet; but sustained only bruises. A Masai who was following Mr. Stanton and was previously warned off, was badly mauled and torn by the lioness when she was hiding in the bush after receiving the first shot.

Nor is the farmer's worst actual trouble with the man-eaters or other predatory types, for fencing is of no earthly avail against the general mass of the game. Juja's twenty thousand acres was once stoutly fenced, and with five strands of barb wire; to-day it is hard to find a two-hundred-yard section of the fence standing intact. Over fences the big buck go like birds, through them zebra chased by lion smash like a whirlwind, and nothing but a wire screen would serve to keep out the little "Tommys," Granti, dik-dik, etc.

Thus it will be seen that proselyting for the S. P. C. A. in British East Africa would be hopelessly uphill work, even for the most zealous.

XIII. THE LUCK OF THE GAME

RETURNED to Juja House Saturday evening, the thirteenth, I found a message waiting me from Clifford and Harold Hill, who until recently have managed Sir Alfred Pease's Theki ostrich farm, and whose own ostrich farm, Katelembo, adjoins Theki on the east and south. Their message advised me that lion had been so thick about their place for a week that they were confident they could show me a chance at one or more if I came over immediately.

Circumstances had compelled me to decline two previous invitations from them, and now this last chance was one not to be lost, for as a rule no section of British East Africa is as thickly infested with lion as the Theki Farm of Sir Alfred Pease and the Katelembo and Wami Farms of the Hill cousins, and few, if any, non-professional hunters have had more experience with lion than the Hills. In the last three years they have themselves killed fifteen lion there and their visiting guests have shot another ten, or a total of twenty-five.

Lucky indeed is Mr. Roosevelt that his initiation into the gentle sport of lion shooting will be at the hands of the Hills; with no other men could he be surer of success or safer against serious injury, for they know the game and have the nerve to play it right.

Both are colonials who have never seen England, South African bred, descendants of families which were among the first British settlers of Grahamstown early in the last century. True to the traditions of their Basuto- and Zulu-fighting ancestors, they were among the first colonials to enlist for the Boer War—Clifford in the Imperial Light Horse and Harold in Neville's Horse, and among the last mustered out.

The war over, seized by the restless spirit of their pioneer forebears, both trekked away north into the wilds of British East Africa, planning there to establish themselves in ostrich farming wherever the wild birds were thickest to which in their youth they were bred, and which in the southern colonies is winning such large fortunes for the initiated.

Slender, sinewy men of iron endurance, quiet and gentle of speech, steady, cool-headed shots at anything that needs lead, but tireless workers on their farm, the Hills have never hunted lion for sport but only as a necessary incident of the day's work.

So, the hour of 4 A. M. Sunday, the fourteenth, found me mounted on Walleye, and followed by Hassan Yusef (riding a mule and carrying my two rifles), trotting away through the darkness and bitter chill of early morning in the African highlands, on a short cut, first through the Athi

Plains and then over the summit of the Machakos Range, to the Hill farm, thirty miles distant from Juja, where I arrived about noon.

Too busy accumulating ostriches and thinning out lion to have any time left for architecture, I there found the Hills installed in two grass huts of the sort natives throw up in a day or two, one the dormitory and the other the dining-room- both windowless because the chinks in the grass walls let in light and air enough; both doorless, because any prowling would-be intruder that might be excluded by a proper door could easily enough force entrance through the flimsy walls.

And there for three days I was made as welcome and as comfortable as ever before in many far more pretentious diggings.

Hanging beneath a thorn tree behind the house, curing, were the four fresh-killed lion skins fallen to Harold's rifle which had prompted them to send for me.

The Thursday of the week previous the Hills had been spending the night with District Commissioner R. W. Humphery, the Chief Administrative Officer of their District of Ukamba, at Machakos Fort, four miles from their farm, helping Humphery celebrate his birthday. At an early morning hour, not long after they had retired, the Hills were awakened by the sergeant of the guard and told that one of their natives had just arrived with word that six lion had broken into their ostrich boma and were killing the birds. Racing for the farm as fast as they could, accompanied by Commissioner Humphery, who had been eight years in the country without ever seeing a lion until, the Christmas Day previous, he had, while out with the Hills, bagged a lioness, and now keen for another — upon arrival they found the lion gone, frightened away by the din made by the natives, and three of their finest birds dead and half eaten in the boma.

Sure the lion would return, the dead birds were left where they lay, the living transferred to a distant boma, and a platform built in a tree that stood in one corner of the enclosure.

The boma was fifty yards square; its wall, built of huge thorn bush piled tightly together, easily ten feet thick at the base and eight feet high. Against all precedent any of us had ever heard of, the six lion had actually torn their way through this most formidable, heavily spiked barrier, pulled and tugged until they had opened a way to the interior.

Friday night the men took two-hour turns on guard upon the platform, but the night passed without incident.

But about 3 A. M. of Sunday morning, on Harold's watch he was roused by movements beneath him, to see, by the half light of a waning moon, the six lion returned, rending the dead birds and quarrelling like cats for the best bits.

Instantly he began firing, and soon the cracks of his rifle were drowned by the deep roars of the lion, mad with rage over this attack by an enemy they could not see. Directly one scented or sighted him and made a dash for the tree, whose platform a good bound might easily have reached, but Harold luckily dropped him with a shot through the spine.

Presently there was silence below. One lion lay, obviously dead, in the moonlight beneath him, but whether the others had gone or were lurking in the shadows he felt so little sure of he kept to his perch till daylight — to find all gone but the one.

However, before noon four of the missing five were located, all severely wounded, in a near-by ravine, and, after a lot of careful work and much hazard, three of the four were bagged.

Early Monday morning we were out, the two Hills, myself and gun bearer, and the Hills' Kikuyu beaters and trackers.

The Kapiti Plains are almost entirely bare of cover, short grassed, bushless, but every donga (ravine) is densely filled with thorn, reed, and weeds, with here and there a water pool of the sort lion love to take to shortly after dawn in the dry, hot season just then at its height, and, to be seen, out of this cover they have to be routed.

Down all their favorite dongas, over the rocky, cave-slit crests of Theki and Wami, through the dense scrub along the lower slopes of the Machakos between Theki and Kitanga, for three days Clifford Hill led his native beaters, while Harold and I, on foot, marched from fifty to three hundred yards ahead of and slightly flanking the line of beaters, one to right and one to left as a rule, but never a lion did we raise. Once we struck fresh sign entering a bit of bush and thought we had him, the incident shown in the pictures where our group is rather closely bunched and advancing to where we thought he lay. But on out of the bush he had passed, over hardbaked ground where he left no further sign.

With more luck than I had ever dared hope for with all other big game, lion are evidently not meant for me — like Director of Surveys, Colonel G. E. Smith, who surveyed the first caravan road from Mombasa to Uganda, who was chief of the Anglo-German Boundary Survey, and has spent the larger part of the last fifteen years in the wildest of British East Africa's wild places, who on these same Kapiti Plains himself killed seventeen rhino in one day—had to do it to protect his safari from their continual charges — but who to this day has never seen a lion.

Tuesday, just before beating the summit of Theki, we had lunch with Mr. Allsop, manager of Sir Alfred Pease's Theki ostrich farm, in his little two-room tin house, which is shrouded in granadilla vines, whose delicious passion fruit was then purpling and should be prime in another month. There I got photographs of the two Arab stallions newly bought by Sir Alfred for Mr. Roosevelt's use, and arrived only the day before, direct from the Soudan, via Mombasa.

Wednesday afternoon, en route back to Juja, Clifford Hill and I visited Kitanga, the new house Sir Alfred is building for the reception of

Mr. Roosevelt, then nearing completion. It is a tin-roofed one-story bungalow, the outer walls built of square gray granite blocks, the partitions of sun-dried bricks, of five rooms, a central living and dining room flanked by four small bedrooms, and sporting two baths. Beautifully situated on a high shoulder of the south end of the Machakos Range, about 6,500 feet above sea level, its broad veranda commands a magnificent view—east over tall round-topped hills thinly clad with wild olives, south across the dim, hazy stretches of the Kapiti Plains and over the rugged crests of Chumvi, Theki, and Wami, the only mountain uplifts that break the plain's monotony, down upon the white splotch in the broad yellow field which represents Kapiti Station, twelve miles away, and on through the purple distance to where, one hundred and twenty miles away, Mt. Kilima N'jaro's 19,000 feet tower so high aloft toward the zenith that it is hard to realize its snow and glacier-clad crest is actually a mountain peak and not a cloud. The view we had Mr. Roosevelt may not get, for Mt. Kilima N'jaro is seldom clearly visible from thereabouts excepting just at the very end of the dry season.

The group of men appearing in the picture of Kitanga, contractors engaged in building the house, are Boer emigrants from South Africa, now farmers living in a close little colony along the slopes of Lucania, a small rugged range lying between the Machakos and the Athi River, and oddly includes three men bearing names famous in Boer history, viz., a Prinsloo, a Botha, and a Joubert, the latter brother to General Joubert, with whom Mr. Roosevelt can exchange campaigning experiences in their mutually native Low Dutch tongue.

Mr. Roosevelt is due to reach Kitanga about April 24. At the Pease house he will probably spend little time, as only small buck are to be had in its immediate vicinity. His lion camp will doubtless be pitched either at Lanjaro, a small spring midway between Kitanga and Theki, or on the Hills' Wami Farm, five miles south of Theki. Thereabouts by May the Hills will be able to show him the surest and safest lion hunting known.

With thirty inches of rain due in April and no more than four inches in May the season will then be prime, Kapiti Plains a waving meadow of short grass, every dry donga a brook, every "pan" a brimming pool of sweet water, the weather so cool that lion then rove or idle on the plains by day, instead of seeking cover as in the dry season, where they may easily be marked down by a man with a telescope on the summit of either Theki, Wami, or Chumvi.

The moment a lion is sighted, the sportsmen will start after him, all mounted. So soon as he sights them, one of the Hills will spur after him, run him to bay, and there circle and worry him at a safe distance while Mr. Roosevelt gallops up, followed by his gun bearer, to within one hundred to two hundred yards, according to his nerve and confidence in his shooting, and dismounts for his shot. In seven cases out of ten the lion charges the pony man instead of the sportsman, indeed is almost sure to if the rider is on a white or gray horse, resembling a zebra. And when he does charge the sportsman, there is always a chance the pony man may head and divert him; but where this strategy fails, then it is a case of shoot quick and straight or take (at least) a rending from carriontainted claws certain to cause fatal blood poisoning if permanganate of potash is not promptly applied to the wounds in such strength that the treatment is even more painful than the wounds.

Just as I was stepping into the gharri in front of Juja House the afternoon of the eighteenth, to go to Mombasa to meet Mr. McMillan, who was due there from India the twenty-first, the following letter was handed to me:

LONG JUJU, March 18, 1909. [British East Africa.]

To E. B. BRONSON, Esq., Juja Farm.

DEAR MR. BRONSON. I saw a very fine lion yesterday morning, also fresh tracks of two small ones, and one was growling around here nearly all night.

I went all around the ditch this morning early; but did not see one. Trusting you are well, believe me, Yours faithfully, W. Marlow.

Thus if Mr. Roosevelt fails of a chance at Theki, it is more than likely the Juja estate can furnish all the lion he wants.

The night we reached Nairobi, Mr. Cunninghame dined with us at Mr. McMillan's town bungalow, where he learned that Mr. Selous comes out as the guest of Mr. McMillan, with whom he is expecting to go on safari for several weeks immediately after Mr. Roosevelt's visit to Juja is finished. Thus, unless they arrange otherwise while shipmates on the Admiral, while Mr. Selous may shoot with Mr. Roosevelt at Theki or Juja he will not accompany any of Mr. Roosevelt's long safaris.

The Juja visit, however, may be deferred to a later date, as Mr. Cunninghame is keen to have Mr. Roosevelt come out with him on a short safari directly he leaves Sir Alfred Pease and before the "big rains" are stopped after certain game which is most easily had during the wet season.

If such a short safari is arranged, it is probable Mr. Cunninghame will take Mr. Roosevelt to Mt. Kenya, a week's march north of Juja, for elephant.

As for the long safari in British East Africa, if the choice is left to Mr. Cunninghame, it is probable it will go by rail from Nairobi sixty-four miles west to Naivasha, there detrain, circle the south end of Lake Naivasha, ascend and cross the precipitous lofty wall of the Mau Escarpment and thence drop into the Sotik country — for there on the Limerick Plains and along the upper reaches of the Amala River is Cunninghame's favorite place for quickly and easily bagging fine specimens of the more abundant species. On this route, in four to five days' march from Naivasha Mr. Roosevelt will be in good shooting. There, moreover, he will be in reach of some of the rarer species; within two to three days' march roan may be had on the crest of Isuria Escarpment, and nearer still, if he has patience and luck, the Chipalungo Forest may yield him a bongo, while two days west of Sotik Boma, on the Rongana, rhino abound sporting horns up to thirty-four inches in length.

The Sotik safari finished, I shall expect to see Mr. Cunninghame march the safari north from Gilgil, probably to and past Rumuruti Boma on the Guaso Narok River, thence swinging west to Lake Baringo for greater Kudu and lesser Kudu, or perhaps instead descending the northern Guaso Nyiro River and following it east along the southern boundary of the great Jubaland Game Reserve, and returning to Nairobi via Nyeri and Ft. Hall.

The time allotted to shooting in British East Africa nearing its finish, I shall not be surprised to see Mr. Roosevelt's safari lead northwest from Londiani Station, through the capital shooting on the Uasin Guishu Plateau, to a look in on the Cave Dwellers of Mt. Elgon, whence its descent to Jinja, the Nyanza head of the Nile, will be easy by one of the excellent roads which Governor Bell's energetic administration has given to Uganda.

The giant white rhino I see in the home press Mr. Roosevelt is keen for, are now about as scarce as hens' teeth, but along the western sources of the Nile, on his way to Lake Albert Edward, through the farther limits of the Uganda Province of Toro, well over toward the Congo, he may have the luck to find one.

If for his journey across Uganda and on north down the Nile to Cairo he follows the usual route, and the only easy one, he will cross the north end of Victoria Nyanza from Kisumu to Entebbe in one of the excellent little steamers of the Uganda Railway, only fifteen hours actual steaming, but passengers are never landed until the morning following the date of sailing. From Entebbe there is an excellent road for one hundred and sixty miles to Hoima, usually covered, in rickshaw or on bicycle, in ten days. The thirty-three miles from Hoima to the Lake Albert Edward port of Butiaba is over such rough going that it must be done on foot, a good two days' march. At Butiaba he will take the tiny Government launch Kenia, on which, for passengers unable to crowd into the engineer's cabin, a tent is pitched on deck. Steaming from dawn to dark and tying up over night, the Kenia covers the three hundred odd miles down lake and Nile to Nimule in five days. From Nimule to Gondokoro, the head of upper Nile navigation, the river falls so rapidly that the entire one hundred and thirty intervening miles must be done afoot, a nine days' march. From Gondokoro one reaches Khartoum by steamer in nine days, and then three days more by rail lands one in Cairo.

Thus the entire distance from Entebbe to Cairo may be covered in thirty-eight days, but it is not likely Mr. Roosevelt will press straight through without a stop. Immediately north of Gondokoro there is capital shooting, including one or two species he will not find in British East Africa, while up the Sobat, a large western tributary entering the Nile roughly midway between Gondokoro and Khartoum, there is probably the best open country elephant shooting remaining in all Africa, and there, I understand, Mr. Cunninghame is likely to take him for a finish of his African sport on royal game.

On Friday the twenty-sixth we left Nairobi in Mr. McMillan's special car for Mombasa, to which he was returning to meet Mrs. McMillan, who was due to arrive there from India the thirty-first.

On Sunday the Melbourne, northbound, and the Oxus, southbound, both of the Cie Mesageries Maritimes, arrived off Kilindini, the west and principal harbor of Mombasa; but since the former had the bad luck to run aground in the narrow channel entrance and the latter lay by to help her, it was not until Monday that both were able to drop anchor in the harbor.

The Oxus brought Sir Alfred Pease, Lady Pease, and their daughter.

While we were at breakfast at the Grand Hotel, Sir Alfred came in and we were introduced. A tall, spare, active man of about fifty, the Hills tell me he is as keen for veldt sport as any youngster. He and his family were hurrying up country by the next train to hasten the completion and furnishing of Kitanga.

Asked if he felt sure of getting Mr. Roosevelt his lion, Sir Alfred replied:

"Well, one never can tell, you know; just depends on a man's luck. Last year during my eight weeks' stay at Theki I personally saw, all told, twenty-seven lion, and yet for the three weeks of the same period my friend Sir Edmund Loder spent with me there, after he had been out three months on safari without getting or even seeing a lion, we failed entirely to show him one."

Yes, indeed, it is all just a matter of "luck," is lion shooting, as few could so emphatically prove as my friend the Cavaliere A. Parenti, a shipmate. Many have read but probably few have credited the story of a lion taking a man from a carriage of the Uganda Railway.

And yet it is true in every detail. Cavaliere Parenti was one of the three men in the compartment in which the man was killed and from which he was carried by the invader. Asked to refresh my memory of the details of the incident, he replied:

"Ah! my God, but I can smell the stench of that lion yet, for I lay beneath him in the darkness on the floor of the compartment during the few seconds he took to crunch the life out of poor Ryall!

"You know, Mr. Ryall, who was then the Superintendent of the Railway Police, our friend Mr. Huebner, and myself, had heard of a man-eater who had killed and eaten several persons between the stations of Kiu and Sultan Hamud, and left Mombasa to hunt him.

"In the night our railway carriage was cut and dropped from the train in the vicinity of his depredations, and the three of us went to sleep, preparatory to an early start in the morning.

"How did the man-eater get in? God knows; I don't; through the open window doubtless.

"The first I knew I was on the floor of the car, beneath some soft, heavy, foul-smelling body; then I heard the crunch of huge jaws and just one low, horrid cry from where Ryall lay in the berth opposite mine. Then the beast was off in a leap through the window and I — I found poor Ryall gone.

"Did we find him? Yes, in the morning, a few hundred yards away — But please don't ask me more, I can't talk of it yet, for the foul smell of that man-eater is ever in my nostrils, poor old Ryall's smothered death shriek ever ringing in my ears."

Yes, and also, as in this preceding incident, just "luck" with whom the sport lies, the biped or the quadruped, as instance, records in the official files of the Uganda Railway proving that eighty-four laborers, chiefly East Indians, were killed and eaten in the vicinity of Tsavo by one family of man-eaters, consisting of a blackmane, a lioness, and three pups, before they were finally exterminated by Colonel Patterson.

And while the files and records of the railway are red with such tragedies, they are also at times lightened with incidents full of humor.

For years and to this day the Station of Simba (Swahili for "lion") has been so infested with lion that they are a constant terror to the resident Hindu baboo (station master). All told, about twenty have been shot from its doors and windows and from the top of the adjacent water tank. Once they got so bad the company was compelled to send there a detail of ten Askaris (native police), but that they failed to afford adequate protection was proved by the fact that the manager received a day or two later the following despatch from his Simba baboo:

"At time of roaring policemen are not so brave; please arrange quick."

XIV. IS CENTRAL AFRICA A WHITE MAN'S COUNTRY?

OF all the long line of national or international expositions inspired by and more or less direct sequences of that with which the Crystal Palace was opened in London in 1851, few if any have been so picturesque and none so weirdly interesting as the first Agricultural and Industrial Exhibition of Uganda, held November 9 and 10, 1908, held at Kampala in a valley slumbering beneath the shadows of Mengo Hill, from whose crest, in 1877, King Mutesa issued orders for the assassination of the first party of pioneers of the Christian faith (members of the Church Missionary Society) that ventured to seek foothold in the heart of far-away Equatorial Africa.

While there were one hundred thousand visitors, many come distances of from one hundred to two hundred miles, the management was spared the vexatious transportation difficulties usually incident to such affairs, for 99,932 (the natives) came afoot, 50 (local officials and missionaries) came on bicycles or in rickshaws, and the remaining 18 of us came from Nairobi by the Uganda Railway and the good ship Clement Hill of the Victoria Nyanza service.

King's birthday morning, November 9, we dropped anchor off the new port of Luziro, deep in Murchison Bay. One little tin warehouse broke the solid wall of forest that lined the shore, one wobbly little pier gingerly reached out a few yards toward deep water to meet our approaching boats, and that was all there was of Luziro.

Come ashore, we found hidden away among the trees perhaps a score of rickshaws, and—would you believe it?— an automobile, a big bus affair with side seats, the Governor's state chariot. Captain Buxton, Mr. Sewall, and I, who were invited to lunch with His Excellency, the Governor, Sir H. Hesketh Bell, K. C. M. G., had no more than begun to congratulate ourselves upon a spin across the Uganda Hills in an auto before our hopes were dashed. Up came an aide who had been conferring with Lieut. Hampden of the Clement Hill to tell us that the expected supplies, which included auto materials, fuel, etc., and a rare lot of fireworks ordered for the fête, the last southbound French mail steamer had failed to land at Mombasa. Instead, it had steamed away south with them for Madagascar—perhaps (who knows?) from a patriotically malicious intent to spoil one British festival in revenge for the checkmate France suffered at Fashoda.

And there stood our steed, come to us pluckily but spent of its last ounce of energy in the coming, sound of body but empty of belly of no more use, with its tanks empty, than its weight in scrap iron!

To be sure the "railway" remained, but unfortunately it was not an available alternative no more use to us than the gasoline and pinwheels bowling away toward an ever-higher-rising Southern Cross, for it then only covered a scant two of the five miles that separate Luziro from Kampala. Moreover, that particular "railway" looked as if you could pack it on your shoulders more easily than ride on it.

It is a "mono-rail system" is Kampala's, of a sort quite largely installed in India in sections where the freight traffic stacks up no more than a few tons a week, and where the people are as little concerned about time as about eternity. Laid along one side of the excellent, wide Kampala road, this lonely rail with its tiny ties looks like a primitive ladder prostrate. There the motive power is cattle. Where mules or horses are available, I am assured the high express speed of six miles an hour is attained. The cars used have two wheels, one of which trundles along the ground like any honest cart wheel, while the other straddles the rail and on it contrives to accomplish a more or less successful rope-walking stunt, usually less. When finished, its time schedule is likely to be, as closely as I could judge, tri-weekly run down toward Luziro one week and a hard try to get back up to Kampala the third week.

Once outside the belt of tall forest that lines the lake, bowling along in rickshaws at close to tram-car speed on down-hill and level stretches, with a sturdy Baganda in the shafts and two of his mates pushing aft, all droning the monotonous but musical chant without which no Central African black can do any sort of toil, we entered a densely settled country where round-topped grass huts were ever peeping out of the banana groves and smiling natives ever peeping out of the huts. The men were decorously robed in long white Kanzus reaching from neck to feet, the women décolleté, bare of neck and arms but otherwise swathed in folds of snowy cotton wound tight beneath the arm pits and over the hips, a most striking contrast to the buxom Kavirondo beauties who are their next neighbors to the east, and who while never more heavily draped of figure than by a slender string of beads circling the waist, are far more virtuous than the Uganda women. Fields of cotton, bananas, cassava, dotted here and there with the graceful fronds of the date palm, stretched as far as we could see from the tallest hilltops.

Passing, toward noon, through the one street of the Indian Bazaar, we were in the heart of Kampala, although one would never know it until told. About us stood the six high hills that constitute it—Mengo, occupied by the boy king, Daudi Chwa, his regents, ministers, and court, the site of their ancient capitol when Lugard first won their confidence; Nakasero, by the English military and civil officials and the boma, or barracks, of the one company of Sikh Infantry and the King's African Rifles, the latter native troops; Nsambya, by Saint Joseph's Mission; Namirembe, by the English Cathedral of the Church Missionary Society; and Rubaga, by the White Fathers.

Descending towards the Exposition grounds, we bumped into another startler-nothing less than an American merry-go-round, and a big one at that, perched on a bench by the side of the road, whirling gayly with a rider on its every horse, waiting native thousands thronging thick about, keen for a chance of a mad gallop this the one only (but never lonely) prototype of Chicago's "Streets of Cairo" or St. Louis's "Great White Way" the modest little Exhibition could boast.

The Exhibition grounds lay in a little valley at the foot of Namirembe Hill and covered a space of nine hundred by three hundred feet.

While impaired by heavy showers, the scene when Governor Bell formally opened the Exhibition was one to dwell always in the minds of all lucky enough to be present.

At the north end of the grounds stood the pavilion of honor, ablaze with the colors dear to British hearts, facing Namirembe Hill and the graceful pinnacles of the English Cathedral that crown it. Grouped at the other end and along the east and west lines stood the Exhibition buildings, all, like the pavilion, walled and thatched with glistening gray elephant grass that made the greensward of the parallelogram look like a vast velvet rug bordered with silver. Drawn up fifty yards in front of the pavilion stretched the grim lines of a company of Sikh Infantry, stern-faced, bushy-bearded, red-turbanned stalwarts; to the right, a company of the King's African Rifles, massive blacks of a dozen different races but chiefly Nubians and Soudanese, uniformed in black jerseys and tall black tarbooshes; nearer still the band. Massed just without the policed lines were thousands of white-robed blacks.

The pavilion itself was a bank of the most brilliant variegated color-the blue and gold of the uniforms of the Governor and his staff; the white and gold of the line officers; the heavily gold-embroidered robes of the native kings and chiefs, some of black broadcloth and some of rich russet-hued bark cloth of native make; the purple and scarlet skull caps of rich Indian merchants; the delicate hues of the Paris gowns of a score of English ladies, wives of the officials; white and black robed Sisters of the Church, black and white gowned brethren of the faith- many of the officers and a few of the officials starred of breast with decorations that told of distinguished services to the State, the decoration that naturally dwarfed all the others, both in magnificence and in demand for space on human topography, being the "Star of Zanzibar," that of one of earth's smallest potentates, the Sultan of Zanzibar.

To the right of the Governor sat the bright-faced boy King of Uganda, his Highness, Daudi Chwa; to the left, his senior regent, Sir

Apolo Kagwa, K. C. M. G., a full-blood Baganda, but, if you please, a belted knight of the British Empire. Near about were grouped, each surrounded by his elder councillors and chiefs, the Kings of Unyoro, Toro, and Ankole, and the Kakunguru and the Saza Chief of Usoga, all feudal lords of his diminutive Highness of Uganda.

The hour of the opening of the Exhibition was justly a proud moment for Sir H. Hesketh Bell, K. C. M. G., the Governor. Of wide administrative experience, great energy, and of exceptional executive ability, in his scant two years in Uganda he has had remarkable success in welding together into a fairly homogeneous whole the previously loosely knit feudal elements of Daudi Chwa's kingdom; and by a great amount of road building, and good road building at that, he has accomplished more towards the opening up of the commerce of the country than all his predecessors. Indeed, at no previous time would the transportation facilities of the country have permitted the assembly of such an exhibition (amounting to four thousand exhibits) of native products, many come from remote points on the Nile, out of the north, and some from far southern Ankole, near to Lake Kivu. Nor, perhaps, at any previous time would tribal jealousies have left such an assembly possible.

After a brief address of welcome to the visiting dignitaries, and of congratulation upon their progress in education and in organized industry, Governor Bell received in turn the visiting feudatories and their chiefs, and the Exhibition was declared open.

Then the dignitaries and the visitors dispersed among the exhibits, viewed the samples of most excellent wheat, corn, cassava flour, chillies, peas, beans, peanuts, rice, yams, ghee (clarified butter), potatoes, rubber, beeswax; of vegetables and fruits; saw the production of coffee in all its stages, from the picking of the berry through curing to the cup; were shown cotton in the boll and in the ginning; marvelled at the native cunning of the basket and mat and cloth weavers, the patience and fair handiwork of the ironsmiths with none but the crudest of tools; stood in dumb surprise before the long line of roundmallet-wielding bark cloth makers, and saw a small eighteen-inch square of tree bark slowly expand to the wide proportions of an ample mantle, the finished product smooth and soft of texture, the color any of many tints from a pale amber to an Indian red; saw all these laughing, singing workers squatting to their tasks-for no Baganda can even contrive to till or crop the soil unless he is comfortably down upon his haunches, and then his hands are helpless unless they are plied in time to the lilt of some tune or song.

While an extraordinary and most interesting Exhibition, nevertheless I recall no native working with any but native tools at native tasks, making and doing the sort of things they have been making and doing from time immemorial, except a few lacemakers taught by mission ladies, and the feeders of the cotton gin; indeed, there was little in the show emphatic of material industrial progress except in the matter of cotton growing, the production of which has increased from the value of $30 in 1904 to $240,000 in 1907-08.

Not the least notable feature of the Exhibition was the youthful King of Ankole, a twenty-four-year-old, seven-foot giant, of an intelligent and most pleasing face. Nor were his principal exhibits less notable in their proportions and attractiveness than was he himself; his cows wore horns that would make the biggest Texas steer look like a two-year-old; and behind him throughout the day trailed a harem of thirty-seven dusky beauties of every tint from ebony to pale chocolate, and of all ages, apparently, from fourteen to four hundred.

A Marathon race was started about three o'clock. The course measured one hundred yards longer than that of Olympia, and not only was the course an endless succession of steep hills, but during the last two hours the runners had to contend with rain and mud so heavy that the white judges on bicycles came in completely worn out. Of the forty-eight starters, none were trained. Nevertheless remarkable time was made, the winner, Kapere, a native of Uganda, finishing in three hours, three minutes, only seven minutes over Olympia time. Only two others finished, one, Rubeni, coming in sixteen seconds after Kapere, and the third, Atanansi, three minutes later. And weirdest of all, the first two, standing for a photo ten minutes after their arrival, showed not the least sign of distress not a heave of flank or a tremor. Obviously, with decent roads and a bit of training, this pair would be tough customers, in any company, over a twenty-six-mile course.

What magnificent reserves of latent energy dwell within the huge bodies of those equatorial blacks, potential to turn every acre of land they inhabit into areas of enormously rich productivity, if only they could be freed of the lethargy within which the ease of their winning a subsistence enwraps them. And yet breakfasting two days later in Entebbe at the excellent Equatorial Hotel of Madame Berti, on purple passion fruit and ripe figs, at a table covered with orchids that would be worth a small fortune in New York, looking off down the perfect roadway, surfaced with red morain, that drives straight through the botanical gardens, and out across the sapphire of the lake to the deep blue of its farther headlands, breathing an atmosphere whose every whiff suffused one's senses with the passive joys of dolce far niente, it was not at all so easy to suppress sentiments of regret that these ease-loving children of Nature must needs be beguiled and bedeviled by white intrusion among them.

Throughout the half-century elapsed since the daring of Livingstone, Speke, Burton, and Stanley made known to the civilized world the vast store of raw riches it holds, its enormous resources under cultivation as a producer, not only of food and clothing but of an infinite variety of trees and plants that supply the rare and high-priced drugs of commerce,

England and the Continental powers have been grabbing greedily for the last square foot they dared appropriate of Equatorial Africa.

And yet to-day, after many years of administrative experience, experiment, and study, the fundamental moot point as to the ultimate value of their holdings remains unsolved.

Is Equatorial Africa—roughly the middle third of the Dark Continent—ever to become a white man's country in anything more than name and administration—a country where white colonists may settle and subsist en masse?

This is the problem that is vexing home Colonial Offices and local Administrative Councils, and that one hears continually discussed by settlers on the streets and in the clubs of Mombasa, Nairobi, Entebbe, Dar-esSalaam, Tanga, etc.

And the problem is all the more intensely interesting from the fact that it is not only infinitely complex but, in many of its elements, without precise parallel.

Of course its nearest modern parallels exist in the conquest and colonization of North and South America. But while in North America the red native was easily displaced and his territory appropriated and occupied through the gradual process of extermination, resultant in small measure from warfare and in large measure from vices and diseases contracted from the invaders, and while the same end was attained in South America partly by ruthless, indiscriminate slaughter, and partly by the blood admixture come of broadcast inter-marriage between invading and native races, on the contrary the native black population of Central Africa (bar the original small Kingdom of Uganda proper, where generations of semi-civilized rule and habit have wrecked morals and reduced the birth rate) increases under contact with and restraint by civilization, and its women are not of types to leave it conceivable that white colonists will mate with them on any wholesale scale.

The black, nearer to the primary brute vigor of the beasts of his native jungle in every physical function than is the white man, the product of untold centuries of adaptation to resistance to the many perils to life that lurk along the equator, endures exposure to sun and other climatic trials and easily recovers from wounds no white man could survive, even eats decaying flesh or fish without being poisoned by ptomaines—so eats without injury or illness of any sort, except that the elephantiasis (a terrible enlargement of the body, usually of the feet or lower limbs), prevalent along the coast and about the lakes, is attributed to the consumption of putrid fish.

The blacks are there, there in uncounted millions, there in population probably more dense than that of the wild tribesmen Caius Julius found occupying Britannia, just before the dawn of the Christian era; and, in like manner, it is easily conceivable, Cæsar and the long string of consuls that followed him through the next four hundred years were, up to the last hour before their final expulsion, constantly debating whether Britannia was ever ultimately to become, actually, a Roman's country!

Is the history of Roman Britain to be repeated in an ultimate expulsion of the white invaders of Equatorial Africa? Doubtless not, literally, and yet that it may be measurably repeated I am much inclined to believe, repeated to the extent of prevention of its occupation by whites in predominating numbers.

While, through bad diet and ignorance of all rules of hygiene more susceptible to ordinary germ diseases than whites, the blacks more hardily withstand them. Inter- and inner- tribal warfare and human sacrifices to heathen gods now stopped —condition. which alone served to prevent a hopelessly dense overcrowding of population in the past — it is only a matter of—years, and not so many at that, until the blacks, fecund as their flowerpot-rich soil, fill all the land from sea to sea. This nothing can prevent except a war of extermination, which modern ethics forbid, or disease.

And in the matter of disease, what is to decimate them? Pulmonary diseases so far are a negligible quantity. Vice and the ills it brings will not do it, for drunkenness and licentiousness and the long train of diseases they engender, which alone served to wipe out the North American Indian, have for generations been widely prevalent among them. Syphilis they apparently make complete recovery from without classical treatment, so local physicians told me. Even the bubonic plague has no chance there now that a competent medical protectorate over them has been established—as witness the prompt eradication of the recent violent outbreak of that disease at Kisumu.

Indeed, of the endlessly long list of known human ills, only one stands as a serious threat to the equatorial black, viz., the sleeping sickness, Trypanosomiasis, for which so far medical science has been able to do little more than give it a name. No more is to-day known of its actual cause or of a cure for it than when, in July, 1891, it stole into Kampala, come from God alone knows where, and quickly showed itself to be the most relentless and stubborn human scourge medical science has ever had to encounter. Within the first twelvemonth it had claimed thirty thousand victims, all natives resident on the islands of Victoria Nyanza, chiefly of the Sessi group, or along the north and west shores of the great lake.

Through the instrumentality of the Royal Society, Colonel Sir David Bruce of the Indian Service, one of the ablest bacteriologists living, spent the year 1903 in a close study of the disease on the ground. But all he was able to learn was that it is communicated by the bite of the Glossina palpalis, a species of the tsetse fly, a small grayish-black chap the tips of whose wings cross in a 66 'swallow-tail" when folded.

Within the infected areas of Uganda, Unyoro, and Usoga, by the end of 1905 a full two-thirds of the population of three hundred thousand people were dead of the scourge, notwithstanding the enforced removal of well natives en masse to a distance of two or three miles back from lake shore and stream sides, beyond the known zone of tsetse occupation; the isolation as rapidly as possible of the sick upon islands of the lake; and the clearing away of trees, jungle, and long grass in the vicinity of Entebbe and Jinja.

Now it is sweeping south along Tanganyika toward Rhodesia, east into German and Portuguese territory, and has already left a wide swath of dead behind it in its march around the north end of Victoria Nyanza, through the Province of Usoga, and into the Kavirondo country, where, already far to the east of Kisumu, it is rapidly ascending the watersheds of the Kuja and Oyani Rivers toward the very heart of British East Africa.

Indeed, when on January 19 last the need of food compelled me to descend into the Oyani valley from the Kisii Highlands, where I had been after elephant, and I there encountered Deputy Commissioner Northcote and Dr. Baker, engaged, with a large party of Askaris (native soldiers), in building hospitals for the care of sleeping sickness sufferers, I was told by them that mine would be the last safari to be allowed to enter the Province of Kisumu, for fear the porters might contract the disease and scatter it north and east through the Protectorate.

Looking down upon the beautiful palm-lined valley of the Oyani, far as the eye could see the country was brown with fields of the ripening metama, gray with the grass-roofed villages, bright with the piebald herds of cattle and sheep of the thrifty Kavirondo, five thousand of whom were then sick of the disease- which means as bad as dead of it, and almost all of whom confront practically certain extermination in the next four years.

Over the entire field of its prevalence, doubtless close to a half-million people are dead of the sleeping sickness since its first observation in 1891.

While crossing the lake from Kisumu to Entebbe, I met Captain F. Percival Mackie, of the Indian medical service, one of Sir David Bruce's large staff of physicians and nurses, just in from India on a two years' detail for further close study of the disease. Sir David had preceded him a few weeks and already had established two hospital camps, one about midway between Kampala and Jinja, another to the east of Jinja, in Usoga.

And there now on the very firing line this devoted but numerically puny little band of soldiers of science stands coolly battling, virtually at death grips, with the monster, the monster that, remaining uncontrolled for yet a few years, is the one potentiality that can quickly and surely make Equatorial Africa "a white man's country"; for while, so far, it has claimed comparatively few white victims, not only do the blacks easily become infected, but all who get it die of it.

Indeed, cutting out, if it so chooses, the economics and the humanities of the local situation, could the civilized world realize what terrible sacrifice of human life might ensue if the sleeping sickness should contrive to steal across to European, American, or Asian shores—and that such disaster is not impossible is proved by the fact that often cases have not developed until months after any possibility of infection, and by the further fact that it is not yet definitely known that the mosquito or some other fly than the tsetse may not communicate the disease, scientific columns would be hastening to the front from all the Great Powers of the world, bent on a joint assault of the enemy before it is too late.

But that the monster will be conquered before it is too late, the vast resources and recent accomplishments in bacteriology, prophylaxis, and therapy leave us every reason to hope, if not to expect.

And then, the monster shackled, what of Equatorial Africa, socially and industrially? Logically, with the death rate by war stopped and by disease checked, the millions of blacks already occupying the central plateau and the lake and Nile basins must go on increasing until, in a few decades, they will number well-nigh all Equatorial Africa can comfortably hold and support; for it is to be remembered that there are enormous areas of the more arid plateaus of British and German East that, while intrinsically rich as the best of our Southern California, Arizona, or New Mexico lands, no native blacks could subsist on if confined to limited sections, and which none but the most scientific modern farming could render profitable.

And, given the survival and increase of the blacks, what, then, the future of the country? Of course, bar the arising of unthinkable conditions, Equatorial Africa must remain, for generations anyway, under white administration—at least until a universal consent is reached to withdraw and let the blacks work out their own problems, which is inconceivable, as meaning certain reversion to stark savagery.

And throughout such period, be it long or short, it is inevitable that many thousands of the adventurous or discontented of all white nationalities will go there as settlers.

What are their chances? Good, capital; none better anywhere, be they lazy or ambitious.

First, with reasonable observance of the laws of sanitation and hygiene, whites may preserve reasonably average good health there, with no greater peril of malaria than one runs to-day in many sections of this country and less danger of pulmonary diseases than our climate is ever threatening. This opinion, I well know, is antagonized by Winston Churchill, but as against him stands the fact that the officials, missionaries, and settlers one meets out there, men and women resident there anywhere from ten to twenty years, are obviously as sturdy, sound, and vigorous a lot on the average as one meets anywhere in the temperate zone. To be sure the little churchyards are not empty of gravestones, nor are they long so empty anywhere else in the world where men have enclosed them. Lieutenant-Governor Jackson, C. B., C. M. G., and C. W. Hobley, C. M. G., of British East; S. C. Tompkins, C. M. G., Chief Secretary of Uganda, James Martin, and Father Laane, all there resident varying periods from fifteen to thirty years, are types of soundness and of physical and mental activity any man of their years would be glad and proud of. Nor are the men here cited exceptions; such types are the rule—possibly, very likely in fact, because, precisely as Joaquin Miller once explained the high type of the average California Forty-niner by contending that "the cowards never started and the weak died on the road," so do few feeble of body or soul ever ship for Central African ports. Of course they (many of them) have "livers"; but, if you ask me, I believe the alleged typical "tropical liver" is less due to conditions climatic than to too frequent impalement by "a peg of whiskey."

Secondly, for that hardy, tireless, stout-hearted but always restless though usually indolent class or type of pioneers of the sort to whom we are indebted for the winning of all North America from savagery—the pathfinders across the treeless plains; the trail-blazers through forests, where danger, if not death, beset them at every step; the venturers in frail bark craft far out over unknown and hostile waters; the trappers and the traders; the men of the coon-skin cap and squirrel rifle; the women of brawn and freckles and fustian frocks; the folk of the log cabin and the little patch of maize and potatoes such Equatorial Africa is a paradise.

Gone are they all, do you say? Gone with the times and conditions that developed them? Never will they be gone so long as blood flows in Anglo-Saxon veins or in French or German for that matter,— and it's a lot we owe them both. Never will they be gone so long as bold spirits are able to find wild places where they fancy they find a larger independence and personal freedom than the teeming centres of civilization afford.

There their beasts may stay fat the year round on the wild feed; no forests must be felled to build and plant; there a man may plant, till, or harvest every day in the year if he likes, or, if he be lazy, so fecund is the soil that a few weeks' work in the fields will keep a family in plenty throughout the year; there, at certain favored altitudes, orchards may be seen standing amid fields of ripening wheat, oats, and corn, wherein apples, plums, apricots, etc., are thriving beside oranges, lemons, bananas, figs, pineapples, pomegranates, papayas, while hard by gardens grow in profusion any and every vegetable it has suited the owner's fancy to plant; there, in otherwise favored sections, the rubber tree, the fibre plant, sisal, cocoa, coffee, and a score of other plants or trees yielding fourfold the crop value of any products of the temperate zone, may be cultivated; there all about, in most parts, wild meat is to be had for the shooting, so one has bought the "small (settler's) license." Ease is there for the easygoing, riches for the industrious.

And, while the local administrations don't yet fully appreciate it, and persist in maintaining ordinances inimical to poor settlers, nevertheless it is precisely people of the type of the old North American pioneers, the folk who arrive scant of belongings, scantier still of cash, but rich in brawn and pluck, the sort that come with a wife and a string of tow-headed children, all workers at something down to the baby in arms, that can be relied on to push out north and south from the Uganda Railway into the wilds, the best possible advance guard for the peaceloving plodders who quickly follow them and for whom they promptly make way as soon as the country is permanently pacified.

The man or family with a few thousands should not go there, for such are usually unsuited to life in the wilds, too often untrained in labor or business. The country has too many such already, who almost invariably fall hopelessly before the temptation of acquiring ten times more land than they have the means to develop and a hundred times more than they know anything about the profitable handling of.

And even the worker who goes there will need to be a pioneer in a double sense, in his system as well as in his practice—for there to-day no white man turns his hand to any form of manual labor, once he has instructed the blacks he employs in their tasks. But such as may go there with the will and spirit of the men of the West and North, may live in ease and plenty at the cost of no more than a fifth of the hard work our own early pioneers had to expend in order to save their young from hunger and shelter them from cold.

To capitalists Equatorial Africa offers rich opportunities, but they can afford and always, properly, prefer to investigate for themselves. I may say, however, that, as the laws now stand, for operations on a large scale one must, to be safe, figure on indentured foreign labor, East Indian or off the Arabian coast, for any form of enforced native labor the laws rigidly forbid in British East and in Uganda.

Their shambas (farms) planted and tilled by their women for the few weeks necessary to furnish the family a season's food supply, few of the native black men know a harder job than idling about their grazing herds throughout the day, weapons in hand, guarding them from attack by lion or leopard. Richer as they are than any equally savage races of history, possessed of all they need, no incentive remains to voluntarily engage themselves as laborers except as they become seized with a greed for the gauds the Indian bazaars display, tempted, but not to a point to lead them to part with their cattle. Thus comparatively few are ever available for farm or other service, and fewer still stay long enough to become fairly adept at such work as they may have undertaken. And yet idle as they do, thieve as they may, no settler owns power effectively to correct or restrain them.

Indeed, it seemed to me the humanitarians of Exeter Hall have been sowing the wind as they never would dream of doing if they themselves were personally familiar with local native life and conditions, and themselves had to toss helpless, as settlers, on the tide of native arrogance their silly clamor for larger license for the blacks has raised, a tide that one day may easily break into a smother of open revolt that will take a good bit of quelling.

To-day no white man, except while on safari remote from any Government boma, may punish a rebellious or lazy black; instead, the culprit must be brought to the nearest boma for trial. Usually it is a sentence to imprisonment he gets in the Nairobi jail or the Mombasa prison, according to the degree of his offence, either about as welcome and wholly enjoyable to the black as is her two weeks' vacation on a Sullivan County farm to a Wall Street Fluffy-Ruffles typewriter. And this when no white man who knows the country will contend for a second that any Central African black can be held to his work except by occasional flogging with the kiboko (whip), or by the dread of it. Argument, kindness, liberality don't go the more of these you hand out, the worse your labor situation becomes. But pay them fairly, feed them well, and let them know they will get the kiboko if they shirk or steal, and no better labor (at the price) could be desired.

Cruel? Inhuman? Perhaps. But please remember there is nothing else for it or so I believe it will in the end be found except to deal with the blacks the` only way they respect, with an iron hand, or to abandon them to their orgies and sacrifices, such orgies and sacrifices as no story that could be told in print could give half an adequate idea of.

But all these labor difficulties I expect to see mending shortly, for the local administrations are alive to existing embarrassments, and settlers are loudly crying for relief the Colonial Office will have to grant send more troops. However, it may eventually come about, whether by some form of coercion or by innoculating him with new wants, only when and as the black is made to work can his moral uplift begin and advance to a point to make education of value to him.

In German East Africa the labor situation is infinitely better, natives respectful and leaping at their tasks till the day's "stunt" is finished—all because Germany suffers from no Exeter Hall type of misguided philanthropists. Nor are the natives in German territory inhumanely treated, either; for knowing an iron heel is ever ready for their necks whenever they do wrong, they seldom invite its application.

XV. RUBBERING IN UGANDA

WHILE now become in many manufactured forms a necessity, rubber is, essentially, a luxury, first, because of the relatively limited supply of the raw material heretofore available, the inaccessibility of its habitat, and the wastefully extravagant, and therefore costly, methods of gathering it; secondly, because it supplies mankind with forms of protection, ease, and comfort never enjoyed before it came into commercial use and for which no substitute has ever been discovered, or, if we may believe the ablest scientists at home and abroad, ever will be discovered.

And yet probably not one out of hundreds of thousands of those who use the 80,000,000 pairs of rubber shoes and boots our factories annually produce, thereby gaining immunity from the many perils of wet feet, or who roll about the world on rubber tires at such ease as nothing but rubber can give to man awheel, has the remotest idea how wild rubber is won and converted into commercial form.

It was my privilege during the lovely equatorial month of November to spend three weeks in the Mabira forest of the Changwe District of the Uganda Protectorate. This forest comprises one hundred and fifty square miles and lies about twenty-five miles north of the equator, extending north from Victoria Nyanza along the west bank of the Nile from that river's source at Ripon Falls, where it issues a booming torrent from the lake, to within two miles of the lower end of its heaviest rapids at Owen Falls.

Returning toward my headquarters in the Ukamba Province of British East Africa from the Uganda Marathon Race and the First Uganda Exhibition, of agricultural and other products, craftsmen's work, etc., held at Kampala, it was my good luck to come to know and gain the friendship of James Martin, for many years and up to a few months ago His Majesty's Collector of the Entebbe District, a man whose name, in nearly every book written of the discovery and conquest of the vast Central African region extending south from Khartoum to Lake Tanganyika and east from the Congo to the Atlantic, figures conspicuously in connection with one gallant deed or another, one tiresome, stubborn, indomitable trek or another to the relief of some imperilled station or the taking of some strategical point in advance of the Germans or French.

Early in the '80's, while General Matthews was Prime Minister to Bergash Bin Said, Sultan of Zanzibar, James Martin served as his aide-de-camp and commanded the Sultan's forces; in 1883 it was he who guided Joseph Thompson from Mombasa to the head of the Nile at Ripon Falls, and thus was one of the first five white men (Speke and Grant and Stanley having preceded them) ever to set eyes on the bold headlands, emerald waters, and mirage uplifted islands of Victoria Nyanza; he who, in '84, served under Sir Harry Johnson in the negotiation of the first treaties with the chiefs about Mount Kilima N'jaro; he who, in '87-8, led a column composed of seven hundred armed Swahilis and only two other white men from Mombasa to and across the Nile to Stanley's relief at the time of his rescue of Emin Pasha, missing Stanley but finding four thousand of the armed ruffians that made up the wreck of Emin's army subsisting themselves by raiding and rapine, captured and brought them to the coast, and saw them safely shipped back to their old master the Khedive; he who, in 1900, signed the first treaty with King Mwanga that gave the Imperial British Company a hold on Uganda, after a desperate caravan journey afoot to beat the Germans, and who, later the same year, escorted Captain Lugard to Mengo and assisted in the conclusion of a final treaty establishing a British Protectorate. He is a bright brown eyed, grizzled and wrinkled but physically and mentally keen and alert old Africander, with a voice resonant as a Baganda war drum, whom all wrong-doing natives have learned to dread and all right-doing have learned to love, and who has himself made more thrilling history than most men ever contrive to read.

James Martin was granted his official pension some years before his normal term of service was expired and is now gathering rubber in the Mabira forest.

Shipmates together aboard the tight little Sybil, from Entebbe, via Jinja, to Kisumu, he hazarded and I was not slow to accept an invitation to come to stay with him at his headquarters in the forest.

Arrived at Jinja just after luncheon of a fine November day, the equatorial sun blazing unblinking out of a vault of cloudless blue but the air crisp and bracing with the atmospheric high wine of a 4,000-foot altitude, we first went ashore for a view of Ripon Falls, the long sought source of the main eastern branch of the great White Nile, and a view of the town.

Out of the generously broad and deep bosom of this vast inland sea whose smiling waters brought us to Jinja, for centuries untold has poured the vitalizing flood that made the valley of the lower Nile the richest known granary of the ancient world, a prize fought for century in and century out, straight on down to this generation, from times long past even before the first stone was laid for the first temple ever reared to Isis.

Napoleon Gulf, from the north end of which the Nile issues, is so shut in by islands it shows no entrance from the town and looks to be a lake; and, as if scrupulously greedy of hiding the source of its great wealth, the Nile has craftily hidden its head in a deep, sharp bend of the gulf where one might easily cruise within a mile of it and, but for its thunderous voice, never suspect its presence.

Scarce more than twenty feet in height of actual fall, Ripon stretches to the majestic breadth of close upon three hundred yards, the water pouring down in smooth, black, oily folds into a hell of seething torment below, save where, at intervals, shrub-crested islands rise out of the great volcanic dyke which, away back toward the beginnings of time, imprisoned the waters of the lake, and through which they had slowly to gnaw their way to give birth to the Nile.

Precisely here will be the head of the railway which, ultimately, will connect with the line slowly creeping south from Cairo past Khartoum. Thus by means of steamer connection with the north terminus of the line pushing from the south and now at Broken Hills in far Northern-Rhodesia, will the "Cape to Cairo" dream of Cecil Rhodes be realized.

And here, midway of the route and therefore of the continent, Nature has conveniently placed power adequate, I should think, to turn all the wheels of several Pittsburgs, and here will be one of the greatest African cities of the twenty-first if not of the twentieth century.

A lovelier climate one may not ask and hope to find. Hot it is in the sun from ten to three, but less oppressive than eighty-eight degrees in the shade in New York, while one may never comfortably sit outdoors at night without an overcoat, or sleep under less than one or two blankets.

To be sure malarial fevers are here, but so were they once, in far more virulent form, in Panama. The tsetse fly still lurks in the noisome shade of jungle and elephant grass along the lake, loaded with the deadly germs of sleeping sickness, but now nearly all sick natives have been removed to islands on the lake and the healthy have been moved back of the known danger zone, while near lake towns and stations the ground has been cleared of all trees and undergrowth and the flies thereby measurably, perhaps, expelled from their near neighborhood.

Aloft of the falls and the rapids below the air swarms with fisher fowl, keen after the finny giants that are ever leaping in the rapids or boldly mounting at the steep falling waters of the falls themselves, while hundreds of crocodiles lie, apparently basking in the sun but alert for victims, on islands and along the shores of the river.

To-day Jinja contains nothing besides the dwellings and offices of Sub-Commissioner A. G. Boyle, C. M. G., and staff of two or three assistants, the post and telegraph office, the police barracks, and a small native village; but, if I am not badly mistaken, before this article can possibly get to press the building of a railway at least forty-five miles north from Jinja to Lake Kioga, a very rich and densely populated district, will be authorized from London and work actually begun, and not many months after another strategic railway line will be pushing west from Kioga to Lake Albert Nyanza and its navigable water route toward Khartoum.

After dinner aboard the Sybil, a forty-foot Baganda war canoe manned by twenty natives at racing pace ferried us the mile across the bay to Bogongo, the landing for Mabira, where we spent the night, lulled to sleep by Ripon's mighty voice, toned down to soft cadence by intervening distance, to sleep so soundly that the quickmounting equatorial sun was half up behind Buvuma Island before we awoke and turned out, to see the mists rising from Ripon's torment a tall cloud of yellowest gold, sharply outlined against its dark olive green Nileside background.

Breakfast over, our beds and luggage were quickly transferred to the heads of sturdy Baganda porters, sixty pounds to the head, and we started in two rickshaws on the fourteen-mile journey to Mabira.

For the first half of the distance the path was heavy, undried from the showers of the previous night, for the season was that of the "little rains," lasting through November and December, during which the days are bright and cloudless but every night there is a downpour. So on we slowly plodded through black mud, shut in between solid walls of fifteen-foot elephant grass on either hand, out of which we sometimes saw rising the tops of the mimosa and of candelabrum cactus.

Throughout the four-hour journey the path was lined with an almost solid procession of natives, travelling single file to the lake, the chiefs striding haughtily along in long, black, short-caped, Spanish-like cloaks, each followed by a band of musicians beating deep-booming drums, twanging at their not unmusical progenitor of the banjo, blowing tirelessly into shrill-shrieking ivory flutes, while behind the band trailed their half-naked chair bearers and porters loaded with their wares.

Stop the drumbeat on a march and instantly a quickmoving column of native porters becomes a dawdling mob; stop their songs in the field or at the rickshaw and at once a group of cheery, hard workers is transformed into slouching, dull-faced idlers.

To right and left along the way we passed small banana plantations and groups of low grass huts half hid among them, the monotony of their dull gray walls only relieved by bright red hanging clusters of drying chillies and by the low, black, oval doorways that give the only access to their smoke-begrimed interiors.

About these hut villages women were idling, or digging in their adjacent shambas. Here in Uganda, more modest than their Kavirondo sisters about Kisumu, who never are clothed more heavily than was Mother Eve herself, all women wear from morn till night most fetching evening dress costume, the laso, wound tightly about the body from the hips to just above the outer swell of the breasts and falling in by no means ungraceful folds to the feet, loose robes of any-many-brilliant colors, usually to the exposure of handsomely turned arms and shoulders no paler wearer of evening dress would be anything but proud of.

But few children are seen, for the Baganda are probably the most conspicuous living exponents of race suicide. Always poor breeders, from reasons of extreme immorality, and in the past recruiting their race by raids and capture of the sturdier women of Usoga, now that raiding has stopped and sleeping sickness has come among the Baganda, their numbers are dwindling rapidly.

At length leaving the elephant grass, we took a plunge into and through a corner of Mabira forest, by a good broad road made as an outlet to Jinja for rubber and timber, a forest beautiful as could be conjured by the most fertile fancy as the last ideal of a tropical paradise. Giant Fecus towered eighty to one hundred feet in height, and slender, graceful Funtumnia Elastica, the prime rubber tree here indigenous, leaped fifty feet without limb or sprout, straight of trunk as a spear shaft, and crested with a narrow and shallow spread of boughs, the long, sharp-pointed tips of whose leaves, silvered by sunlight filtering through the taller forest canopy, look like the gleaming spear points of a waiting Baganda war host. Portly, straight-growing mahogany and other forest tree growth of infinite variety are there, many wound from ground to top with mighty parasitic vines of a sort that, serpent-like in habit as in appearance, often finish by crushing and smothering the very life out of the tree itself, after first feeding and fattening at its expense, until naught remains of its once magnificent proportions and virile life but a shrivelling, rotting core within the thick vine folds that have wrought its ruin. Everywhere are thick festoons of delicate flowering creepers that, high aloft, look fine and fragile as lacework, broad-leaved plantain-like fern growths nestling tight to giant boles high aloft, and, lastly, those very spirits of all plant life, the air-feeding orchids, beautiful, intangible almost as a spirit, drooping idly from lofty boughs. It is a forest noisy with the merry chatter of monkeys and brilliant with the flitting of parrots, swarming with timid, tiny duyker antelope a scant eighteen inches long, a forest at first glance all smiles and beauty and charm for every sense, and yet a forest whose dusky recesses are as sinister of oblivion as the very grave itself.

Peril, deadly peril to life, attends your every step. Powerful-jawed and sharp-toothed python often eighteen feet long, lie along low-lying limbs, watching for quarry. Green and black mambas fast as a good pony are ever slipping about through the undergrowth. Indolent cobra de capello and puff adders are always to be closely watched for, as too lazy even to try to get out of your way, their bite certain death in a few minutes (if instant remedy is not at hand) like that of the mamba, and their colors blending so perfectly with prevailing forest hues that rarely do any but natives see them until right upon them. Gigantic hippos at night roam far back from the still pools of the larger streams they pass the day in. At any turn of a path through either forest or tall elephant grass a mob of buffalo may sweep down upon and over you, though usually when in mobs and unattacked they pass you by, but come suddenly on a lone bull, or wound one, and usually you confront a finish fight, with a mighty beast quick of foot as a panther, armed with sharp horns often of more than four-foot spread. Hideous crocodiles, hated alike of man and beast and sparing none, the giant Nilotic sort close to twenty feet long, lie near swamp or stream margins so log-like that even natives have stepped upon them before seeing them, only to be laid helpless before the cruel jaws by a sweep of the mighty tail. Lastly, all about swarm crowds of mosquitoes and flies, often charged with malarial infection that, apparently, all must ultimately fall prey to who escape the reptiles and the beasts.

A very hell amidst heaven is a Nileside forest, and yet, with all its hazards, a place where white men may go and come unscathed for years, as have indeed such men as Lieut.-Gov. Jackson, C. B., C. M. G. (now of B. E. A.), ex-H. M. Collector James Martin, Chief Secretary S. C. Tomkins, C M. G., Sub-Commissioner A. G. Boyle, C. M. G., and others of their fellow empire builders in Equatorial Africa, if only they know their way about.

Emerging from the forest toward noon, before us on three close-clustering hills rising three or four hundred feet out of the valley, stood the Mabira headquarters buildings, on one side the executive offices, on another Mr. Martin's bungalow, on another the staff quarters, while down to the left, in a bend of forest near the stream, nestled the factory buildings, where the crude latex (milk) is washed, coagulated, and boxed in hundredpound packages for shipment to market.

The most modern methods are here employed, tapping being done with locally devised tools considered an improvement on those used by the Para rubber planters of Ceylon, and washing and coagulation by scientific methods, which, through perfect cleaning, etc., adds largely to the market value of the product.

A rubber tree is nine years in maturing in the forest, but may be tapped for from one-quarter to one-half pound by the seventh year; after eight years, by full tapping top to bottom the trees should yield three-quarters to one pound to the tree.

The hundred and fifty square miles of this forest are subdivided into blocks of four square miles, with broad paths along the base lines between blocks, and many narrow tapping paths penetrating each block. Trees are carefully searched out and counted in each block as fast as surveyed, until now five hundred thousand full-bearing trees have been tallied, with much land still unsearched, and hundreds of thousands of Nature-sown seedlings coming on.

Tapping is done in the rainy season, which here means ten tapping months in the year. But tapping can only be done when trees are dry. However, since nearly all the rain falls at night, tree trunks are usually dry enough for tapping by 9 A. M. The tapper finishes his tapping shortly after midday, bringing his day's take of latex (of anywhere from one to five pounds) to his local station in the evening, whence it is carried early the next morning to the factory at headquarters.

So far the maximum number of tappers used is about five hundred, the remainder of the total of two thousand blacks here employed being engaged on road and path making, factory labor, clearing land, and planting Para rubber or other crops, and on the completion of headquarters and station buildings.

Since April, 1908, about twenty-five tons have been shipped, thus assuring a total yield this year of not less than seventy tons, worth in London an average of at least four shillings per pound ($1) or, gross, $80,000, which as nearly as I can estimate is produced at a total outlay, including new machinery, buildings and freight duties, and administrative expenses, of $60,000, thus leaving $20,000 as profit on a total cash investment to date not much in excess of $100,000.

Next year, the third, with installation of new machinery, factory and station construction, road making, etc., all finished, the output should be an increase of fifty per cent to one hundred per cent on that of this year and expense should lessen at least twenty-five per cent; and I can see no reason why after the fourth or fifth year the forest should not be shipping between one hundred and fifty and two hundred tons per year.

Moreover, rubber making expense is sure to continue to decrease through revenue derived from fuel and timber sales. The forest is full of superb woods, especially the muvule, which is much like the best walnut timber, and Nysambia, which closely resembles good beech in appearance and quality. While remote from large markets for profitable shipment in wholesale quantities, local demand for timber and fuel can probably be relied on for profit sufficient to cover a part of the cost of maintenance of roads and paths through the forest and to the lake.

Monday morning there arrived at the factory five hundred pounds of latex as the product of Saturday's tree tapping, a thin, milk-white fluid which at the factory is poured into big tanks; Tuesday, seven hundred pounds, and Wednesday, nine hundred and twenty pounds came.

Given average good quality in the latex extracted, and here it produces fifty per cent in net rubber of its gross weight, the profit in rubber making lies in its rapid and economical washing, by which it is cleaned of all foreign substances, contained resins, etc.; its coagulation and pressing into thin sheets or ribbons which at a glance show buyers their absolute purity in net rubber; its drying, smoking, and packing for shipment.

Oddly here, in these equatorial African jungles, whence heretofore rubber has never been gathered and made except by the most crude, wasteful, and uncleanly native methods, and while over ninety per cent of the vast Brazilian, Central and South American product is even to this day, after a generation of experience, still taken and prepared for market by unsuperintended Indians at a waste in one way and another of more than a third of its value, here in Central Africa the last resources of science are employed to produce chemically pure rubber at minimum cost.

Generally in Africa and in Central and South America coagulation of the latex is obtained only by rubbing lime juice or other acid along the incisions in the tree trunks, or by catching the latex in cups and fetching it to camp, dipping broad, thin, paddle-shaped blades of wood in the latex and holding it in the smoke of burning palm nuts until coagulation is finished, and repeating this process until a thick "ham" is so accumulated. In both processes no contained resin is eliminated, much bark, dirt, and even stones are often incorporated in the mass, and a high moisture content remains, leaving the manufacturer always buying more or less of a pig in a poke and paying freight on a lot of waste material.

But a new era opened in rubber production a decade ago with the demonstration in Ceylon that rubber forests may be successfully and profitably grown from artificially planted seed. And as from year to year more capital had to be poured into these plantations to insure their proper care and the sound maturity of the trees, chemistry began to be ransacked for improved methods of coagulation and mechanical art for better tools and machinery for tapping the trees and cleaning and curing the rubber, with the result that the cultivated Para rubber of Ceylon fetches in the London market from eight to twenty-two cents a pound more than the best fine hard Para taken from wild trees.

And now here in the heart of the Uganda Protectorate, within a few miles of the scene of Stanley's heaviest fighting thirty years ago, and in a region where the pacification of the country has only been accomplished by almost continuous punitive operations by the stout-hearted little staff of British civil and military officials who, with a handful of Soudanese and Sikhs, have taken and held the country for the Crown, operations that often involved heavy fighting, and have continued down to a few months ago, here in the equatorial wilderness the best Ceylon methods have been materially improved, both in tapping and coagulation; better tools have been devised for stripping the outer bark off a desired incision line, a hooked blade that cuts an even depth and width, and a set of spur-like roller blades for quickly running along incision lines and tapping the latex cells, while prolonged experiment here by Chemist John Hughes has at last yielded a dawa (chemical formula) which coagulates the latex almost instantaneously at a cost of one-tenth of a cent per pound.

When work begins in the morning a bucket of boiling water, the hotter the better, containing a scant ounce of the dawa, is poured into a Nysambia trough made on the place, three feet long, about eight inches wide, and eight inches deep, into which is immediately poured five pints of latex. Instantly the yellow resins and foreign substances are eliminated and taken up in suspension by the hot water, and within one and one-half minutes a thick mass of clean rubber is formed which is carried to and passed three times through steam-driven rolls that press out the moisture and give it form, from which it comes out a beautiful milk-white strip of what the market calls "crope" rubber, ten feet long and six inches wide, deeply stamped with diamond-shaped figures, the centre of each diamond thin, the outlines thick, that at a little distance make the ribbons look like strips of lace,- about two and one-third pounds, the product of five pints of latex.

These strips are hung in a steam-heated drying room until all moisture is expelled, then matured or "cured" in the smoke room, in the creosote-laden fumes of a wood fire, which renders it proof against all forms of attack by bacteria and consequent decomposition.

From the smoke room the strips issue of the palest amber tint and are folded and packed, under high pressure, in hundred-pound boxes for shipment.

Thus Monday's latex is by the next succeeding Monday converted into the highest type of commercial rubber and on its road to market, where, as now cleaned and prepared, the product of these wild Funtumnia Elastica trees is commanding as high a price as the best cultivated Para.

And notwithstanding prevailing high export duties and unreasonably excessive freight rates between Mabira and Mombasa, I can see no reason why within another year this product should not be laid down in London at a cost well inside of forty cents per pound.

The first week of my visit I spent in and about the factory and offices. The third day, the big native chief of Kioga District arrived, attired in a well-fitting Norfolk jacket, and boasting a silver watch chain, a nickeled policeman's whistle, and sandals for decorations, followed by his ministers, court band, and a hundred nondescript followers. Returning from the Exhibition at Kampala, he stopped to pay a visit to his old friend Martin, who employs some hundreds of his subjects, and to see the wonders of the new rubber factory.

After the inspection Mr. Hughes handed him a bottle of ammonia to smell, as a sample of the dawa used in coagulation. At the first whiff he nearly threw a back somersault and then, as salve for his wounded dignity, proceeded to compel every last one of his followers, down to the meanest porters, to take a stiff whiff of the bottle, holding the noses of several tight to its mouth until they were near strangling.

Of evenings, dining in a bungalow heavy with the sweet scent of the scores of rose bushes and violet beds that hedge it round about, what with my host's fascinating stories of stirring incidents of the early days of Uganda empire building, delicious curries so hot they would make Hades feel like a skating rink, weird Arab dishes, "muscatis" and "pillous," that would conjure new joys for the most blasé gourmet, lettuce and water cress tender as true charity, palate-tickling combinations of tomatoes and anchovy paste, fresh pines juicy and sweet (almost) as the lips you best love, and Chianti that makes you want to kick somebody's hat off, Mabira has taken permanent lodgement among the dearest treasures of my memory.

Indeed, if, after death, my spirit contrives to have quite its own way, more than likely any interested will find it wandering in some dusky nook or bright glade of the Mabira forest, near to Kiko's smiling face and not far from the red bungalow on the hill.

The last week of my visit to Mabira was spent in a tour of the forest with my host to the outlying stations, from Mbango, the headquarters, to Kiwala, to Wantarunta, to Lochfyne, etc., stations usually eight to twelve miles apart, each in charge of a canny Scotch forester, with a Goanese clerk and timekeeper and Goanese gang bosses.

The journey was very comfortably made, the host in a rickshaw and I on a tall, gray, country-bred pony, through miles of beautiful forest cool of midday and chill of evening, through patches of open country and elephant grass in the burning sun, across swamps ringed round with tall, feathery date palms and wild figs, along the wide belt of papyrus reeds that for miles fill the entire channel and valley of the Seziwa River, the Nile's first important tributary, from the west below Ripon.

And whether along the forty miles of twelve-foot main road or the two hundred miles of base line and still narrower tapping paths, the latter sometimes fifty yards apart and sometimes a thousand, according to the plenty or scarcity of tapable trees, ever about us rose the tall silvergray shafts of the Funtumnia, sometimes standing singly, sometimes in close clusters of a dozen or twenty, each bearing the brown scars of the tapper's knife.

One could follow the running, singing, laughing band of Baganda tappers into the dusky forest glades to their work if his wind held out and he could keep his neck from entanglement in the thick network of vines that canopy the tapping paths, and the dread of snakes thicker here than even in the worst dreams of the most bibulous—out of his mind, but to photograph them at their work the shades forbid.

The station buildings are usually set on well-cleared hillcrests, the superintendents' houses neat bungalows, roofed with tin, whose walls, lintels, and door and window frames are made of the bamboo-like stems of the elephant grass, bound together with strands of fibrous bark, quickly and cheaply made, but snug and cool.

Of evenings, the near-by native hut villages are ringing with the shouts and laughter and all sorts of merrymaking horse play, including wrestling matches not widely differing from or inferior to the Græco-Roman style.

Not content with Mabira's native wealth hundreds of acres about Mbango and the outlying stations are cleared and planted with Para and Funtumnia, with sisal, cocoa, coffee, croton-oil plant, indigo, citronella, cassava, bananas, sweet potatoes, pines, papayas, crops that, in the thick black loam that makes all Uganda like to the most luxuriant garden, yield in profits per acre two to four times that realized on temperate-zone farming.

Nor is this work in any measure groping or experiment, for it is under the direction of Ernest Brown, formerly an assistant in the botanical gardens of Entebbe, where for years careful study and demonstration have been going on to prove what commercially valuable tree and plant life thrives best here. There it has been proved that, while the Castilloa Elastica of Central America apparently matures well it yields no latex; that Para trees 4 years old may measure at 3 feet from the ground up to 18 inches, and 16 at 6 feet; 7-year-old trees up to 27 inches at 3 feet and 231 inches at 6 feet, and at the latter age may be relied on for pound to the tree, while after 9 years they are good for 1 pound; that sisal produces 3 per cent of net fibre against the prime yield of 3 per cent in German East African coast plantations, where sisal planters are netting profits up to 80 per cent.

These are dry statistics, perhaps, at first glance, but vital to rubber and fibre manufacturers and users of our own country, vital to our ever swelling surplus capital seeking safe and profitable employment abroad, absorbing to the thousands of the more adventurous of our younger generation, sons of the men who tackled and tamed the trans-Missouri region and whose blood cries out for chance of like exploits and opportunities.

For myself as an old pioneer of wild places, and recalling how twenty-five years ago we used to hustle and compete for arid tracts of grazing land at fifty cents to two dollars an acre, in northwest Texas and New Mexico, lands valueless for anything but grazing and that would carry no more than one head of cattle to fifteen acres, how the farms of the eastern and central States had to be hewn out of solid walls of forest and in many places the soil delved for among rocks, in a climate where a year's work had to be crowded into half a year to keep man and beast from perishing during the other half, it is tremendously impressive to see in British East Africa lands that will easily carry a head of cattle to each acre and keep them fat, or, here in Uganda, millions of acres under no heavier growth than elephant grass whose every square foot is rich and moist as the soil in a nursery pot. This land, besides its high-priced tropical products, grows in big yield (at one point or another, according to altitude and rainfall) most of the grains, vegetables, and fruits of the temperate zone. These lands are available to all comers at two rupees (sixty-six cents) the acre, often at less, while native labor is so abundant at four to six rupees a month that no white man here ever turns a finger to manual task, labor rightly handled that gives the employer quite as much as the average day labor at home, while good East Indian carpenters, iron workers, wheelwrights, masons, etc., are available at fifty to sixty-five rupees, or sixteen to twenty-one dollars, per month!

To be sure it is not all beer and skittles here. Freight rates are shockingly exorbitant, but so were they once on the Southern Pacific and other Western roads; land and other laws are crude and need a lot of mending; the Colonial Office is greedy and none too considerate of the settler. But against all this the local administrations, here and in British East, are doing all for the development of the country that could be expected while the Colonial Office persists in entangling all local officialdom in a bewildering maze of East Indian bureaucratic red tape, and settlers are sending up persistent cries for saner laws, simpler official forms, cheaper freights, and more rational taxation not much longer to be denied even by the mustiest and thriftiest of the Crown's colonial bureaucrats.

My visit ended, I reached Bogongo a day ahead of the next mail steamer.

Rising at dawn and taking a shotgun for birds and a heavy .38 pistol on the chance of a crack at a crocodile, I started in my host's great sixty-foot canoe for a cruise along the reeds of the lake shore and to get a view of Ripon Falls from the west.

Just as I was stepping into the canoe, near at hand uprose a true Nile ibis and a lovely, lavender-hued, crested crane. Dropping them with a right and left, I sent them to the house for approval, and three hours later had the ibis, beautifully roasted, for breakfast, dark, tender meat, in flavor much like prairie chicken, while the crane was condemned for everything but personal beauty.

As we glided gently along through alternating patches of lotus pads, reeds, and still shallows, never have I seen predatory life active in such varied forms and on such colossal scale.

Beneath me in the shallows big fish were darting savagely after the little ones. Above, a sort of black and white kingfisher poised stationary, with chin bent tight to chest, sharp beak downpointed, fierce little eyes hungrily searching the depths forty or fifty feet below him, wings beating so rapidly to maintain his poise you could scarce see them, and then down straight at his quarry like a lump of lead he would drop, disappearing entirely under water for a second or two, to rise full or empty clawed, according to hunter's luck.

Along the lake shore the air positively swarmed with insect life, chiefly flies individually so small you can scarce see them. Often in mid-lake for miles gray to black columns may be seen rising several hundred feet from the water that look like the smoke of freshly stoked steamer fires, but which are really swarms of tiny flies, which, once your vessel runs into them, shut out all view like the densest fog, and, if at night, extinguish all lights.

All about me on the lotus pads dainty little lemonhued birds were hopping about industriously picking for their insect breakfast, while aloft, at times, the air was fairly black with swallows darting hither and yon like the aërial corsairs they are, to whom all flies are prey. V-shaped flights of black divers big as wild geese were ever passing, or groups of them standing on the little rock pinnacles that rise a few feet above the water near to the falls, wings extended "spread eagle" fashion and lazily flapping, apparently a sort of "warming up" for a deep plunge after passing fish.

Distant, narrow, black lines on the water that disappeared as I advanced were the heads of crocodiles, too wary to permit of near approach by boat.

Returning soaking wet from a half-mile walk through bush and long grass, from the old Stanley crossing to Ripon, to get a snapshot of the west end of the falls, out in the lake nearly a mile from shore we sighted a big hippo bull, floating, full length exposed, near two small jutting rocks covered with divers.

I tried to slip in for a close camera shot, but when within a hundred yards he dropped all but his head below water, and fearing to lose him altogether, I so snapped him.

Meantime, the canoe having drifted to within some eighty yards, the fancy struck me to have a try at him with my pistol, the upper third of his head being in full view. The first shot was a trifle too high, but at the second I thought I had him, we plainly heard the "smash" of the ball upon or into the great bony head, my boys yelled "Piga! Piga!" (Hit! Hit!), and with a snort he rose full body out of water and plunged down, leaving a narrow red ribbon of blood twining among the bubbles.

Then for about an hour he rose at minute to half minute intervals for air, but only for an instant's exposure of the tips of the nostrils, which, try hard as I could, gave me no chance of landing another shot, sometimes driving to right and left in his dives, again in circles, too much dazed to follow usual wounded hippo tactics of a rush for shore and the reeds.

My only chance of hitting him again lay in a square charge of the boat, which often the hippo makes, with full head exposure as he rushes open-mouthed and at an eight-knot pace for a crunch of your boat gunwale. If on such a rush one waits until he is within a few feet of the boat, a deadly shot is not difficult. But no such charge did he make. Once he rose within twenty feet of us, but apparently by accident, for it was only for a second's exposure of great nostrils that looked like the business end of a young double-barrelled cannon. Nor were the next few seconds, until, having passed squarely beneath us, he rose two hundred feet on the other side of us, overcharged with comfort, for one of the worst things a hippo can hand you on Nyanza is to rise beneath the canoe, usually smashing it and upsetting you into water swarming with crocodiles as the air is with fowl.

After an hour of these frequent rises and dives he disappeared, dead I am forced to believe, though, notwithstanding I had the water watched till night, he did not rise. Of course since the affair finished a scant halfmile above the falls, an undercurrent may have swept him down, or, maybe, hippo have the "funnybone" in the head and it was that I hit, for rarely will a head shot from the heaviest rifle kill a hippo unless driven straight into the brain through nostril or behind the eye, and to have so scored with a pistol at the distance is rather too much to flatter oneself.

However, all this happened only yesterday, the yesterday of this writing, and perhaps a wire may bring me in the next few days news of a trophy retrieved worth while, for Provincial Commissioner A. G. Boyle, C. M. G., of Jinja, kindly promised to have his Askaris watch and search waters and shores.

XVI. THE HAZARDS OF THE GAME

LIKE most other things, sport is essentially relative. Doubtless all true sportsmen will agree that the greater the hazard of limb and life one incurs in any sport, the greater, the more fascinating, the sport becomes.

Who that has ever battled with an outlaw bronco or held a head-strong, half-broken hunter to his work across stiff country, could drive a trotting race and find it better than tame? Who that has run the Gatineau's boiling rapids and thundering chutes in a canoe could get much of a thrill paddling about Lake Placid, wondering if he is ever going to get a "bite"? What scarred centre rush, hero of a score of terrible tussles that sap the last ounce of nerve and muscle in a man, could find a satisfactory quickening of the pulse in a game of ninepins? Who that has known the fierce joy of pulling his very heart out on his varsity crew could long abide a house-boat? Who that has held the wheel of a ninety-horse-power racing car through the thrills and perils of a long-distance race, every sense alert and strained to the breaking point from start to finish, could get his own consent to ride a gymkhana donkey race?

And, judged by such standard, compared to the best big game shooting North or South America ever afforded, that of Africa towers aloft in all the scornful majesty characteristic of a "tablestake" poker player watching a game of "craps." Not only will the African rhino, elephant, buffalo, and lion carry comfortably quite as much lead as even the grizzly bear, and the two former much more, but they are far quicker to charge and faster of pace. The grizzly you can outfoot, if you can't kill him, by running transversely to the slope of a steep hill. But even on a good Basuto or Somali pony you are not safe against the charge of a lion with less than forty yards' start,— and not in one out of a hundred lion encounters does the sportsman have a horse beneath him or at hand.

The habitat of the lion is wherever his subjects, the game, are thickest, on the low bush veldt near the coast, on the high veldt of the interior. He is more than the King of Beasts, for he is far and away the first true gentleman of his court. As a rule he seeks no trouble with man, and usually he will do all that could possibly comport with his kingly dignity to avoid it. Often he will leave his feast on a fresh kill at man's approach. Seldom if ever do lions become man-eaters, deliberate, predatory raiders of villages or camps for human food, until so old they have found difficulty in taking even zebra, their easiest prey, and through stress of hunger or by some unhappy chance have learned that man is easier and perhaps (who but lion know?) tenderer still. But once he gets the knowledge and the taste, woe to belated night travellers through his bailiwick, woe to villagers or night campers unprotected by a thorn zareba (fence) he cannot leap, for so softly and silently does he steal upon his victim, so crushing deadly is his grip upon the neck, so mighty his strength in tossing his kill across his shoulders and slipping easily away with it, that very often naught of his raid is known until those sleeping near awake to find an empty bed, and blood along a spoor which plainly shows he has bounded away with their comrade in mighty leaps, free and light as those of a cat crunching a mouse.

So not long ago on the Guaso Nyiro died young McClellan. After a good day's sport he retired, alone, to his bed, surrounded by the tents of his escort and the sleeping forms of his porters. Twenty feet in front of the tent blazed a great camp fire. Back and forth through the centre of the camp paced an Askari sentry, rifle on shoulder. Along came a hungry man-eater. While unseen until too late, the facts proved that he must have thoroughly prospected the camp, for along its outskirts lay easy picking, the sleeping natives. But, perhaps surfeited with black meat, or inspired by the pride of his royal blood to disdain it while rarer spoil lay near, straight to the Bwana's tent he penetrated and into it entered, all so cunningly that his presence was unsuspected until bounding off with McClellan's limp body across his shoulder, and partly blinded by the firelight, he cannoned into and bowled over the Askari; and when the next day the headman of McClellan's party brought to the scene Deputy Commissioner Collyer from his near-by station of Rumuruti, the body was found near camp, unmarked save for the mangled and broken neck. Doubtless the Askaris' random shots had frightened the lion away, and cries and drum beatings kept up all night by the natives had served to prevent his return.

Nor was it more than a few weeks later, when Deputy Commissioner Collyer was on safari in the same neighborhood, that a lion entered his camp, slipped his paw beneath a tent and caught a Kikuyu by the ear, tearing away the lobe and a part of his cheek. The yells of the victim stirred the camp to shooting and shrieking that made Leo retire. But he scored all the same, a few days later the Kikuyu died of shock.

While ranked along with his third cousin, the leopard, as vermin in even the closest protected sections of Africa, as a marauding outlaw all comers are free to shoot without a license, nevertheless, in his prime he is a foeman well worthy of the best man the love of sport brings against him. Come face to face with him at three to ten paces at the turning of a bush, pass in the tall grass within a few feet of a hidden lioness and her cherished tawny pups, pursue or wound him when he is temperately retiring, usually at slow and dignified pace, from the proffered gage of your presence, and it is far worse than an even chance that you confront a case of kill or be killed; for, once he charges, usually it is a battle to the death, with odds against you even though he receives a mortal wound before,— as in his customary tactics, his claws are in your shoulder and his white fangs leaping at your throat. For while few sportsmen are killed outright, on the spot, by lion in these days of high power rifles, once a lion has mauled you with his carrion-tearing teeth or claws, nothing can prevent death of blood-poisoning but the immediate and most thorough disinfection of the wounds, if this is lacking, an early amputation, where a surgeon can be reached.

As chiefly a night prowler, like all predatory savages, biped and quadruped alike, it is just hunter's luck when you get a chance at a lion.

Of six months spent in the plains and bush of British East Africa, a full forty days, all told, I occupied exclusively hunting lion in country where they had been thick about our camp every night, often when they had sought entry to our boma, twice when they had made kills within a few yards of where we slept, without yet getting sight of one.

I have followed their fresh spoor through long grass and mimosa thickets where one could not see more than the length of a gun barrel; trailed them into their very caves and stood, expectant, while my shikaris tried to stone them out or taunt them to action with buzzing Somali expletives; risen before dawn, forded crocodile-infested rivers in the dark, stumbled through bush and hidden bowlders to some den marked down the day before, and there lain concealed until an hour or more after dawn in hope of sighting them on return from their night's foray, but all without avail.

At first I found it most nerve-racking work, but now I don't seem to mind, whether because I'm getting used to it or because repeated failures have left me skeptical of each new start, I don't know. Indeed, I was beginning to harbor fears that, like Tartarin de Tarascon, my lionslaying must ever remain merely a hyper-heroic figment of my dreams, until a few days ago I learned that Ronan Wallaston Humphrey, the District Commissioner at Machakos Fort, twenty-five miles from Juja Farm, where I am a guest, a keen sportsman who has shot about everything else, was in the country eight years before he saw his first lion; and that another equally keen sportsman, Chief Secretary S. C. Tomkins, C. M. G., of Uganda, here twelve years, has never yet seen a lion except from a train. So that, while I can as little count on eight more months in the lion country as, at my age, I can venture to count upon eight more years on earth, my hopes have revived.

And why, indeed, should not one hope, when, in the short space of eighteen months, no less than twenty men, sportsmen or settlers all, have been killed or badly mauled by lion within a radius of thirty miles of Juja Farm, and twelve lion have been killed within three miles of the farm in the same time?

The Lucas tragedy was characteristic. Lucas and Goldfinch were partners in a farm on the western slopes of Donya Sabouk, ten miles from Juja. One day the pair jumped a lion, in tall grass near the Athi River, which retired at their approach. After him they raced on ponies, Goldfinch in the lead. But Leo's retreat was only a stroke of strategy, he sidestepped them into concealing long grass, only to leap upon Goldfinch and his horse as they passed, sinking his right fore claws in the pony's right flank, his left in Goldfinch's left thigh, his rear claws tearing at the pony's hind quarter.

The mixup was such that Goldfinch could not bring his gun to bear on the lion and that Lucas did not dare to shoot from the saddle, so, jumping from his pony, Lucas ran forward to his partner's aid. But their watchful enemy was not so easily to be taken in flank, for before Lucas got to a position where he could safely fire, the lion leaped upon him and began rending him. No more was he down, however, before Goldfinch, badly torn though he was of the lion's claws, slipped from his horse, ran in, and gave the lion a shot through the heart that laid him dead.

Yet, while scarce a minute had elapsed since he first struck Lucas, Leo had taken his toll; Lucas was so badly mauled that, what with the delay in getting him into the Nairobi Hospital and the severity of the wounds, the surgeons found naught but an amputation could save his life. This Lucas stubbornly refused, vowed he would rather die than live as a maimed man.

And die a few days later he did, in a manner typical of his dauntless soul. The evening the surgeons told him he could not last the night out, to his bedside he summoned two of his closest pals, "Daddy" Longworth and another. And there throughout the night they sat, Lucas bolstered on pillows, drinking whiskey and soda; Lucas toasting them a long life, they him a Happy Hunting Ground in the next world, until, just as the first pale flush of the brief tropical dawn began to dim the candles, the two watchers suddenly realized they were looking into the face of a dead friend. For Lucas it was about the nearest approach conceivable to active participation in his own wake.

In the history of East African lion shooting, nothing is more heroic than the conduct of the Somali shikaris. Far and away the finest native race of this continent, with a strong strain of Arab blood, light of complexion, wavy-haired, often with little of negroid cast of feature, tall and slender, scrupulously clean of dress and habits, Mohammedans all, at home nomads with their flocks and herds, abroad the Jews of the Dark Continent, traders wandering in small bands from one tribe to another between the twentieth degree of north latitude and the fifteenth degree south, the Somalis are faithful and true to their salt. No sahib who treats them half decently is likely to find cause of complaint of their fidelity,—they are as ready to die for him as most others are ready to desert where peril threatens.

No one can know the Somali and not be inspired by a profound admiration for his religion. For its exemplars, Mohammedanism has done three things that, not to make comparison, let us say uplifts it high among religious cults; it makes an absolutely temperate people, who never know the taste of liquor in any form; instead of filling them with a dread of death, it not only makes them reckless of it but inspires them to seek it in battle, as divine warrant of everlasting abode beside the sweetest waters and beneath the best-loved shade of the most fecund date palms of Allah's celestial abode; it makes a scrupulously devout people who, five times a day, remove their sandals, bathe feet and hands, spread rug or wrap, no matter what the presence, and, facing Mecca, for ten or fifteen minutes engage in prayer, so pray a few yards from your camp fire, in a crowded street, upon a thronged railway platform, adoring, rapt, oblivious to the world, its joys and sorrows, its benefits and threats, first standing, then kneeling, then bending and touching the forehead to the earth.

Cultsmen these of a faith no intruding propagandist can win them from. Indeed, I am told by a recent high official of the National Bank of India's branch at Aden that a friend of his, a missionary of the Church of Scotland, a physician missionary at that, a man of the highest attainments, and of untiring devotion to his task, for nine years treated an average of twelve thousand Mohammedans a year, healing their wounds, relieving their pains, on the sole condition that each should attend his services and listen to his pleas. Scrupulously they kept faith, come they did and listened,— but, after nine years the facts forced him to admit frankly he had not won a single convert to his creed.

All this may seem a digression from my subject, but nevertheless, to the missionary, the "benighted" blacks are the biggest game this Dark Continent affords.

Only a few days ago, with Djama Aout and Hassan Yusef, Somali shikaris, I followed the absolutely fresh spoor of a lion to the mouth of a cave into which the spoor entered, a cave high enough of roof to admit of entry of two or three men, standing, a distance of probably eighty feet. On into it both Somalis started, and when I protested their folly, they simply replied: "Inshallah (God willing), we come back." And into the cave they went, one carrying my second rifle, the other nothing but his skinning knife, in as far as they could get, tossed stones into the dark recesses beyond and in every way invited a charge, which, luckily for them, was not made.

The experience last February on the Theika, eighteen miles north of Juja, of Geoffry Charles Buxton typified the wonderfully fine fibre of the Somali, and, incidentally, his own. One morning he left camp at dawn with his Somali shikari, he himself carrying a doublebarrelled .577 cordite rifle, his shikari a Mauser. When out from the camp no more than half an hour he sighted a big black-mane about a hundred yards away, leisurely retiring from his approach. Bush so thick and grass so high he could not get a good opening for a shot, Buxton raced in pursuit until he came within fifty yards and, himself winded, halted for a shot. At the same instant Leo, evidently decided he had drawn sufficiently on the reserves of his patience, stopped and turned, tail angrily lashing, head up, and eyes blazing his royal wrath.

With a steady aim Buxton sent a great, heavy .577 ball crashing into his quarry, a shot that entered just inside the front of the shoulder, ranged through the lion from end to end, and dropped him quivering in the grass. Had Buxton left him, the lion would have been dead in ten of fifteen minutes, but, notwithstanding he knew he had delivered a mortal wound, keen he should not lose his trophy, Buxton fired again, and, with little to see of the recumbent body, missed. This last shot, however, proved quite enough for Leo and nearly too much for Buxton; it roused the dying jungle monarch to action—he rose and charged.

And at this crisis, while hurriedly throwing a spare shell into his empty gun, Buxton observed that its stock (broken shortly before in an encounter with an elephant and mended with string wrappings) had become so loose it was unserviceable, a dilemma to try the nerve of the steadiest man. However, lacking time to grab his spare gun from the Somali, as the lion rose at him, holding the .577 loose alongside him, Buxton fired,— and, naturally, missed.

Then in another instant the dauntless pair were at death grips.

Sure the lion was already carrying a wound he could not possibly long survive and that he must win the fight if only he could save himself for a few moments, knowing his only hope lay in keeping his feet and holding the lion off, as they came together Buxton rammed his empty rifle barrel down the lion's throat, down until three-fourths its length was within the mighty jaws, where the wood work beneath the barrel close up to the trigger guard is still deeply scarred by the lion's teeth.

Then ensued a struggle unparalleled, I believe, in the history of lion hunting, between a dying lion fighting to the last and a man who knew himself to be as good as dead if for an instant wind or nerve failed him.

Instantly he received the thrust down his throat, the lion sank two claws into the inner right forearm that held the rifle, four and six inches above the hand, sank them into and nearly through the arm to puncture of the other side, and this hold he held until both went down. Thus dragging at the arm that held the gun, the lion really helped hold it to a firmer, deeper thrust that hurt so much he shrank back from it, but, with an advancing enemy whose grip the nigh paralyzing pain of his wounds did not suffice to lessen, he could not escape it.

And there they swayed and struggled, each literally staring death in the face, Buxton, indeed, now sure he was gone, for the fetid odor of putrescent meat told him the lion's carrion-rending claws that held his arm were laden with poison of the deadliest.

Meantime the beast was tearing the man to ribbons, the hind claws slitting his legs, those of the loose fore paw digging at the hand that held the rifle. But flinch the man did not, dared not, and knowing him well, I believe would not had he dared.

Luckily, just as Buxton was near to going down of sheer exhaustion of the struggle and the shock of his wounds, help came from his Somali shikari.

This man from the start of the struggle had been trying to shoot the lion with the Mauser, but could not discharge it. Buxton of course supposed the gun was in some way jammed, but at the finish it proved the gun been set at "safe," and this, through excitement, the Somali failed to note.

At length, and just in the very nick of time, the Somali dropped the gun and literally sprang upon the lion's back, so hitting its ears and pounding it about the eyes with his bare hands that it whirled to reach him and all three went to earth together, the Somali beneath the lion; beneath both, the Mauser.

Thus at last released, Buxton painfully rose, gingerly pulled the Mauser free and with it blew the lion's brains out, all done so quickly he saved his faithful follower from fatal wounds.

A people you are apt to become fond of, are the Somalis, when you come to know them well.

Dr. H. S. Hall, the resident physician of Juja Farm, got to Buxton just in time to save his life. With iron nerve, Buxton had cauterized all the thirteen wounds with pure crystals of permanganate, and thus himself had saved himself from poisoning. But some of the crystals bit into and opened an artery, and only a tight tourniquet saved him from bleeding to death until, five hours later, Hall came, tied up the artery, dressed his wounds, and brought him here to Juja Farm, where he lay through several weeks of slow convalescence.

Some men are, constitutionally, greedy. In September I met Captain Buxton out on another lion hunt, notwithstanding his right arm was still heavily bandaged!

One of the finest lion trophies I have seen out here is that of A. B. Duirs, late of the Imperial Light Horse, one of the first nine men to gain entry into Mafeking at the time of its relief, a ten and one-half-foot black mane skin without any visible mark of the wound that killed it.

One Sunday morning last summer he was out alone stalking an impala buck on the Komo, two miles from his home on the N'durugo, six miles from Juja. Suddenly, when almost near enough for a sure shot, some lucky instinct prompted him to glance to his right, to see, not thirty yards away, another hunter stalking the same buck he was after, a big black-mane; and no more had he turned than the lion discovered him and instantly began the snarling and tail lashing that preludes a charge. Realizing that it was a case of strike first and true, he dropped on one knee, took careful aim, and dropped His Majesty stone dead, the ball entering a nostril and ranging back into the brain!

Oddly, the safest lion shooting of all, bar unsportsmanlike shooting at night from within a thorn zareba over a donkey bait, or from a treetop commanding a water-hole, is where the sportsman is afoot on a naked plain where there is nothing to climb more substantial than a sunbeam and no hole to crawl into bigger than a wart-hog's. Under such circumstances a pony man runs the lion to bay, while his chief approaches at another angle, afoot. So run to bay, the lion invariably charges, charges desperately, but nearly always at the pony man, and not infrequently catches and downs man and horse where carelessness has brought them nearer than a hundred yards.

Often one sees their fresh kills, a month ago I saw one of the freshest. I was driving in a gharri from the farm to Ruero Falls, over a stretch of short-grassed, level plain, presently entering a region of long grass. And into the long grass I had not driven more than a hundred yards when I caught a glimpse of a dead zebra, a hundred to one a lion's kill. So over to it I walked, to find a carcass still warm, eyes not yet glazed, blood still freshly flowing and not a wound on it save two deep claw digs on the right shoulder, and the flesh of the neck immediately behind the ears torn away and the spine crushed, just at the base of the skull. The zebra was not dead three minutes; doubtless I should have seen the attack if I had been looking that way, and probably old Leo was then watching me from a near-by thicket or out of near concealment in the grass.

Without disturbing the kill, I drove the remaining three miles to the falls, stopped there an hour, and then drove back within about a mile of the kill, where I left gharri and driver and proceeded to carefully stalk the kill, sure the lion would be returned and gorging himself.

It was aerie work by one's lonesome, going through grass shoulder high, with clumps of mimosa on all sides, every step a convenient ambush of the sort Leo loves, and the picture of the zebra's yawning wound and crushed spine persistently intruding before my eyes. However, resentful of previous failures, I kept on till I had the carcass in view at about fifteen yards, only to discover Old Cunning had not returned. Then for an hour I crawled about through the grass and bush in a wide circle of the kill, only in the end to score another failure.

My host McMillan is more lucky, or more probably a better hunter, for he seems to get lion when he likes, has a dozen or more to his credit. On safari last spring on the Guaso Nyiro he spoored a lion into an old abandoned Masai kraal, overgrown with tall grass. Slipping softly about the eight-foot high enclosure, trying to locate his quarry, suddenly a line of waving grass caught his eye, and then just as he stood alert to get a bead, the lion rose in a mighty leap at the fence crest, for once a bit too slow, for a perfect snapshot caught him aft, ranged through him and out of his head, and added one more to the big game trophies that, well set up, make the "Jungle" of a certain house in Berkeley Square look like a wholesale invasion of that end of London by militant African carnivora.

Mombasa, standing on a bold, high headland between its tiny north harbor, that well served all purposes of old Arab and Portuguese days, and its broad roadstead to the south called Kilindini, now almost exclusively used; ringed round with tall brown coral cliffs all honeycombed and sharp pinnacled; well-nigh hid beneath broad-spreading mangoes and the lazily nodding fronds of palms which, wherever found, are the very sign manual of one-time Arab dominion; defended without by a perilously narrow harbor entrance through the jagged jaws of a broad belt of surf-beat coral reef; defended within by a grand old coral-walled fort, that for centuries has added its shrill tenor drum-beat to the hoarse bass beat of the surf as a challenge to all strange comers. Mombasa enjoys a climate and occupies a position of great natural military strength, commanding a trade route that leads to such rare prizes that for a thousand years it has known less of peace than of war—the prizes sought, slaves and ivory.

Times and times unnumbered has Mombasa been captured and sacked and changed sovereignty. Chinese and Persians, Japanese and Arabs, Turk and Christian in turn contended for it to the death, and up from the far south and over all in the sixteenth century rolled the ruthless tide of the vandal Zimba invasion, only to fall later before a wily Portuguese alliance with warlike native neighbors.

For three years, from 1696 to 1698, the Portuguese garrison of this grand old fortress withstood an uninterrupted Arab siege, only in the end, wasted by famine and bubonic plague, to see their flag cut down and themselves fall to the last man by infidel scimitars.

Then thirty years elapsed before the Portuguese regained Mombasa, only a few months later to be permanently expelled by the Imaum of Muscat.

And Arab ever thereafter Mombasa has remained, for, technically, the town is held to-day by the British only under concession from the Sultan of Zanzibar.

From Mombasa the narrow-gauge Uganda Railway climbs toward the high central plateaus as rapidly as its shockingly slow service permits; at 100 miles, 1,800 feet elevation is reached; at 200, 2,300 feet; at 327 (Nairobi), 5,450 feet; at 484, 8,340 feet, whence descent is rapid to 3,650 feet at Port Florence on Victoria Nyanza, 584 miles from the coast.

The country on both sides of this railway from its one end to its other is literally alive with wild game, although little is seen of it till the first one hundred miles is traversed and the low bush veldt left behind, or after the more thickly settled Kikuyu country north of Nairobi is entered. But between Voi and Nairobi train passengers are seldom out of sight of hundreds, usually in sight of thousands, from the tiniest dik-dik antelope, slender, delicate, and diminutive as an Italian greyhound, to towering giraffe and massive lion. Indeed, only a few days ago a large herd of elephant crossed the railway just east of Voi, trekking from the bamboo forests of Mount Kilima N'jaro to fresh pastures in the north.

On my first journey up from the coast, no more than two hundred yards from the station of Kiu, a great lioness crossed the track just in front of us, walking slowly away south and no more than thirty yards from the track as we passed. Stopped in the station, a Boer emigrant took a shot at her from a car roof, but apparently missed.

The extraordinary present abundance of game both north and south of this section of the Uganda Railway is due to the fact that all the vast territory extending from the Tsavo River to Escarpment, a distance of two hundred and thirty miles, and from the south line of the track to the German border, embracing about eleven thousand square miles, is a carefully preserved game reserve, preserved as jealously as the Yellowstone Park, while immediately southwest of it in German territory is another reserve of the same size. Unfenced, shut in by no impassable streams or mountains, the game is free to wander out of and into the reserve at will; but like the shrewd stags of a Scotch deer forest, so well does the game seem to know the very boundaries that mark for them sanctuary, that little do they leave it except in periods of local drought or as crowded out by overstocking, so well do they know the immunity of sanctuary that, shooting from trains being forbidden, timid antelope, wary giraffe, and even lion and rhino often idle within a stone's throw of the track.

And since from the Tsavo to Kapiti Plains, one hundred and fifty miles, there is absolutely no white settlement north of the track, and from Kapiti west settlers are few and scattering and practically all within a narrow belt of forty miles, naturally the heavy out movement of the game is northward, while yet other thousands are pouring down into this central open region of Ukamba and Kenya Provinces from north of the Guaso Nyiro River, out of the Jubaland and Sugota Game Reserves, that together total an area of thirty-eight thousand square miles.

The region lying between the Athi and the Tana Rivers is the centre of this sportsman's paradise, although equally good and varied shooting is to be had southwest of the railway in the Sotik country. Close upon a halfhundred different varieties of big game are here to be had, each in their favorite type of country: elephant during the dry (and hotter) season, in the dense bamboo thickets of high mountain slopes and during the rains in the bush veldt and elephant grass country; hippo in the streams, or from dusk to dawn feeding along the banks; rhinos, any old place, on plain or hills, in bush or open; most buck and antelope, preferably in the most open level plains; duyker and dik-dik in long grass, out of which they pop right under your feet, visible only for the instant of each leap, artful little dodgers most men would be more apt to get with buckshot than with bullet; reed buck, among the scrub of steep, rocky hillslopes; leopard everywhere, but seldom seen and rarely killed unless by trapping.

Elephant are to be found within at the most a week's march of almost any camp in the Protectorate, as also are most of those now rarer prizes, sable antelope, roan antelope, oryx, eland, Kudu.

By many sportsmen the buffalo is considered a far more dangerous antagonist than the lion. Loving the shade and concealment of papyrus swamps, dense forest and fifteen-foot elephant grass, buffalo are seldom seen until you are within a few yards, often a few feet of them. Mobs of buffalo seldom charge you deliberately but, when startled by scent of you or by a shot, they stampede; often the mob comes thundering straight upon you and you are lucky indeed if by rapid close shooting you can turn them.

The real danger with buffalo is with the wounded or in an encounter with a lone bull. The latter will often charge you from no more provocation than the fact of your presence. Recently an officer of the King's African Rifles was spooring an elephant near Mount Kenya when he sighted a lone buffalo to his right. Keen for his elephant, he made a wide detour to the left of the line of spoor, to avoid chance of having to defend himself against the buffalo. When well past the point where he had seen the buffalo he returned to the spoor, but before he had followed it thirty yards and before he could turn or spring aside, with a cleverly executed rear charge, the buffalo, which had been quietly stalking to intercept him, caught him on its horns and tossed him upon the flat top of a mimosa tree, where, luckily, he lodged comparatively unhurt. And there up the tree the doughty old warrior held him till nightfall!

A wounded buffalo is infinitely more dangerous when he runs from you than when he charges, for in nine cases out of ten, after a dash that may be of a few hundred yards or a mile, he revengefully circles back to an interception of his own trail, stands hid in grass or thicket until his pursuer comes plodding all unconscious along the trail, and then is out and upon him.

And yet fierce as is the temper of a lone bull, savage his cunning, irresistible his great charging bulk, I believe him far less dangerous than the lion, he has less speed, lacks the lion's poisoned weapons, and is a much bigger target; and this opinion is substantiated by the indisputable fact that at least ten men are killed or mauled by lion to one by buffalo.

While easily stalked, the rhino is a most nasty customer, as most men will agree who have hunted him especially Benjamin Eastwood,

Chief Accountant of the Uganda Railway, who was mauled and tramped by one to the near loss of his life and the actual loss of one arm above the elbow.

If the rhino gets your scent, almost invariably he charges, often, probably, from sheer curiosity, only that doesn't make him any more easily disposed of. Moreover, he runs and turns at a speed incredible of his vast bulk. Either shoot straight or stand absolutely motionless, when, with his bad sight, there is a possibility he may mistake you for a tree and veer past you.

Indeed, this latter is the safest tactics in the crisis of any and all charges, stand fast and still, even the unwounded lion sometimes swerves in his charge and retires before a man with nerve to so await his coming.

Where you sight your rhino first and can get the wind of him, it is perfectly easy to stalk within even five or ten yards and land a shot where alone you can be sure of a kill, four inches back of the eye into the brain pan, into the spine between neck and shoulder or midway of the body and in line with the centre of the foreleg into the heart. And none of these shots are possible except with a hard-nose bullet, no soft nose will penetrate his thick hide to any vital part.

Doubtless the most exhausting and nerve-racking work the African sportsman encounters is in the pursuit of elephant. Not often are they to be found except by following their own narrow paths between walls of bamboo thicket, jungle tangle, or elephant grass so entirely impenetrable to the hunter that escape from the path is impossible. So meet an approaching frightened herd and chance of escape is practically zero. Rarely does one see elephant until within a few yards of them. Often one will find himself squarely in the middle of a feeding herd, will hear them breaking limbs or tearing up roots, within five or ten feet of him, on all sides, and yet without seeing one! Like any youngsters, the totos, the babies, are playing about the outer edge of the herd. At the first alarm, the mothers rush trumpeting about for their young, and it is in such a position the hunter's greatest danger of elephant lies. Imprisoned in bush through which they easily crash, man and beast are practically in collision before there is time for the man to stop him with a vital shot in the chest, the only vital spot in a charging African elephant, or even time for the elephant, from surprise or fear, to swerve. Otherwise safely armored by the massive bone structure of the head, the elephant's comparatively tiny brain is only to be reached by a side shot in the orifice of the ear, while the sure shot for the heart is midway of the body and in line with the inner side of the foreleg. Indeed, I have known several elephants to retire, leisurely if not comfortably, with two or three balls in the temple which had failed to reach the brain, whether to ultimate recovery or death was never learned.

The vitality of the elephant is enormous, as in fact is that of all

African game, down to the tiniest buck.

But occasionally a white man comes along with a vitality as astonishing as that of his quarry. Of this Craig Helkett, an officer of the First King's African Rifles, is a wonderful proof.

Out for a few weeks' sport with elephant before going on leave, he gave one a mortal chest shot at such close range that it was upon him before he could deliver a second shot, passed one of its great tusks first transversely through his stomach and then through his thigh, picked him up with its trunk and tossed him far to one side into the bush, and then lurched away to die. And, miracle of miracles, though it was nine days before his men got him to Entebbe and surgical aid, he is making a safe recovery.

Still for the experienced and prudent elephant hunter, the sport is comparatively safe. Mr. Bell, an Englishman who has been for the last five or six years shooting elephant for the ivory, as a business, and who has to his credit the probably unparalleled bag to one gun of over five hundred head, says he has never yet been charged. Only a fortnight ago he came into Entebbe from a four months' safari in the Congo country with the tusks of one hundred and eighty big fellows. Deducting the period of the journey in and out, this remarkable kill must have been made within no more than six weeks' actual shooting! And one day alone he bagged eighteen! No bad business with ivory at two dollars and a half a pound and an average tusk weight of probably one hundred pounds per pair!

Asked by a friend of mine how he had contrived to so long come off unscathed, Bell replied, "I never shoot until I get my big tusker right; if I find myself amid a big herd, I manage to slip out and bide my time; patience will always get you a big tusker right, and then you have it your own way," and, indeed, "patience" is the watchword of every notably successful big game hunter: waiting to "get them right."

Hippo are rarely to be had in daylight hereabouts, although they are plenty in the larger streams and positively swarm in the lakes of less than 5,000 feet altitude. They are easiest to be had by cruising at dawn in boat or canoe a few yards out from landings for their favorite grazing grounds, where a fair breast or shoulder heart shot may be had as they enter the water, or by lying in wait on land on moonlight nights for them to come ashore. On the water at dawn or of a night they often rise near you, and in such position the only sure shot is through a yawning nostril into the brain. They are trophies well worth while, their great teeth, finer ivory than that of the elephant, making beautiful mirror or picture frames. On water they are beasts to have especial care of, for they sometimes charge you and sink your canoe with a crunch of the jaws or rise under the canoe and spill you into crocodile-infested waters.

At the African home of my host, William Northrup McMillan, at Juja Farm, twenty-two miles from Nairobi, and in the heart of the great

Athi Plains, all the East African game abounds in thousands, except rhino and elephant, sable and roan antelope and oryx-and the latter are to be had within two to five days' journey hundreds nearly always in sight from the veranda of the house. I have lighted a cigarette in my room at daylight and gone out and killed a big Wildebeeste bull before the cigarette was finished. In fact, the twenty thousand acres of the "farm" so swarm with game after the rains that before the dry season is half over the grass is eaten short as on an overcrowded cattle range, all from the overflow of the great game reserves north and south of us. But notwithstanding their great numbers, it takes marksmanship to get game on the Athi Plains,—for they are bare of cover and it is unusual to get a shot at anything but lion or hippo short of three hundred to six hundred yards.

The heavy-bore rifles are now practically obsolete among African sportsmen, the four, eight, and twelve bores and even the .577, whose chief merit lay in the fact that they sometimes kicked you out of the way of a charging beast. Few now use anything heavier than the English double-barrelled .450 cordite, and I and many others find the .405 Winchester the most satisfactory of all for all-round African work, although the 30-30 is heavy enough for anything except a few of the bigger fellows, while not a few, Bell and, I understand, Selous included, prefer to trust in the higher velocity and flat trajectory of the pencil-like .256 Mannlicher for even elephant. While I have not yet tried the Mannlicher, I believe it is no more than probable its devotees are right, for such is the extraordinary vitality of all African game that the more lead you throw into them the faster and farther they run, unless you get brain, heart, or spine. I have myself in a two-mile pursuit of a two hundred and seventy-five pound wounded hartebeeste bull put nine big .35 Mauser bullets through him before finally bringing him down, and a few days ago Captain Dugdale and First Officer Hampden of the S. S. Clement Hill, on Victoria Nyanza, put twenty-two .303's into a hippo before getting him.

Even the smaller antelope, slender and delicate though they appear, must be hit in brain, heart, or spine, no matter what the calibre of your gun, or you lose them.

Not a few American sportsmen besides McMillan have had their fling at African big game, notably Astor, Chanler, John Bradley, and Max Fleischman, and more are sure to come.

The journey may be made most comfortably. By. arranging close sailing connections, the German Lloyd steamers from New York to Naples and the well-served German East African line thence south fetch you to Mombasa in thirty days, and two days later you can be in Nairobi, all at a cost well within $500, or at Marseilles one may connect with the steamers of the Compagnie Messageries which sail once a month via Suez for all East African ports to Mombasa, and for all island ports thence south to Madagascar and Reunion.

Nairobi, the seat of government of this Protectorate, now has a total white population of eight hundred and fifty, including the military and police, while its highly variegated assortment of colors, ranging from pale saffron to ebony, numbers eleven thousand. Its streets, especially about the Indian bazaar, are thronged with Orientals and native savages, the former as weirdly picturesque in the variety and styles of their costumes as are the latter in the scantiness or entire lack of any costume at all. Grave Sikh constables, bearded and turbaned; Parsee merchants and clerks in long black coats and flattopped skull caps; Hindu mechanics, turbaned and often carrying water pipes half as big as a foot bath; coast Swahilis in long, nightgown-like kanzus of thinnest muslin and embroidered white skull caps; flowingrobed Arabs with sashes stuck full of enough life-taking steel to arm a half-dozen men of any other race; tall, slender, graceful Somalis in khaki jackets, turbans, and flowing waist cloths; Goanese merchants and clerks in white drill; Indian women and children wearing more brilliant colors than even a kaleidoscope could boast, and Kikuyu women with nothing on but a flapping, slipping skin or length of begrimed "Americani" (cotton cloth) which sometimes covers the back and sometimes does not, sometimes shrouds one end of the body and sometimes the other, a cover so scanty as to leave little to the imagination except the privilege of conjecture why they bother to wear it at all; tall, lithe Masai warriors, their hair in flapping red ringlets, had of a mixture of red clay and castor oil, a skin loosely looped about both shoulders or over one, short swords stuck in their belts and in their hands spears with narrow blades three feet long; gallant Kikuyu dandies with the lobes of their ears split and stretched to hold anything from a tomato can to a porcelain marmalade jar, or, if a bit épris by civilization, swaggering under a battered helmet or strutting about in nothing but a faded and fragmentary but tightly buttoned frock coat; red-blanketed Wakamba, their upper teeth filed to points sharp as pins, these once eaters of their enemies and of their own dead, as are still several tribes within ten days' march of here; and here and there the khaki-clad figure of a European, helmeted and putteed, looking isolated in this jostling savage throng as a vagrant cork upon the sea.

Nor are the vehicles and the beasts that draw them less varied than the people. An Irish jaunting car drawn by a sixteen-hand Missouri mule is followed by a two-wheeled pleasure cart with a body much the shape but twice the size of a theatre wagon, painted in daubs of every gaudy color the builder could command, drawn by a pair of hump-necked bullocks that jog along at a clumsy but tolerable pace, the European lady and children inside bouncing helplessly about, wondering, I imagine, whether heads or elbows are to get the next bump.

Then along is apt to come dear old John Boyes, King of the Kikuyu, in an American buggy drawn by two Abyssinian mules so diminutive I am puzzled why so kindly a soul as he does not stow the mules under the buggy seat and pull the trap himself.

Next, one is likely to see approach at slow, lurching pace a pair of camels, hitched tandem to the high two-wheeled cart of some Somali trader, the camels' faces wearing the ghastly expression of equal parts of double distilled agony and concentrated extract of despair that always makes the mere sight of a camel's face run one's temperature down to congealment of the very fountains of content and joy. Follows a great Transvaal trek wagon, rattling and groaning along, pulled by anywhere from five to twenty yoke of cattle, a Hindu's cart pulled by two dome-necked bullocks, the driver roosting on his heels upon the tongue of the cart, tight and safe as a fly on a wall, or a rickshaw drawn by a donkey and crowds of rickshaws propelled by "boys."

Despite its raw appearance, Nairobi possesses an excellent hotel, which at certain seasons is crowded with safari parties, for here alone are the safari parties organized. Twenty such parties went out in October and November, ten are now at the Norfolk Hotel, and forty or fifty more are expected during December and January. The usual party consists of two men, occasionally of only one, sometimes of three or four. Not a few ladies come out, and some shoot.

Probably half the sportsmen coming out here are of the British or Continental nobility. The more brilliant planets of the titular firmament, princes, dukes and earls, abound, while its lesser lights, lords, counts, and barons, are here thick enough to form a "milky way" were it not for the fact that theirs is, by preference, a whiskey-and soda way. Here are the names of a few of those either now here or who have been here in the last few months. Duchesse de Aosta, Prince de Furstenberg, Prince de Chimay, Duke de Penaranola, Marquis de la Scala, Earl of Gifford, Duke de Alba (Aide-de-Camp to the King of Spain), Duke de Medinacoli, Lord and Lady Waleran, Lord Bury, Lord Wodehouse, Sir E. and Lady Plowden, Sir Charles Kirkpatrick, Count Palffy, Count Zichy, Baron Kervyn de Leltenhone, Baron von Uklanski, Baron and Baroness de Bethune, General and Mrs. Allenby, Colonel Yardley, Colonel Colville, Professor Agassiz, and Major Dalgety.

The sportsman need bring here nothing but his guns and ammunition. Newland, Tarlton and Co., Limited, the Boma Trading Co. and Will Judd make a specialty of furnishing safari parties and do it well. A safari for one man will consist of a white safari leader, usually a good shot and familiar with the country and the run and habits of its game, a headman, gun bearer, cook, mess boy and tent boy (all Somalis), and twenty to twenty-five shenzi (savage) porters, each carrying on his head a sixty-pound load—tents, beds, provisions, etc., all furnished, including food, at three hundred and fifty to five hundred dollars a month. Horses, mules, liquors, etc., are, of course, extra. Horses here are scarce and dear, thanks to the tsetse fly, a Somali pony worth no more than thirty dollars in Texas bringing readily two hundred dollars, while Abyssinian mules, tough, wiry, and good roadsters but little bigger than a donkey, sell at one hundred and fifty dollars. The "big" game license, which allows you to kill from one to ten head of about everything afoot or a-wing, costs two hundred and fifty dollars.

Every one is asking how long the big game here can last. I should say certainly no more than four or five years in anything like its present abundance and easy access. About 1,200,000 acres have already been taken up by white settlers, stock raisers, and farmers, who find it difficult and in some places impossible to maintain fences. Buffalo and zebra especially go through barb wire as if it were no more than thread. As a result the settlers have been so actively urging changes in the game laws permitting them to shoot at will trespassing game that a few evenings ago, at the St. Andrews dinner of the Nairobi Caledonian Society, the Governor, Colonel Sir James Hayes Sadler, stated that while he agreed that sport was in a way a mainstay in the making of British manhood, public game preservation must not be permitted to impede the development of the country by white settlers, and further said that changes in the game laws in this particular were under consideration. Give the settler a free hand, and a year or two will see easy shooting ended within seventy-five miles of the railway, except on big estates like Juja and Kamiti, whose owners are likely to preserve them indefinitely as shooting boxes.

Any American sportsman keen for a chance at African big game shooting while still at its best should not long delay coming, but I don't believe any one now living will live to see African big game actually exterminated.

For at least the course of this generation there will remain plenty of places where the active enthusiast can get his elephant, lion, rhino, hippo, buffalo, and most of the antelope family except a few of the rarer species. Indeed, not even two or three generations will see the swamps and jungles of the Congo, the Zambesi, the Tana, the Juba, the Lake and the Nile basins, etc., or the forest recesses and bamboo thickets of Central Africa's taller uplifts, generally occupied, save as now by natives, or in any considerable measure tamed; and until so occupied and tamed they must remain a safe breeding region and retreat for all sorts of the bigger game which is most sought.

Portuguese East Africa and the Congo are full of fine shooting, though not so varied as here. Moreover, the climate of both sections is far more dangerous than that of British East, and neither offers any facilities for safari provision.

German East Africa, Matabeleland, Northern Rhodesia, Somaliland, and Abyssinia offer capital sport, but all under either less convenient or less safe conditions than here.

And, even yet, far south in Cape Colony, the Transvaal, Basutoland, and the Orange Colony, it is a poor sportsman who cannot take a few days off and slip away to a quiet bit of bush or nook of plain where he can bowl over a few buck or even an elephant.

THE END

www.ingramcontent.com/pod-product-compliance
Lightning Source LLC
Chambersburg PA
CBHW070629310726
48982CB00001B/212

* 9 7 8 1 9 6 3 9 5 6 5 2 8 *